# Castles, Catnip & Murder

## A Dickens & Christie Mystery

### Book V

## Kathy Manos Penn

Paperback ISBN: 978-1-7370117-1-2

eBook ISBN: 978-1-7343226-2-0

Large Print: 978-1-7370117-3-6

*For Puddin', the calico kitty who not only cleans my desk, but also provides inspiration for Christie's sassy personality.*

*We cannot cure the world of sorrows, but we can choose to live in joy.*
-JOSEPH CAMPBELL

# Acknowledgements

The idea of a yoga studio in Astonbury was inspired by my years of taking yoga in Dunwoody, Georgia. For over a decade, I attended weekly classes—much like Leta, never quite managing a true home practice.

My longtime instructor, Kathy Koenigsburg, was the inspiration behind Leta's devotion to her own teacher. When I decided to make a yoga retreat central to this book, she was my first call. Though she generously offered guidance, any mistakes related to poses or the retreat's flow are mine alone.

Kathy was both a resource and an inspiration, and I'm deeply grateful.

# Contents

# CHAPTER ONE

*Mid-August*

"ARE WE READY TO LEAVE? Have you packed my food?" Christie meowed from her perch in my suitcase.

Dickens cocked his head and barked. "What is your problem? Leta never forgets the food, and she packs my treats too. We're pros at this travel thing."

He was right. He'd been my companion on plenty of trips, but this was a first for Christie. The two went back and forth in this vein as I considered my wardrobe for the trip to the coast. *Leggings, shorts, tops, sundresses, yoga clothes, sweaters, a sun hat or two—maybe a jumpsuit. That should do it.*

I enjoyed the chatter of my four-legged companions and treasured my secret ability to "talk to the animals." Secret because I'd learned not to let on to family or friends that I was a female version of Doctor Dolittle. The few times I mentioned it as a child, I got a pat on the head and comments about my vivid imagination. I had kept quiet about my talent ever since.

It was a good thing I'd googled the weather forecast, as Cornwall was in the midst of a heatwave with highs in the eighties. Typically, the temperatures never rose above the sixties—Fahrenheit. *How many years will I have to live here before I think in Celsius?*

Smiling, I turned to my demanding black cat. "Patience, princess. We don't leave until Saturday morning, and I'm getting my ducks in a row ahead of time. Then I'm headed to yoga class, but you don't get to go today."

Though I was pleased Christie was excited about the trip to Tintagel, I still wasn't convinced it was a good idea. A yoga retreat for Wendy and me was one thing. Taking Christie was another.

How I'd let Rhiannon talk me into using Christie for cat yoga classes at her studio on the High Street was a mystery to me, but Christie turned out to be a natural. My feisty feline was a sociable thing and did exactly as expected—walked over and under people as we did downward dog and other poses and chose a select few to lie on when we ended the class in our corpse poses. Rhiannon's clients loved the experience, but I was still hesitant about taking my girl out of town to a yoga retreat.

Wendy and I parked in front of Let It Be Yoga at the same time. We'd met a year ago when I moved from Atlanta to the idyllic village of Astonbury, and we'd become fast friends. Our shared passion for books, yoga, and shopping sparked an instant bond.

Her face lit up when she saw me. "I'm so excited about our trip, I can hardly wait, and Mum's been packing for days."

When Rhiannon invited the two of us to attend a yoga retreat in Cornwall, we leaped at the chance. What could be better than yoga and Tintagel all in one trip? Wendy had vacationed there in April with her then-boyfriend Brian, but the trip had led to the demise of their romance, and she was eager to visit again with me—a fellow English major. It didn't matter that I'd taught only four years to her thirty. We were both avid readers and were wild about King Arthur.

Upstairs in the studio, Rhiannon waved to us. "Guess what? I spoke to Guin last night, and she's arranged a special session of chair yoga for Belle and Ellie. What do you think? Won't they be surprised?"

Wendy clapped her hands. "They'll love it. They're excited about visiting Tintagel, and I'm sure they never thought of taking a yoga class." Rhiannon and Guin met at the Iyengar Yoga Institute years ago and now put on annual yoga retreats together.

When Wendy and I saw the pictures of Knight's Rest with its yoga studio, cottages, and pool, we thought Belle, Wendy's mother, would enjoy accompanying us to spend time on the coast. Our next thought was that she'd enjoy it even more if our friend Ellie came along. We booked a cottage for the two to share and had visions of them alternating between touring the area and relaxing while we focused on yoga.

I smiled as I imagined Belle and Ellie's reactions. "I can't fathom how Guin can be so organized. I'm still surprised she's carrying on with the yoga retreat so soon after her loss. How's she holding up?"

Guin's younger brother Arthur had died at Tintagel in July. He was famous not only for his research and archaeological finds, but also for his books and entertaining lectures. How he'd found time to teach at Cardiff University, lead digs, write, and keep up a lecture schedule, I'd never know.

Rhiannon shook her head. "When you meet her, you'll understand. I've always imagined her and her brothers as a trio of Energizer Bunnies. She had a small yoga studio in the village of Tintagel, but when her parents died and left the family farm to her and her brothers, she threw herself into turning Knight's Rest into an intimate resort while her youngest brother Gareth developed the family's lavender farm. Between the two of them, they've built a thriving business. Staying busy plus her daily yoga practice is what keeps Guin centered."

"And Arthur?"

"He was the boy who always had his nose in a book. The way Guin tells it, there was never any doubt he'd go to university, but his passion for archaeology and Arthurian legend meant he spent plenty of time back home in Tintagel. He traveled the world, kept a flat in Cardiff as his home base, spent months on digs in the Middle East and England, and returned to Knight's Rest whenever he got the chance."

As more students arrived, Rhiannon broke off our conversation to greet them and explain that they'd need bolsters and blocks for today's class. Wendy and I gathered our props and sat cross-legged on our mats. The session focused on hip openers—perfect for me since I'd spent most of the previous day at my desk, legs crossed, writing. I felt refreshed and ready to tackle the day when class was over.

Tossing our mats in our cars, Wendy and I headed up the street to Toby's Tearoom, our usual destination after yoga. It was a gorgeous summer day in the Cotswolds, just right for sitting outside with a scone and a vanilla latte. The brightly colored umbrellas out front were set off by planters filled with white roses. Since Toby had hired Jenny as a barista the previous year, she'd proven to be a goldmine of ideas. She was forever surprising him with things like the white roses or colorful handmade holiday decorations, and it was a treat to see what would greet us as the seasons changed.

We grabbed a table, expecting Rhiannon would be right behind us. Fifteen minutes later, she appeared with an uncharacteristic scowl on her face. I glanced at Wendy. "I'm not sure I've ever seen Rhiannon frown—have you?"

"Nope. Wonder what's up."

When our friend brought her tea to the table, we asked and were surprised at the answer. She'd had a call from Gemma, our local Detective Inspector.

"I'm trying so hard to be patient with her," she said. "I know her schedule isn't her own and I've been flexible about her canceling on me at the last minute, but it's getting more and more difficult to plan around her."

I blinked in surprise. "What do you mean, 'canceling on you?' For yoga or what? Don't tell me Gemma's been taking yoga with you."

"Yes, she's been a private client for several months. I'm just out of sorts now because she's called to cancel her afternoon appointment for the second time this week. It wreaks havoc with my schedule."

Wendy posed the obvious question. "So, why are we just now hearing about this?"

Her question elicited a big sigh from Rhiannon. "For some reason, she wanted me to keep it to myself. I put it down to her keeping her professional and private lives separate or something like that. It wouldn't have been a big deal, except . . . except the cat will be out of the bag when you see her at Knight's Rest. That doesn't feel right to me, but my lips were sealed."

"Knight's Rest?" I exclaimed. "Gemma's going to the yoga retreat?"

My relationship with Gemma was difficult *and* difficult to describe. I was friends with her parents, Libby and Gavin, who owned the Olde Mill Inn, and Gemma lived in the guest cottage on the property. Mostly, we encountered each other at cocktail parties at the inn and at village events—until, that is, my unfortunate discovery of a dead body behind the cricket pavilion in Stanway. Unfortunate was putting it mildly, especially as I'd had several similar experiences since then, and each time, I'd somehow found myself involved in a murder investigation and at odds with Gemma.

Wendy looked from me to Rhiannon. "This should be interesting."

Despite the fact that Wendy and Belle were my partners in crime, so to speak, I was always the one who bore the brunt of Gemma's irritation. It was always me she chastised and ridiculed. We three had no experience in sleuthing and no business sticking our noses into police business, as Gemma was quick to remind us—and yet, that's exactly what we did.

Oh, we always had a good reason, and from time to time, Gemma appreciated our insights—even invited our input—but more often than not, she wanted us out of the way. She didn't hesitate to ask what I'd observed, and she grudgingly admitted that, for some reason, people shared information with me much more readily than they did with her. Wendy thought my work experience in conflict management made me a good listener, that people responded to that. Whatever it was, folks tended to confide in me.

I blew out my breath. "Well, as long as we don't stumble across a dead body, we should be fine."

Rhiannon looked aghast. "Heaven forbid. The questions about Arthur's death are already enough of a cloud over the retreat."

Tilting her head, Wendy studied Rhiannon. "Now, what does that mean? Questions?"

"I shouldn't have said anything in front of you two. Let's just say his fiancée has doubts about Arthur's death being an accident, though that's what the authorities have concluded. And, please, let's leave it at that."

Wendy and I took the hint and didn't push Rhiannon to elaborate, but that didn't mean we weren't curious.

# CHAPTER TWO

As I WALKED TO the Book Nook for our monthly book club meeting, Dave called from New York City. "Hey there. How's my brown-eyed girl?"

I never failed to smile when he described me with the title of my favorite Van Morrison song. Once upon a time, I could also be described as brown-haired, but as the gray strands increased, that was becoming a stretch.

I calculated the time as 1:15 in the afternoon in New York City and pictured him sitting at his desk in his Manhattan apartment. "Your girl is fine. Headed to the bookshop."

"I'm jealous. *The Once and Future King* has to be one of my all-time favorite books. There's something magical about it that's stuck with me, or maybe it's all the King Arthur movies I've seen. Let me guess—*First Knight* is your favorite, right?"

I laughed. "Now why would you think that? I have to admit I love *Camelot* for the music as much as the story, but Richard Harris doesn't hold a candle to Sean Connery in the sexy department. And when you add Richard Gere to the equation? Yup, *First Knight* is number one."

He knew me so well. It was nearly a year since I'd met Dave at a cocktail party at the Olde Mill Inn. A recent widow, I wasn't ready to date, much less to fall in love, but that's what happened. It wasn't love at first sight, though our common interests meant we hit it off pretty quickly. Dave was visiting the Cotswolds in search of material for an Arthur Conan Doyle article he was writing. I still marveled at how our long-distance relationship had blossomed, and I blushed every time I referred to him as my boyfriend.

He chuckled. "That's tough competition for a guy. I'll just have to believe you love me for my brains."

He was right *and* wrong. He was an accomplished writer who'd won accolades for his articles in the *Strand* and *The New York Book Review*, and he was busy writing a book titled *Barrie and Friends* about the author of *Peter Pan*. Our mutual love of reading and writing was a large part of the attraction, and though I wasn't in his league as a writer, he was always gracious about the columns I wrote for small local papers in the States.

"Don't sell yourself short. Sure, you can be a bit of a brainiac, but I'd say you qualify in the tall, dark, and handsome category too." Just saying that made me stop midstride and picture him in his tux. *Takes a girl's breath away*.

"Aw, Tuppence, you do know the way to a man's heart."

He'd called me that ever since we'd dressed as Agatha Christie's sleuthing couple Tommy and Tuppence for a costume party. My subsequent escapades with Wendy and Belle ensured the name stuck. And after our adventure during the Chipping Camden Literary Festival in April, Dave had earned his stripes as Tommy.

Our easy banter made our daily calls a joy. Neither of us took it amiss when the other one was too busy for a long chat or had to cut a call short. "Yes, Tommy, I try. Now, I'm opening the door to the Book Nook, so I've got to say goodbye. I'll call you tonight. Love you."

After I chatted with Beatrix, the proprietor of the shop, and admired the displays on the counter and in the window, I was still early enough to snag three seats together. The bookshop cats, also named Tommy and Tuppence, were stretched out in the window as though studying the books and posters.

Wendy arrived soon after I did and spoke with a few friends before joining me. She leaned over and whispered, "Are you packed and ready for our trip?"

"Yes. I can't wait. I was already excited, but tonight's discussion of *The Once and Future King* is the perfect send-off."

As we chatted with other book club members, we sipped wine and eyed the snacks Beatrix had set out. Wendy and I were forever watching our weight, and the thought of soon wearing swimsuits at a coastal resort put paid to any thoughts of sampling the cheese and crackers. We noticed Gavin had no such qualms. He filled plates for himself and our friend Ellie and joined her in the row behind us.

Just as Beatrix strode to the front of the room to open the meeting, Rhiannon slid into the third seat we'd saved. "Phew," she exclaimed, "Made it."

It was Wendy's turn to lead the talk on our monthly book club selection. When Beatrix introduced her as our eminently qualified speaker, Wendy leaped up holding a copy of the book. Beatrix's description was apt, as she had not only taught high school English but had also offered a summer class on Arthurian legend at a junior college before returning to Astonbury.

"Let's see a show of hands. Who believes King Arthur existed?" All but a few participants raised their hands, and the rest followed suit when Wendy amended her question to, "Okay, who *wants* to believe?" That got a laugh as more hands shot up.

What ensued was a lively discussion mixing elements of King Arthur movies with the books we'd read. Many of us had seen Disney's *The Sword in the Stone* and the musical *Camelot* at the movies as children. *Says something about the average age of this group.*

Not many had read T.H. White's *The Once and Future King* until now. Somehow, I'd picked up that White had derived his version of the tale from Malory's *Morte d'Arthur*, which I'd read in college, but I didn't know his interpretation was influenced by his perspective on World War II.

Most of the group had read Mary Stewart's *The Crystal Cave* and what had been billed as the feminist version of the tale, *The Mists of Avalon*.

Gavin Taylor, our lone male participant, stroked his goatee and chuckled. "I feel like an outsider tonight. I vaguely remember Libby being glued to the telly for *Mists of Avalon*, but that's about it. And I've never heard of Mary Stewart."

Pointing at him, Wendy said, "But I bet you can tell us who starred in *Camelot*, right?"

"Of course I can—Richard Harris and Vanessa Redgrave. Can't recall the fellow who played Lancelot, though."

Cries of "Franco Nero" erupted with comments about how sexy he was.

"Of course, this tidbit has nothing to do with the book," Wendy elaborated, "but did you know he and Vanessa Redgrave fell in love during the filming of *Camelot* and later had a son together? And, of course now, after other relationships through the years, they're married?"

Behind me, Ellie cleared her throat. "But back to T. H. White . . . "

How appropriate for the dowager countess to put us back on track. Knowing Ellie, I suspected she had a signed first edition of White's book tucked away in her library at Astonbury Manor.

I realized I'd been only half-listening to Wendy as I anticipated our trip. I tuned back in as she said "Close your eyes. When you saw that 'Candle in the Wind' was the title for the last section of White's book, what came to mind?"

Several participants spoke at once. "Princess Diana and Elton John's song."

Gavin raised his hand. "That's what I thought too, but then as I reflected on the rise and fall of Camelot, I saw it was a fitting description for the brief span of Arthur's reign. And just think, that has to be why Americans liken John F. Kennedy's abbreviated term as President to Camelot, right?"

Humming the tune from the movie, I laughed. "I can't help myself. The song keeps running through my mind. Wasn't it Jackie Kennedy who first connected the two not long after JFK died?"

Ellie chuckled. "Yes, it was. I've heard it described as a calculated move on her part to preserve the memory of her husband. She emphasized in an interview that JFK enjoyed listening to the cast album, especially the last line of the title song—where Arthur asks us to remember Camelot as a fleeting moment in time when things were nearly perfect. She was one smart woman."

Wendy threw up her hands. "You stole my thunder, Ellie. I didn't think anyone would know it was Jackie who planted that image in our minds. When the movie came out several years later, JFK's legacy was forever linked to Camelot." Grinning, she pointed to Beatrix. "I'm getting the signal it's time to wrap up for the evening. Don't forget to check out the selection of King Arthur books Beatrix has for us."

We moved en masse to the display table filled with novels and scholarly works about the legend of King Arthur. Rhiannon picked up *Finding Camlan* and handed it to me.

"This book makes me think of Guin's brother. The main character is an archaeologist who's spent his career searching for traces of King Arthur. It's a mystery and a romance rolled into one."

Flipping through the pages of *Finding Camlan*, I smiled. "I suppose as an Arthurian scholar, Guin's brother had an affinity for Tintagel. Did he work on any excavations there?"

Rhiannon rolled her eyes. "The most recent one in the 21st century? Yes. In fact, he led it, and it was quite a feather in his cap. I recall him saying he wished he could travel back in time to the initial excavation of the 1930s, and he all but cried when he spoke of the site reports being destroyed by a Luftwaffe bombing raid on the archaeologist's house during the war. Still, Arthur's findings of remnants of fifth- and sixth-century buildings and fragments of wine and food containers from Northern Africa and Gaul far surpassed what anyone could have envisioned."

"I imagine his family is quite proud of him. Do they share his passion for all things King Arthur?"

My friend hesitated. "It's a bit of a family thing. Their parents named all three children after characters in the legend. Arthur was first, then Guin or Guinevere, and finally Gareth."

"Okay, Guin and Arthur are obvious, and I recall Gareth was a knight of the round table."

Rhiannon laughed. "If you want to impress Guin, mention that Gareth was Arthur's nephew and was accidentally killed by Lancelot when he came to rescue Guinevere from being burned at the stake. By the time this trip is over, you may hear more than you ever wanted to know about the legend and the ruins of

Tintagel. Guin's invited a guest speaker on the topic for Saturday night."

"I can't imagine I'd ever get tired of learning about Arthurian legend. I assumed there wouldn't be a lecture when I heard Guin's brother had died. Wasn't he on the program as the speaker?"

"Yes, it would have been Arthur, but Guin was able to get Dylan Porter to replace him. He and Arthur taught together at Cardiff University and Dylan took the reins at the Tintagel dig when Arthur started spending more time in London organizing the Arthurian Exhibit at the British Museum."

Just then, I saw Gemma walk in the door. She waved and went to the front counter, where Beatrix handed her a package. Our local Detective Inspector seemed to be in good spirits.

I was surprised when she came over and draped an arm over Rhiannon's back. Gemma wasn't a hugger, and this was as close as I'd seen her come.

"Rhiannon," she said, "I apologize again for missing our sessions this week, but gaining those several hours in my schedule allowed me to wrap up the loose ends on a big case. Now, I can go on this trip without anything hanging over my head."

Observing their interaction, I was struck by the difference in their demeanors. Both were slender blondes, but Rhiannon, tall and lithe with wavy shoulder-length blonde hair, was the epitome of grace and calm. I saw her as a tall version of the Fleetwood Mac singer Stevie Nicks.

Gemma was more athletic and wore her blonde hair in a ponytail. Energetic and wound tight were words that came to mind. Come to think of it, even in social settings, she never quite seemed to relax. *I suppose they're both well-suited for their chosen professions.*

"Gosh, Gemma," I said, "I don't think you've been on vacation since I moved here last year. You went on that leadership training course in December, but that's hardly a vacation."

"You're right. I can't tell you how much I'm looking forward to a week in Cornwall. Since I moved back from Oxford, I haven't had more than a long weekend off, and I've learned I have to be hours away so I'm not called back at the drop of a hat. This will be a real treat."

"Are you a King Arthur fan too, or are you going more for the yoga?"

"I've seen *Camelot*, of course, but I can take or leave anything beyond that. And goodness knows, there was no way I was going to get through *The Once & Future King* at over 600 pages." She held up the package she'd picked up at the counter. "That's why I asked Beatrix to order the audiobook, though it's thirty-three hours long. I thought I'd start on the drive down and then lie by the pool with it. That's my plan—lie by the pool, take two classes a day, and stroll around the lavender farm. Sounds like heaven to me."

"To me too, except I'm eager to get beyond the book and soak up all things King Arthur. Wendy and I plan to take a guided tour of the ruins, and I'm looking forward to the lecture Saturday."

"The guided tour might be fun. It'd be great exercise anyway. Maybe I'll tag along. If Rhiannon's friend Guin doesn't expect too much from me in regards to her brother's death, I'd enjoy that."

Wendy walked up in time to hear the last line. "What about his death?"

Gemma muttered, "I shouldn't have let that slip."

"But you did," I said. "So, what's up?"

Rolling her eyes, Gemma explained, "She and her other brother were about ready to accept it was an accident until Arthur's fiancée expressed some doubts. She'll be at the yoga retreat, and, realizing I was a DI, Guin asked if I'd take some time to hear the girl's concerns. I have to be careful so I don't step on any toes down there. It's not my place to get involved."

Wendy looked at me. "Did you hear that, Tuppence? Sounds as though the fiancée needs a good listener, someone to help her work through what's bothering her."

"Not on your life, Wendy. We don't even know these people."

"Uh-huh. Who did you know in Chipping Camden when you and Mum and Ellie got involved?"

Gemma groaned. "Oh, bother. Don't you two even think about going all Agatha Christie on me."

*For once, Gemma and I are on the same page.*

# CHAPTER THREE

WHEN I OPENED THE door Saturday morning to let Dickens out, Watson greeted me with a meow and a stretch. The handsome tabby was a recent addition to Astonbury Manor and visited Christie several times a week.

Christie glanced up from her puddle of milk. "I looked for you last night when Leta came home. Where were you?"

Watson wrapped himself around my legs before butting his head against Christie's. "I came by, but all the lights were out. Anyway, I'm here now."

Watson was a wanderer. He briefly resided at the Olde Mill Inn when Gemma brought him home from a crime scene, but he kept making his way to the manor house. We were all convinced he was attracted by the chef's homemade animal treats. Whatever the reason, he'd taken up residence there. I thought perhaps he preferred Astonbury Manor because he didn't have to compete with Paddington, who'd long been top cat at the inn.

My flirt of a cat reached out a paw and patted him on the nose. "A good thing too. We leave for Cornwall today. Will you miss me?"

Watson licked her between her eyes and then lapped up the rest of the milk. I took that as some sort of answer.

Taking my coffee mug, I joined Dickens in the garden. I stood by the goat willow tree and stone marker Ellie had given me in the spring. The engraving on the bronze plaque affixed to the golden stone read, "In Memory of Henry Parker."

We were riding bicycles on a sunny April day in Atlanta when my husband was struck down by a speeding car. Determined to carry on, I resumed my career and, if anything, worked longer and harder than I had before. That approach did little to fill the hole in my heart. While I was focused on work, I could forget about what had happened, but grief never failed to find its way into the precious little downtime I had.

Henry used to complain that I wasn't spontaneous, that I took planning to unbelievable extremes, so he would have been as surprised as I was when I decided to take early retirement and move to England. We'd visited the Cotswolds on vacation and toyed with the idea of retiring here. In my heart, though, I knew Henry never would have done it. Rent a villa in France or cottage in the UK for a month, maybe, but move overseas? Never. For me, it was a dream come true.

"Henry," I said softly. "Dickens and Christie and I are going to Cornwall. Can you believe it? You and I loved exploring Tintagel, and I'm looking forward to doing it again. They have a new walkway, for which I'm sure short people everywhere are giving thanks." No doubt it was exaggerated in my memory, but a few of the steps carved into the cliff had seemed thigh-high and been a challenge for my short legs.

Dickens nudged my calf and barked. "Leta, Henry's not here. Who are you talking to?"

With my free hand, I rubbed his head. "No, he's not, but I think maybe he hears me."

My white dog cocked his head as though he wasn't quite sure. I knelt in the cool grass and rubbed his belly when he rolled over. Just like the Great Pyrenees I'd had before him, Dickens was a fiend for belly rubs. Despite his diminutive size, my dwarf Pyr had all the traits of the full-size members of his breed. He was good-natured and gentle, born to protect . . . and to bark. With Dickens around, I was safe from walkers, cyclists, and falling leaves.

We both stood and returned to the kitchen, where I shooed Watson on his way, over Christie's protests. "Christie, you and I need to have one last discussion about this yoga thing before we leave."

"What's to discuss? I meow and purr and look pretty, and I crawl on people and maybe knead one or two if I especially like them."

I knelt and touched her chin. "Look at me. That's all well and good, but there's one more thing. Remember?"

She ducked her head. "You mean that thing about not wandering off? I can explore the courtyard and the cottages, but that's it?"

"Exactly. Even if the Knight's Rest cat takes off and wanders the whole farm, you are not to go with him. I have your word, right?"

Dickens added his two cents. "I'll keep an eye on her, Leta. Besides, why would she want to go anywhere without us? We're her family."

I wasn't sure, but I thought Christie may have rolled her eyes. *Can cats do that?*

She stood on her hind legs and patted my face with her paw. "Dickens is right, Leta. I'd never leave you. You belong to me."

"Aww, that's sweet! Now, let's get a move on."

In short order, I showered and threw a few last-minute items in my suitcase, including my copy of Jill Paton Walsh's *A Presumption of Death*. Dickens pranced impatiently while I placed Christie's backpack on the floor of the mudroom so she could crawl in. She adored her backpack and poked her head from the top as I fastened the seatbelt through the straps. Dickens had a special harness in the seat next to her. "All ready?" I said as I backed out of the driveway.

Wendy was waiting outside when we pulled up to Sunshine Cottage, the home she shared with her mother. "I can't believe how excited I am. You and I haven't been on an honest-to-goodness girls trip since you moved here. You can't count that overnight to Oxford nor the trip to Dartmouth last year. The Oxford weekend was cut short, and most of our time in Dartmouth was devoted to detective work. This trip to the coast is for pure pleasure."

"You're right, and I do love a good girls' trip. In the States, I traveled all the time with my girlfriends, much to Henry's chagrin. Pre-Henry, a few of us even took weeklong bicycle vacations in different parts of the country. After that, Henry and I went on cycling trips in Europe. It would take some doing for me to manage a whole week of cycling nowadays, though."

Wendy looked aghast. "Don't even think of getting me on a bicycle, but I bet you could get Peter to go. He's been intrigued by your descriptions of cycling in France and Greece."

It was Wendy's twin, Peter, who'd gotten me back on my bicycle after Henry's accident. I'd shipped it over from the States but hadn't worked up the courage to take it for a spin until Peter had it tuned up for me. Now, he and I cycled twenty miles or so most Sundays. My improvement on my bike mirrored my grieving process—some days were more difficult than others, but I was steadily gaining strength.

Loading Wendy's suitcase and yoga mat into my car, I laughed. "No worries. A few days of yoga, time exploring Tintagel, maybe a day trip down to Penzance—this week at the coast is all I need. Now, is your mum all set? She and Ellie aren't departing until lunchtime, right?"

The Astonbury contingent would arrive in piecemeal fashion. My refurbished London taxi was full to the brim with two four-legged passengers plus Wendy, so Ellie and Belle were traveling in Ellie's Jag. Eager to arrive in time for the optional late-afternoon class, Wendy and I wanted to get on the road early. Rhiannon had gone down Friday to help her friend Guin prepare for the retreat, and I didn't know Gemma's plans.

With the radio tuned to the Beatles station, Wendy and I commented on our favorite songs and how we enjoyed them as much or more than we had in the sixties. I recalled how thrilled I was when an older cousin gave me three Beatles albums for Christmas one year. I could still recite the titles—*Introducing the Beatles, Something New,* and *Beatles '65*—and Wendy couldn't believe I didn't own any more until my parents gave me The White Album as a birthday gift.

Laughing, I explained how the Beatles were a line of demarcation between Henry's musical taste and mine. "I'll grant you he was older than I was, but for some reason, the British invasion didn't do a thing for him. And you know Don McLean's song 'American Pie?' I joked that Henry *really did* believe the music died when Buddy Holly did, and the group he couldn't get enough of was the Kingston Trio. That's why the two times I saw Paul McCartney, it was with girlfriends, not Henry."

Four hours later, we turned into the long gravel drive leading to Knight's Rest. The white wooden sign was emblazoned with the red Knight's Rest logo—a knight on horseback with his shield and lance. Fields of lavender greeted us as we wound our way toward the stone buildings in the distance. Below us, I caught a glimpse of a pool sparkling in the sunlight, surrounded by a semicircle of small cottages. A barn stood off to the side flanked by sunflowers nodding in the stiff breeze. Beyond the postcard scene, I spied what looked to be a large family home and a smaller barn. Farther down the cliff, I could see more lavender fields and another cottage, this one midsize, and what I thought might be a small garden shed. A sign pointing toward the barn said "Registration."

Wendy and I exclaimed over the setting, and Dickens stirred and stood up. His bark woke his snoozing sister, who craned her neck out of the top of the backpack. Both seemed entranced by the change in scenery.

I beamed at Wendy. "Oh my. This is even better than the photos. I wonder which cottage is ours."

As I pulled up to the barn, a willowy grey-haired woman in yoga attire opened the door. She was followed by a youth in shorts and a white t-shirt with the red logo.

"Greetings. I'm Guin, and this is my nephew Art. Once we get you checked in, he'll help you with your luggage."

We introduced ourselves, popped the trunk, and unlatched our four-legged companions. "Guin," I said, pointing to Christie in her backpack, "meet your newest employee. She's ready to be a yoga cat. Dickens, on the other hand, is here to make new friends and get plenty of belly rubs."

While Guin rubbed Christie's nose, Art embraced Dickens. "What a great dog. I'd say he's a Great Pyrenees, except he's so small."

Dickens licked Art's face and barked. "Hey, don't start with the small comments. I'm plenty big."

My boy was a tad sensitive about his size, but would soon get over it if Art paid him enough attention. I grabbed Christie in the backpack and followed Guin inside while Art intermittently played with Dickens and unloaded the luggage.

The rustic outward appearance of the barn gave way to an updated interior with the look of a lodge. With its two-story vaulted ceiling, the reception area was open and inviting. It was finished in a mix of stone and dark wood, and the registration desk sat beneath a loft bordered by a wooden railing. I imagined the area had once held bales of hay, but now the narrow walkway fronted two doors. One was labeled *Office* and the other *Conference Room*.

Behind the desk stood a young blue-eyed girl with almost white-blonde hair. She smiled as we entered. "Welcome to Knight's Rest. I'm Elaine."

Guin explained this was her niece, Art's sister. Elaine turned to the old-timey cubbies on the wall behind the desk and pulled two keys from the one labeled *Iseult Cottage*. Handing us the keys and a folder containing a list of the cottages with their assigned guests and a schedule for the afternoon and evening, she wished us a pleasant stay.

As I perused the schedule, Guin elaborated. "Rhiannon tells me you two are avid readers and King Arthur fans, so I think you'll especially enjoy tonight's lecture. Dylan is a professor at Cardiff University and is overseeing the dig here at Tintagel." She tickled Christie's chin. "Do you think Christie will be interested?"

"Pfft," Christie meowed. "I'm interested in food, naps, and laps to climb in. If that means I have to listen to someone speaking in the background, so be it."

Laughing at Christie's loud meows, Guin suggested we stop by the yoga studio to meet Archie before we settled into Iseult cottage. Wendy remained behind, oohing and aaahing over the books displayed on the shelves in the reception area, as I followed Guin down the hall. We passed a dining room, a snack area with a fridge and bowls of fruit, and two restrooms before stopping at an open door. Inside, we found Rhiannon in the Viparita Karani pose—legs up the wall—with a large grey cat by her side.

Christie had lots to say. "So, this is the other yoga cat? He's sitting in his Buddha pose, isn't he? What do you think, Leta?"

Archie looked our way. "Shhh. Don't mention Buddha. Guin already has me on a diet."

*Reminds me of how carefully I watch Dickens's intake.* I placed my backpack on the floor and unfastened Christie's leash. "Christie, mind your manners. This is Archie."

Creeping out, she paused, stretched, and approached Rhiannon. Archie studied the princess as she pawed the wavy blonde hair spread like a halo around my friend's head. When Christie deigned to give him a head bump, the grey cat purred.

Guin smiled at me. "Looks as though all's well with the cat yoga staff."

Without moving a muscle, Rhiannon said, "I never had any doubts. They're both pretty sociable."

*Yes, but Christie's also pretty darned snooty.*

I found Wendy outside, where Art and Dickens stopped playing ball long enough to drive us via golf cart to our cottage and place the luggage in our rooms. A young woman emerged from Vivienne Cottage next to ours as we stood in the doorway taking in the view. Funny how I so readily classified people I thought to be in their thirties as young. When did that happen, I wondered? Whatever her age, she was a slender curvy brunette attired in a lavender flowered sundress. Her hair was piled on top of her head in a loose bun.

She approached with her hand outstretched. "Hi. I'm Caryn Darby, and you must be Wendy and Leta. You look exactly as Rhiannon described you. Plus the cat and dog are dead give-aways."

We exchanged greetings and learned that she lived in London and worked at the British Museum. She'd come down on the Night Riviera Sleeper earlier in the week and been picked up at the station in Truro.

When Wendy asked whether she'd visited before, Caryn hesi-tated. "Um, yes."

"How did you find the classes?" I asked. "Wendy and I take two classes a week in Astonbury, but we're not good about home practice. I hope we'll be able to keep up."

She took a deep breath. "I take classes near the museum in London, but actually, I haven't taken yoga here. I'm, I mean, I was . . . engaged to Guin's brother Arthur, and I've visited a few times."

*Way to step in it, Leta.* Both Wendy and I murmured con-dolences before Caryn moved off toward the barn. Inside, we plopped into the two comfortable chairs and wondered aloud what Caryn's concerns might be about her fiancé's death.

"Seems to me it would be painful to come here so soon after the accident," I said.

Wendy nodded. "I wonder if she already planned to be here or she made a special trip. If Guin and her brother—Gareth, isn't it? If they've accepted Arthur's death as accidental, maybe Caryn just needs to talk it through. Could be she's working through SARA."

*S-shock, A-anger, R-rejection, A-acceptance.* SARA stood for the stages of grief, something I'd personally experienced. "Possibly. Maybe she's accepted his death but can't come to terms with the how. It would be interesting to know details about the accident. Did he fall from the ruins? Was he at Merlin's Cave for some reason and got caught in the pull of the tide? The one newspaper article I read didn't explain any of that."

*Typical. No wonder Gemma called me a Nosey Parker. Already, I want to know more. And Wendy is right there with me.*

# CHAPTER FOUR

ATTIRED IN NEW YOGA duds purchased for the retreat, Wendy and I exited our cottage. Christie was on my back, and I planned to leave Dickens inside, but he darted out the door and ran to the pool where Art was straightening chairs.

"Dickens, dang it, come back here."

Art called to me as Dickens pranced around him. "If it's okay with you, he can stay with me. The last guests have just arrived, and after I put their luggage in their cottage, I'll take him to meet my dog Merlin. He's in the lavender fields with my dad."

Dickens jumped up and gave a joyous bark. "A new friend! Say yes, Leta, say yes."

If Rhiannon thought Christie was sociable, I wonder how she'd describe Dickens. He never met a stranger and thought all the dogs in the world—and people too, for that matter—were waiting to be his friends. My boy was the poster boy—or dog—for the William Butler Yeats quote, "There are no strangers here; only friends you haven't yet met."

"Thank you, Art. As you can tell, Dickens thinks that's a grand idea. Just send him back when you've tired of him."

Belle and Ellie were checking in when Wendy and I entered the barn. They'd enjoyed their leisurely drive from Astonbury and were ready to put their feet up by the pool and relax until dinner.

Christie meowed hello and extended a paw toward Belle, who tapped her playfully on the nose. "You sure are talkative, little girl. Are you nervous about your star turn?"

Swatting at Belle's finger, Christie meowed, "Me, nervous? Surely you jest. I'm ready to meet all the yogis."

Belle, of course, had no idea Christie had answered her. She laughed as Christie continued to meow and crane her neck to see over my shoulder.

Assuring our friends we'd see them for dinner, we moved down the hall. I rubbed my lower back and hoped the ache caused by the four-hour drive would soon be gone.

Rhiannon directed us to pick up bolsters and blankets in preparation for the restorative class that would soon start. As Guin greeted students from the front of the room, I spied Gemma already set up. When we were all present, Guin and Rhiannon welcomed everyone and introduced themselves. They asked us to follow suit by sharing our names and where we hailed from. When it was my turn, I introduced Christie too.

Guin wrapped up by explaining the role of the cats. "Who's taken cat yoga before, or maybe goat yoga?" As half the class raised their hands, she continued. "We think you're in for a treat because we have two special guests with us. This grey boy is Archie. Expect him and his new friend Christie to wander over and under you, purr in your ears or beneath your chin, walk across your backs, or whatever strikes their fancy. We make no demands of them. We ask only that they share their calming influence with us. Perhaps they'll visit each of you, but you never know. They may pay special attention to only one or two of you."

As if on cue, Christie approached Archie, who sat near Guin in the front of the room. The two circled each other in what appeared to be a choreographed dance until Christie turned her nose up and moved to Gemma's mat. Quiet laughter and murmurs erupted at their antics. For a moment, Archie surveyed the room before meandering over to crouch beside the woman from Cardiff, who'd introduced herself as Morgan. We had nine students and two instructors, and I hoped our feline partners would spend time with each of us over the next few days.

We began with the comfortable cross-legged seated position, Sukhasana, breathing deeply and striving to clear our minds. The beauty of a restorative class is moving through only five to six poses and holding them for a longer time than you do the poses in a typical class. Guin led the class, and she and Rhiannon together helped us stretch and relax into the various positions.

As we moved into the legs-up-the-wall position we'd found Rhiannon in earlier, I saw Christie follow Caryn to the wall and nudge her hand. Caryn smiled as she scratched Christie's head and was rewarded by Christie stretching out lengthwise along her side.

The next position, the reclining Bound Angle Pose with a bolster beneath my back and blankets beneath my knees, was one of my favorites. I noted Christie was still with Caryn and had her sleek black head resting on Caryn's feet as though to keep them warm.

By the time class ended at four, I was in heaven. My tight shoulders had relaxed and the ache in my lower back had disappeared. Guin reminded us that dinner would be served promptly at seven, followed by a lecture on Arthurian legend at eight.

Wendy and I agreed that time in the sunshine by the pool and leisurely showers were next on the agenda.

I waited for Christie to follow me, as she'd stayed by Caryn as she rolled up her mat. "Leta, I think she needs a friend."

When I picked the princess up, Caryn turned and smiled. "She's a sweetheart, Leta. I'm glad you brought her."

"If this keeps up, Caryn, you may find her at your door tomorrow looking for her morning milk, but if not, we'll see you in class."

*I should tell Caryn about Henry's accident. Perhaps my opening up to her could pave the way for her to work through her feelings.*

There was no sign of Dickens when Wendy and I exited our cottage at 6:30 in anticipation of a glass of wine before dinner. Instead, we found Archie curled up in the chair outside the door.

Chuckling, Wendy knelt to scratch between his ears. "Have you come to visit Christie?"

In response, Archie pushed past her and darted to the kitchen, where Christie was daintily dipping her paw in the water bowl. The two cats meowed greetings and rolled on the floor before Christie led the way to the couch.

I glanced at Wendy. "I wonder if she's thinking of two-timing Watson."

We wove a tale of feline romance as we strolled to the barn. Belle and Ellie were in the dining room and got a kick from our description of the cat encounter. Though she was smiling, Belle leaned heavily on her cane and moved a bit more gingerly than usual as she settled into a chair.

Gemma appeared with two glasses of wine and handed one to Belle. "There you go, that should help."

Belle must have picked up on my questioning look. "Leta, don't look so worried. It's just my arthritis acting up. I'll soon be distracted by dinner and tonight's speaker, I'm sure."

Leaning in, Wendy hugged her. "Mum, I can always count on you for a positive outlook. Tell me, how do you like Knight's Rest? Is it everything you wanted it to be?"

Belle's blue eyes twinkled. "Yes, dear, starting with the name of our little bungalow. How can you not be enchanted with a stay at Igraine cottage? Ellie and I are wondering what we'll do when Uther Pendragon knocks on our door tonight."

My wine went down the wrong way at that comment. I had a vision of Uther wrapped in a dark cape trying to explain to two little old ladies that he was lost and looking for his lady love.

Wendy must have been thinking along the same lines. "I always thought you had to have a willing suspension of disbelief to imagine that Igraine mistook Uther for her husband when he snuck into her bedchamber that night. Seriously? No matter what magic Merlin wove, she never twigged to the fact it was another man in her bed? No matter, their night of illicit passion resulted in Arthur's birth."

Sipping her wine, Gemma laughed. "I tell you what. If a tall, dark handsome knight knocks on your door, please direct him to Guinevere Cottage."

I looked up to see Rhiannon approaching us with a lanky blonde man who bore a striking resemblance to Guin. *He could be a tall, blonde, handsome knight.*

"Let me introduce you to Gareth, Guin's brother. He's the driving force behind the lavender farm."

Ellie commented on his namesake's place at Camelot's round table before we embarked on a discussion of the lavender business. He seemed equally at home chatting about King Arthur and lavender crops.

At dinner, the Astonbury contingent split up to socialize with the other participants. Belle and Ellie shared a table with two sisters from Dartmouth—Penny and Sue. Wendy found herself at a table with the after-dinner speaker, Dylan Porter, his wife Morgan, and Gareth Knight. We'd seen Morgan in yoga class and commented on her porcelain complexion and strawberry-blonde hair but hadn't picked up on her relationship with our speaker. Gemma and I sat with Guin, and Rhiannon shared a table with Caryn and a mother and daughter from Boscastle.

Gemma and I complimented Guin on the restorative class and explained that we both felt much less tense as a result. Our host laughed as I relayed Belle and Ellie's comments about Igraine Cottage and the likelihood of Uther showing up and Gemma's offer to entertain him if he did.

Chuckling, Guin tilted her head. "Gemma, does that mean there's no romantic partner in your life?"

"Not at the moment and not for quite a while. There was when I worked in Oxford, but not since I moved to Astonbury."

That was news to me. *I wonder which came first, the end of the relationship or the move home.*

We chatted about the "dreaming spires of Oxford" before Guin turned to me. "Now, Leta, tell me more about you and Dickens and Christie. With that accent, you can't have been in the UK for long."

"You're right. I've been here around eighteen months, and Dickens and Christie joined me last September." I shared the story of Henry's accident and how I'd made the sudden decision to retire early and relocate to the Cotswolds. "I had friends who thought I was crazy to do it, but it was the right move for me. I haven't had a single regret."

Gemma smiled. "Your timing was perfect. Schoolhouse Cottage came on the market just as you started househunting, and it may be the most charming cottage in Astonbury."

I had to agree with her. "I love my cottage, perfect in so many ways for a word nerd and former English teacher. It's easy to imagine schoolchildren seated at their desks in the two large rooms downstairs. And when my neighbor's son comes by to ring the bell, I can see them lining up to come in the door."

As dessert was served, Guin leaned in to speak softly. "Gemma, I know I asked you to speak with Caryn, but Leta, I think it would also do her a world of good to speak with you. I can tell she's having difficulty seeing how she'll go on without Arthur, and hearing how you've built a new life could help with that."

She elaborated after we both assured her we'd be happy to help. "Gemma, as a detective inspector, I hope you can help her process what we know about Arthur's accident and come closer to accepting we'll never know every piece of the puzzle."

Turning to me, she went on. "That's one step, but she also needs to work through her grief. I tried to get her to see a counselor in London, but she resisted. She needs someone to talk with. I hope I'm not putting you on the spot, Leta."

I was surprised when Gemma responded. "Guin, Leta's the right person. She's a gifted listener. I'm not sure why, but people tend to share their deepest thoughts with her. I think maybe they sense she genuinely cares about what they have to say. I agree. She'll do Caryn a world of good."

*Will wonders never cease? She just paid me a compliment.*

Elaine and Art cleared the tables as Guin invited her guests to take a short break, grab another glass of wine, and settle in for the evening's presentation. She suggested we switch tables too so we could mix and mingle. Gareth led the way to the front of the room, followed by two men carrying a large model. They placed it on a round table to the left of the podium. To my surprise, Dickens wandered in behind them.

"Dickens, you decided to return?" I called.

Gareth looked up. "I wondered who he belonged to. He's been with my son and his dog all afternoon. Even shared Merlin's dinner."

"Why doesn't that surprise me? My boy never misses an opportunity for a meal, do you, Dickens?"

He barked. "Wait until I tell you where I've been. I had fun."

It seemed all my companions were enjoying them-selves—both the two-legged and the four-legged. When I moved to a new table near the front, Caryn joined me and Dickens squirmed in between us. With a chuckle, she knelt to rub his belly as Belle sat down.

"Belle, have you met Caryn? I'm going to have to keep an eye on her. Christie's taken a liking to her, and if she rubs Dickens's belly much longer, they may both go home with her."

Belle told Caryn she had first dibs on my animals, and they chuckled over how easygoing my cat and dog were. *Easygoing? Dickens maybe, but Christie? Little do they know.*

As Dylan Porter moved to the podium, the men who'd come in with Gareth approached our table. The shorter of the two motioned to the chairs next to Belle. "Hi, I'm Martin Pascoe and this is Colin Carmody. May we join you ladies?"

Belle and I murmured "of course" and introduced ourselves. Caryn nodded but remained silent, making me think she already knew them. Martin had greying curly hair and weathered skin, and I pictured him as someone who worked on the water, perhaps a fisherman in this coastal village. He had a compact wiry build and was the first man I'd seen today who was under six feet tall. His younger companion was on the tall side, as were Dylan, Gareth, and Art.

Colin sat a camera on the table and explained he was the unofficial photographer for the dig. With his freckles and shaggy blonde hair, he reminded me of a thirty-something version of Opie from *The Andy Griffith Show*.

"And how does one come by an interesting job like that?" I asked.

"The short version is I worked at a photography studio in London and decided to take a sabbatical. I envisioned being a travel photographer, but that didn't quite pan out. When I camped here for a few weeks and peddled a few of my shots to tourists, Martin noticed, and before I knew it, I had a job of sorts."

When Belle asked Martin about his role, he elaborated. "Around here, it pays to be a jack-of-all-trades. Scholars like Dylan direct the dig and study the findings. The student volunteers play in the dirt. I've worked with the volunteers in the past, but nowadays I conduct tours, and I manage the warehouse where we catalog and store the artifacts."

Colin added, "When he says jack-of-all-trades, he means it. I take pictures and produce postcards, but I also work at the warehouse and occasionally get roped into answering the phone at the tour office."

Our conversation broke off as Guin introduced Dylan Porter. He began his presentation by paying tribute to Arthur Knight. "I'd much prefer to be here tonight listening to Arthur give this talk. He was my friend and colleague for over twenty years, and I find it difficult to imagine a world without him. He was inspirational and indispensable to archaeology and the study of Arthurian legend. I have big shoes to fill tonight." His eyes glistened when he lifted his glass. "To you, Arthur. We miss you."

Guin and Gareth were seated together at a nearby table and seemed moved by Dylan's words. I glanced at Caryn. She sat stone-faced, her eyes wet with unshed tears, her hands clenched on top of the table.

Despite his caveat about big shoes, Dylan was an engaging speaker. To me, he looked the part of an archaeologist. With his toned, tanned biceps showing beneath the short sleeves of his khaki shirt, I could imagine him squatting at a dig, brush in hand, delicately cleaning a pottery shard. His ginger beard and unruly mop of ginger hair completed the picture.

He began by assuring us that the Dark Ages weren't dark atop Tintagel. The discovery of 5th and 6th-century walls revealed the presence of a large dwelling surrounded by smaller buildings. The inhabitants lived the high life, as evidenced by signs they feasted on pork, fish, and oysters served on fine tableware from as far away as Turkey. They drank from Spanish glassware, and they imported olive oil in amphorae from southern Turkey or Cyprus. Historians had now dubbed the era Cornwall's First Golden Age.

He shared fascinating details of fragments they'd uncovered—not only pottery, but also pig, cow, and sheep bones. "Everything we've found suggests that the Tintagel clifftop was part of a major post-Roman settlement and very likely a royal site with trading links extending from the Celtic Sea to the eastern

Mediterranean. As for who lived there, I'd love to tell you it was without a doubt King Arthur's mother, but alas, I've no evidence to support that claim."

That line got laughs around the room and comments about Uther Pendragon and Igraine. When the laughter died down, Dylan took questions before wrapping up.

"Thank you for being such an attentive audience. If you enjoyed tonight's talk, please look for my book coming out later this year—*Archaeology and Arthur*. I think you'll find it intriguing." He pointed to Colin at our table. "Many of the photos in it were taken by Colin Carmody, our talented photographer, and you'll find a binder of those and others up here next to the podium."

Dylan continued as both Colin and Martin stood. "Now, I invite you to gather 'round to see the scale model we brought. My colleague Martin Pascoe, who's been part of the dig since the beginning, will point out the highlights and answer your questions. And, before we leave tonight, if you'd like to schedule a tour of Tintagel with one of our team, Martin's the man to see."

Belle pushed her chair back. "I'd best look at the model, as that's as close as these old bones will get to the ruins. You and Wendy will need to bring back lots of photos."

Ellie came over to help Belle up, and the two walked to the model. As I stood, I noticed Caryn was making no move to get up.

I touched her arm. "Caryn, are you okay?"

"It was difficult to hear Dylan make that presentation. It should have been Arthur, and that comment about King Arthur's mother? That was Arthur's signature line. He closes—closed—all his lectures at the British Museum with it."

I put my arm around her shoulders and hugged her. "This has got to be a difficult visit for you. It's so soon, and I know how I felt only a month after my husband Henry died in a cycling accident."

Her eyes filled with tears. "I'm not sure it was an accident."

*Oh my, here we go.* "Caryn, why don't we get something to drink and sit outside? I'm happy to lend an ear."

Her face didn't exactly light up, but she nodded and stood. "I've got my favorite blend of tea at my cottage and a jar of Gareth's lavender honey. Let's meet there in twenty minutes, okay?"

I let Wendy know where I'd be, and she said she'd be with Ellie and Belle, waiting for Uther to arrive. "You'll be a help to the girl, and maybe you'll find out what's up with her doubts."

At our cottage, Archie and Christie lying side by side in the sitting room reminded me of a double quotation mark. Christie lifted her head and stretched her legs, and Archie stood and arched his back before meowing goodnight. *And that's why it's called cat pose in yoga.*

I was knocking on the door to Vivienne Cottage when Caryn came running up. "Sorry, I got held up," she apologized. "Oh, you've brought Dickens *and* Christie."

I sat my squirming cat down inside while Dickens inspected Caryn's cottage. "Just like ours," he barked, "but her perfume is different."

Christie sniffed. "Of course it is, you silly dog. Still, I think Leta's is extra special."

*Nice to know my fussy feline approves of Shalimar—my signature scent.*

When Caryn asked how I took my tea, I told her tea with honey sounded heavenly. I noticed two colorful tins on the counter in the kitchen nook, both labeled in a jaunty script. The navy blue with the moon and stars was labeled 'K'night and the pale blue with a sunrise said Day.

Her eyes followed my glance and she smiled. "Arthur gave me two sets for my special tea blends. I usually keep one in my office at the museum and one at home but thought they'd be perfect for storing my tea on this trip. It's silly how particular I am about tea. We'll have my chamomile lavender honey blend tonight. It's lovely the way Gareth's honey intensifies the flavor."

We took our delicate cups to the Adirondack chairs outside her door. I couldn't get over seeing the chairs here in the UK, and I thought they suited the surroundings.

Christie stood with her paws in Caryn's lap before leaping up and making herself at home. "She needs me, doesn't she?" asked my girl.

Leaning over, I stroked Christie's head and smiled. "I'll soon be jealous if you keep this up. At least Dickens is content to lie by my side for the moment."

Caryn smiled as Dickens barked. "Only because Caryn doesn't have a free hand for my belly."

To ease into the conversation, I asked Caryn to tell me how she met Arthur.

"I met him several years ago at the museum, but I was getting over a broken heart and didn't think of him as a romantic interest. For me, the timing was off. He told me later he knew right away I was the one and he was waiting for me to figure it out. And I did. We've been engaged eighteen months now. We hadn't set a date, what with his hectic schedule and my job at the museum, but we were getting there."

All I had to do was nod and the story poured out. Wendy called this my pregnant pause technique. I'd never thought of it as a technique, though it stood me well in my career both in my conflict management role and as an executive coach. Listening wasn't something many people did well.

I learned Arthur had given up his role on the dig at the first of the year to focus on two things—the Tintagel exhibit he was mounting at the British Museum in partnership with English Heritage Properties and putting the finishing touches on his latest book, *Tales of Tintagel*. That shift allowed him to spend more time in London with Caryn.

"Arthur's publisher rang me as I was packing for the retreat because she was hoping I could locate his latest draft."

Caryn explained that the two were long-time friends, dating back to when she edited his first book. She moved up the ranks, and when she opened a small firm of her own, he followed her.

"Arthur always said he couldn't imagine working with anyone else. I'd lost track of where he was on this latest book, and I was touched that she wanted to publish it posthumously. When I found his edits along with a few fact-finding emails, she was ecstatic, and I was comforted by reading Arthur's words. When I closed my eyes, I could almost hear him reading aloud."

*Poor girl.* "I imagine it was a bittersweet experience. And his colleague Dylan has a book coming out too. Were he and Arthur also close friends, as Dylan mentioned?"

"Oh yes. They met at university as undergrads and were inseparable. They taught together, took their students on digs in Turkey and the British Isles, and collaborated on papers. They claimed they complemented each other. Arthur saw Dylan as brilliantly intuitive, a man who could read a scholarly paper and see an entirely new concept or theory, something no one else had considered. What he struggled with was explaining it so others could grasp it. Arthur was the linear thinker, methodical and organized, the one who was good at pulling Dylan's disparate thoughts into a cohesive whole."

She seemed on the verge of laughing. "Dylan's students tease him about being absent-minded, and one even presented him with an old DVD of the movie, *The Absent-Minded Professor*. Arthur joked that Dylan wouldn't have survived in the days of pen-and-paper notes because he could barely keep track of his computer files. They had fun with each other."

She looked reflective. "Maybe that's why the title of Dylan's book, *Archaeology and Arthur*, seems familiar to me. It sounds like something Arthur would have suggested. I wouldn't be surprised if he did." Her eyes filled with tears. "It's not fair! Arthur should be here too."

When she'd composed herself, I posed another question. "You said Arthur gave up leading the Tintagel dig. Did he also resign from his position as a professor at Cardiff University?"

"That hadn't been decided. He toyed with the idea of retiring until the university granted him a leave of absence. They weren't pushing him for a decision."

I rubbed Dickens's belly when he nudged my hand. "He sounds like a fascinating man. I wish I could have met him."

That was Caryn's signal to tell me more about Arthur's career, the courses he taught, the digs he'd led, the lectures he'd given in England and abroad.

*With all that going on, I wonder what he was doing back in Tintagel.* "So, was he visiting family the weekend of the accident?"

"No—I mean, well yes, but that wasn't why he came down. He'd been grumbling off and on about the boxes of artifacts arriving from Tintagel—'shoddy work' was his phrase—and he was especially angry about a recent shipment so when he said he was making a quick trip to see Martin and Dylan, I joked he was a fussbudget." Her tears gave way to anger. "He died because he had to micromanage Martin and Dylan. If not for that, he wouldn't have been here. He wouldn't have died."

"And seeing them tonight brought those feelings to the surface. I'm so sorry, Caryn." I couldn't help myself. A yawn escaped.

Caryn sighed. "Thanks for listening, Leta. Guin keeps telling me to let the anger go, but I can't. Maybe someday. Sitting here with you and Dickens and Christie and reminiscing . . . well, somehow I feel a little bit better. Can you tell me one thing before you go? Does the ache ever go away?"

I patted her hand. "Not entirely, but as time passes, I'm better able to focus on happy memories rather than the gaping hole Henry's death left in my life. Let me rephrase that. Remembering the good times rather than lamenting what might have been . . . that's turned the huge hole into a tiny tear. And I've found room in my heart for a new relationship. Dave will never take Henry's place; instead, he's a new chapter in my life."

We stood and hugged before I shooed my four-legged companions to Iseult cottage. *She'll survive this,* I thought, *but it will take time.*

In no time, I was tucked in bed talking to Dave. "You can't believe how charming it is. All the cottages are named for female characters in King Arthur's world, and ours is named Iseult. Tonight's lecture was the perfect setup for the Tintagel tour Wendy and I are taking tomorrow."

"When do you get time for yoga? Isn't this a yoga retreat?"

"Yes, and today's restorative class was just what the doctor ordered after the long drive. You should have seen Christie. She was a star."

He listened patiently to my tales of Christie's antics before inquiring about the lavender farm. "When do you take that tour? I imagine the scenery is reminiscent of a Monet painting."

"Yes, it is. As we drove in, the glimpses of lavender in the distance, the sparkling pool—words can't do it justice. Let's just say, if I had any artistic tendencies, I'd pull out a canvas and brushes, but given that stick figures are a stretch for me, it's not a temptation."

My perceptive boyfriend could tell I was running out of steam. "I hear you yawning, so I'll let you go. Just one last thing. Tell me you packed your purple spray and your siren?"

I sighed. "Yes, I did. You know I keep one of each in the car and attached to the strap on my purse. Don't you think you're being a bit over-protective?"

"Not at all. Two women driving rural two-lane roads can't be too careful. And if you and Wendy get a hankering to do a pub crawl, it can't hurt to be cautious."

I chuckled. "A pub crawl? You *do* have a vivid imagination! Never mind, I promise to be careful."

"That's all I ask. I love you, Tuppence. Sleep tight."

As I drifted off, Christie snuggled behind my knees, purring. I had to admit that my activities over the past few months gave Dave a legitimate reason for concern, but a yoga retreat? Unless I pulled a muscle doing a headstand or warrior pose, I thought I was plenty safe.

# CHAPTER FIVE

THE NEXT MORNING, I was sitting on the side of the bed when Wendy poked her head in the door. "Ready for a coffee? I made a small pot, thinking we'd get more at the barn."

Wendy was as addicted to coffee as I was, claiming she'd grown to love it in her teaching days in North Carolina. Belle slept in most days, so Wendy fixed a pot of coffee for herself every morning and then brewed tea for Belle.

"Let me grab a cup, and then I'll wash my face and get dressed."

"Tell me you're not putting on makeup."

"No way. We may be at a resort, but there's no need to get all fancied up for breakfast and yoga. I'll do that before we go on the tour, though I'm not sure why." A memory flashed into my head. "Well, I do know why. My mother once said to me, 'Aleta Petkas, I hope you're not one of those women who goes to the grocery without makeup.' You should have seen her face when I told her I was, so I can't imagine what she'd say if she thought I was taking a tour that way."

Leaving Christie behind with the requisite puddle of milk in her dish, we took Dickens with us to the barn, where we ate a light breakfast of fruit and yogurt. Then, we three took a stroll around the property.

Dickens was fired up. "Look, Leta, a bird flew up out of the field. And there's a rabbit. Did you see it?"

Wendy was amazed at his running back and forth. "I've never seen him like this. What's up with him?"

"It's the wide open space. He's off-leash and he can run and frolic to his heart's content. When we're in the village or walking to see the donkeys, he's good about staying by my side."

"Well, he's certainly entertaining. Now, you were asleep when I got to the cottage last night. Tell me about your visit with Caryn. Do you think talking to you helped her?"

"I think it did, a little. Grief isn't something you cure in one conversation, but getting her to talk about how they met and how he loved his career steered her away from the pain—at least for a moment or two. I think reminiscing is part of the process, focusing on the happy past rather than the present pain."

Wendy nodded. "Good. Maybe when Gemma speaks with her about the accident, she'll move closer to acceptance, though I know it's not a linear process. It's two steps forward and one step back until you get all the way there."

As Guin took us through ninety minutes of standing poses, I felt my leg muscles quiver with the strain. Her class seemed slightly more intense than those we took with Rhiannon—more of a take-no-prisoners style. I followed the same yoga instructor from studio to studio for ten years in Atlanta because I thought no one compared with her. When I moved to the Cotswolds, I didn't expect to find anyone to take her place, and I felt fortunate to find Rhiannon, right there in Astonbury.

To Christie and Archie, the intensity of the class made no difference. They wandered from student to student, rubbing against ankles, strolling beneath us as we held triangle pose, and playing with our hair when we went up in shoulder stand.

Wendy and I made an executive decision to fluff and dust after yoga instead of doing the full shower routine. We were sure to be hot and sweaty after touring Tintagel on this warm summer day, and we were both such planners, we had our day mapped out—the tour, some shops, a dip in the pool if time allowed, and then a quick shower before our afternoon yoga session.

Archie had again followed us to Iseult Cottage, and he and Christie were curled up together on my bed. *What a life.*

As I changed into shorts and a sleeveless top, I checked in with Dickens. "You want to go with us, right?"

He cocked his head. "Is Merlin going too?"

"No, he's staying here. Does that mean you'd rather play with Merlin than go with me?"

"Uh-uh. I'm with you, Leta. I can chase rabbits and eat dinner with Merlin when we get back."

With that settled, I met Wendy in the kitchen, where she was putting apples and bottles of water in her small backpack.

Rhiannon was waiting for us in front of the barn. "Do I get to share the backseat with a handsome dog today? I couldn't ask for a better date."

When she reached to scratch my boy's ears, he barked, "Of course you couldn't. Just ask Leta."

The mother-daughter duo, Lilith and Lilly, were riding with Penny and Sue, the sisters from Dartmouth. It made sense that Caryn and Morgan were staying behind. Morgan told us she knew the tour by heart after listening to Dylan day in and day out, and she was looking forward to time on her own by the pool. After my evening visit with Caryn, I didn't have to ask why she wasn't joining us.

"Rhiannon," I said. "I'm curious. Why is Morgan staying at Knight's Rest rather than in town where I assume her husband is lodging? At the only retreat I attended in the States, all the guests drove or flew in. None were local, so I don't know what the norm is."

"That's Guin's doing. Morgan planned to attend as a day guest, but in Guin's typical generous fashion, she invited Morgan to stay overnight gratis. She didn't go into detail but alluded to Morgan having a hard time lately and said a full retreat experience would do her good. I have the impression there may be a money issue too."

I wasn't surprised when I caught Wendy glancing at me. Knowing what she was thinking, I cut her off at the pass. "I hope the retreat helps her, then." *I've been told I tend to take care of others before myself, and I've already signed up to comfort Caryn.*

Guin had arranged a special tour for us, and we were delighted to see our guide was Martin, who we'd met the night before. Awestruck by the stunning sight of the bridge, we stood quietly while we waited for the other foursome to arrive.

Something about its span prompted me to double-check that Dickens's leash was secure. "We want to be extra careful you don't trip, fall, or wander off. You and I have never been anywhere like this." He must have sensed my concern, because he gave me a reassuring lick.

When we were all present and accounted for, Martin reintroduced himself and handed around brochures. He asked who had visited previously, and it turned out we all had, but it had been before the bridge was installed. Even Wendy, who'd visited in April, had to access the island the old way, by first walking down from the village and then climbing the steep steps to the island.

We both laughed about how challenging the steps were for short folks like us. Lily, who was about 5'7", commented that the steps were a challenge no matter your height.

Martin pointed out the architectural highlights of the mainland courtyard we stood in before explaining the gap between where we were and the ruins on the island. "At one time, these two pieces of land were joined by a natural land bridge. Its collapse in the fifteenth or sixteenth century took the central part of the castle with it into the sea."

As he led us across the bridge, he invited us to imagine a castle suspended there instead. Wendy was especially taken with the view, perhaps because it was only four months since she'd been there. "It looks so different from this perspective. I can just see people going to and fro, so busy with their daily lives they were oblivious to the beauty of this clifftop."

Martin picked up on her comment. "You're probably right. In the fifth and sixth centuries when it was part of a key trading route, it would have been plenty bleak and dreary, no matter the oils and tableware coming in from the Mediterranean. Even when Richard, Earl of Cornwall, purchased the island and built his castle in the 1200s, it wasn't exactly the lap of luxury—by today's standards, anyway."

Arriving on the island, we stopped to survey the stone entryway. I thought about Iseult Cottage and asked a question. "Martin, will we see the walled garden built by the Earl? I understand there's some connection to the legend of King Mark of Cornwall and the love story of Tristran and Iseult."

Penny added, "Look here, Leta. The brochure says there are stones around the garden that tell the story. And I also read Richard may have been inspired to purchase the land by Geoffrey of Monmouth's *History of the Kings of Britain*. Just imagine. In the 1100s, Monmouth's writing gave birth to the tale of King Arthur being conceived here."

I wondered how frequently Martin had a gaggle of literary ladies on his hands. He seemed to take it in stride, sharing arcane bits of history and legend as we explored the ruins. He pointed out where some of the more recent archaeological finds were uncovered. "Here's where the fragments of the red slip ware bowl were unearthed and over here is the site of another significant discovery—a stone inscribed with Latin and Greek letters, even some Christian symbols, dating from the seventh century."

When we reached the bronze statue of King Arthur, Dickens barked, "He needs a dog to keep him company." It was comical to watch him weave in and out of the sections of the cape that surrounded the main body of the statue.

Our last stop was a trench where several students were carefully working. "Hi, Martin," one called. "Would you care to show your group a few of the items we've found today?"

"You know I would. That's why I brought them this way. Ladies, listen up and let these dedicated volunteers showcase their work." We were enthralled. None of us had ever been to a dig, so this was the experience of a lifetime.

We were listening to explanations of the tools they employed to carefully reveal fragments of pottery and animal bones when I glimpsed a familiar face. Colin was approaching with his camera hanging around his neck. He snapped a few shots from a distance and then crouched to aim his camera at a volunteer's hands holding a brush.

Stretching her hand out, Wendy greeted him. "I'm Wendy Davies, and I admired your photos at Knight's Rest last night. Do you ever get tired of watching all this?"

He tilted his canvas hat and grinned. "Not on your life. The work they do is amazing. I like to think that my visual record, limited as it is, goes some way toward letting the world know what goes on here."

With a shy smile, Rhiannon held out her phone. "Could we get you to take a picture of the three of us?"

Waving her hand away, Colin directed us to stand near an unoccupied trench. "I'll go you one better." Before we knew it, he moved Rhiannon between Wendy and me and stood back. Clicking away, he circled us and directed us to move our heads and hands to different positions.

He pulled out a business card and handed it to Rhiannon. "Here you go. Email me at this address, and I'll send you the best of the bunch. No charge."

We thanked him profusely and returned to the group as our tour was wrapping up. I looked at my friend. "That was brilliant, Rhiannon. I felt like a model in a professional photo shoot."

Back on the mainland, Martin bade us farewell, but Rhiannon, Wendy, and I hung back with Dickens to tell him again how we'd enjoyed the tour. Wendy surprised me when she issued an invitation. "Martin, would you care to join us for lunch or at least a pint? I know you're working, but . . . "

"What a generous offer. How can I possibly turn down three lovely ladies and a handsome dog? Would you prefer a pub or a café with a view?"

We opted for the view, and he escorted us to the Beach Café. We oohed and aahed over the breathtaking vista of the castle and the bridge as we enjoyed the food, the pints, and the chance to catch our breath. Dickens glued himself to Martin's side as though he knew he was the best bet for a snack. Sure enough, it wasn't long before Martin's hand disappeared beneath the table.

Before long, the conversation drifted to life in modern-day Tintagel. We compared our experience of living in Astonbury with that of living here. It turned out Martin had lived in Tintagel all his life and had gone to school with Arthur and Guin.

"Arthur and I were friends as lads and the bond stuck." He laughed. "Even though he turned uppity when he went to university and became well known in the world of archaeology and research. Truly, I'm joking about the uppity bit, but it was good fun to tease him when his professor tone took over. It only took a few pints for him to get back to the old Arthur."

Rhiannon sipped her pint. "How long did you work with him at the castle? I mean, the dig is fairly recent, right?"

"Yes, but I've worked on and off at the castle in some capacity since I was a lad. Both Arthur and I did. He was fascinated by the legend and the literary aspect, while I dreamed of being the next Indiana Jones. I wasn't cut out for university, so becoming an archaeologist was never realistic. Having Arthur and Dylan for mates has been the next best thing. What they bring to the table in expertise, I easily match in enthusiasm."

I nodded. "It must have been a terrible shock to hear about the accident."

He downed a large slug of his beer. "I was right gutted. When we were lads, everyone called us Mutt and Jeff. I guess you know I'm Jeff, the short one, and we were inseparable. People needed a new name for us when Dylan came along, and we became the three musketeers. We were that close. What the stupid git was doing in the water at Merlin's Cove at high tide is beyond me. He knew better."

Thinking about what Caryn had shared with me, I dug a little deeper. "Could he have been meeting someone?"

A guarded look came over Martin's face. "Funny you should say that. He was supposed to meet me in the cove the next day. We had a pint at the Malthouse with Dylan and Colin and a few of the volunteers from the dig, but Arthur wanted a private talk. So we agreed on eleven on the shore. I wouldn't have been surprised to find him wading to Merlin's Cave that morning. He often did that."

Wendy and I were good at tag-teaming. "Is it Merlin's Cave or Merlin's Cove? I'm confused."

"Most tourists speak only of the cave, but the pebbled beach and the waterfall north of it make up the cove. You can access it by taking the cliff path or the steps with the railing before you come to the entrance to Tintagel Castle."

"I had no idea," said Rhiannon. "That was a good question, Wendy. It's a beautiful spot, no matter what you call it."

"Aye, and we spent lots of time there. As kids, we explored and messed about. Later, it became our place for more serious talks. There's something about standing on the shore looking through the cave that makes for introspection. We call it our thinking spot."

It was my turn. "We three don't have a picturesque place like that in Astonbury, but we have a favorite pub. We always meet at the Ploughman. Bet that's the way it is here. It's like going home."

Martin sipped and smiled. "You're right. When Arthur came home, it was always the Malthouse for us, and we introduced Dylan to it. Morgan wanted to branch out, but she could never talk the three of us into it."

Wendy laughed. "You mean you guys let her into the inner circle? Must have been hard being the only girl."

"Well, when I was younger, I could have done without my sister tagging along, but when she and Arthur were dating, I was overruled. And when she married Dylan, she became an official member of the club."

*His sister! And she had a thing with both men.* I felt Wendy nudge my leg with hers, and I imagined she was thinking the same thing I was.

Martin must have picked up on our body language. "I guess that sounds odd. She didn't date 'em at the same time. She and Arthur didn't last long after he went to university, and the summer he brought Dylan home with him, it was all over but the shouting. She and Arthur seemed more like chums when they were together, but with Dylan? She fell and fell hard. Fortunately, it was mutual."

*That's how it was when I met Henry.* "Gosh, Martin, I can only imagine how hard Arthur's death has been for all of you. We only saw a few headlines in Astonbury. Did they ever figure out exactly what happened?"

His smile disappeared. "I don't think we'll ever know. I mean, you hear someone died in a road accident, and you can picture it. If I'd heard an excavation caved in and he was buried in the debris, even that would be easier to accept."

We all expressed our condolences, and true to form, Dickens put his head in Martin's lap as though to comfort him. Thanking him again for the tour, we started uphill to the car.

Wendy paused. "As long as we're here, do you want to visit Merlin's Cave? Not because it was the scene of the accident, but to see the carving."

She was referring to the bearded face carved into a stone near the mouth of Merlin's Cave. I'd seen it on my trip with Henry, but it was worth a second visit. The cave was a sea cave and passed completely through Tintagel Island from the east to the west. That's likely why Martin found it unbelievable Arthur had visited at high tide. Growing up here, he would have known the beach was off-limits and the cave would fill with water.

We retraced our way to take the steep rocky steps to the shore and then carefully picked our way through the rocks to Merlin's Cave. Something about clambering over rocks had always scared me. On rafting trips in the States, when we had to exit the raft and climb over boulders to avoid shallow water, I was the last one to make my way to the waiting raft. Compared with me, Wendy and Rhiannon were scampering over the rocks.

The carving was of a bearded face, only slightly larger than a human head, and it made me think not only of Merlin but also of Dumbledore from the *Harry Potter* series.

Carefully picking my way back to shore, I saw a man standing on the rocks. He had his hand over his eyes and was staring out to sea, and he looked familiar. *Oh! It's Dylan Porter.*

He shook himself as though deep in thought and turned toward shore before catching sight of me. "Hi. Didn't I meet you last night?"

I reintroduced myself. "Yes, I heard your presentation at Knight's Rest and enjoyed it tremendously. And we've just had the pleasure of a tour with Martin."

Dylan nodded. "You were lucky, then. We're all passionate about the dig, but I think Tintagel is in Martin's blood." He looked around. "Did Morgan come with the yoga crew?"

"No, she's relaxing by the pool. I imagine after growing up here, she didn't need another tour of the castle."

"You'd be surprised. She still likes to visit, but after hours when the crowds are gone. Me? For all the revelations up top, this spot is my favorite. This is where I do my best thinking." He paused, and in what seemed an afterthought, added, "Arthur and I used to work out our knottiest problems standing right here."

*The three of them. This was their thinking spot.* We chatted for another moment before he took his leave, saying he needed to get back to work.

I watched my friends snap photos of each other in front of the cave until finally they waved and scrambled over the rocks toward me. They teased me about leaving them to talk to a tall stranger. They'd been too far away to recognize him. As I explained it was Dylan Porter, I wondered aloud why we didn't see him at the dig. We concluded the boss didn't have to be there every moment.

As we climbed to the car park, Rhiannon touched my arm. "You didn't seem too sure on your feet back there. Are you okay?"

I explained about my deep-rooted fear and laughed. "Probably years of therapy could help me understand why I feel that way."

"As good as your balance is, that's not the issue. Maybe someday, a memory will surface that will explain it. On a different note, I couldn't shake the image of Arthur among those rocks at high tide. Why would he have gone there?"

Wendy had more questions. "I haven't heard anything about the coroner's report. Do they think he waded in and was caught in the tide or that he fell from the top where the castle ruins are?"

I shuddered. "I've watched too many police procedurals on TV, and if there's any truth to those, the condition of the body would have indicated which it was. I wonder whether the family knows."

The conversation tapered off as though our questions were too morbid for the beautiful day. We were panting when we got to my car, and Wendy handed around the bottled water.

Rhiannon looked at her watch. "Ladies, we have enough time either to catch a few shops or squeeze in a swim before the afternoon session. Probably not both. Pick your poison."

It didn't take long to choose time at the pool. We all agreed we were too hot and sweaty to enjoy ducking in and out of shops, and since we were here for the rest of the week, we figured we could pop into the village another time.

A refreshing dip in the pool was just what the doctor ordered. Dickens positioned himself beneath my lounge chair in the shade, and I lowered the seatback so I could lie stretched out, enjoying the sensation of the breeze and the sun on my wet body. There was something indescribably delicious about relaxing, almost snoozing, by a pool. The only thing missing was the sound of waves on a beach. *I should suggest a beach trip to Dave—maybe to Florida or the Outer Banks.*

My reverie was interrupted by the ringing of my cell phone. I barely opened my eyes as I answered, "Hello."

"That sounds like a sleepy greeting. Are you napping?" *Speak of the devil.*

"Not quite napping, just near nirvana lying by the pool. I was thinking we need to add a beach trip to our travel list."

"I could go for that, especially if there's a bikini involved."

*What a horrid thought.* "Surely you jest. This tummy hasn't seen the sun in years, so if a two-piece is a prerequisite for a trip, you're out of luck."

He laughed and said all the right things about how good I'd look in a skimpy suit before we moved on to where we might go. We tossed around ideas like the Greek Islands, somewhere in the States, maybe Bermuda. The possibilities were endless for a couple who lived on opposite sides of the pond.

I yawned. "So what are you up to today? Writing, research, a day of leisure?"

That got a laugh. "A day of leisure? You must be kidding. Though I suspect plenty of people think we freelance writers have it plenty easy. No, at the moment, I'm planning a trip to the University of Texas in Austin to view the unpublished J.M. Barrie play in the Harry Ransom collection there."

He'd told me about that discovery when we first met. It was buried in the collection of donated documents, and its existence was unknown until someone stumbled across it. It was seen as a spoof of Arthur Conan Doyle's Sherlock Holmes stories. Since Doyle was one of Barrie's friends, I imagined Dave was considering a chapter about it in his book *Barrie & Friends*.

"And you, sweetheart? What's on your agenda when you pull yourself away from the pool?"

"Only yoga and dinner. We spent the morning traveling back in time to the days of King Arthur. Too bad there's not a movie night planned. Watching *Camelot* would be a treat." I told him about the tour of Tintagel and promised to send photos.

Imagining myself as Guinevere to Sean Connery's King Arthur, I drifted off again until Wendy called to me. "Come on, Sleeping Beauty. Time for a shower if we're going to make it to yoga."

Wendy, Christie, and I arrived at the barn a few minutes before class. As we passed Guin at the front desk, we thanked her for setting up our special tour and told her how much we enjoyed it.

Rhiannon was on her own in the studio, instructing the guests to get blocks and straps. Gemma was set up by the mother-daughter duo Lilith and Lily, and they were regaling her with bits about the tour. Before gathering our props, Wendy and I rolled out our mats near Morgan. *Funny, she looks almost forlorn.*

I spoke to her as I arranged my blanket and assumed the cross-legged Sukhasana pose. "Good afternoon, Morgan. How was your day?"

"Oh, relaxing. How was Tintagel?"

"Delightful. It was the perfect combination of stunning scenery and intriguing information. I'm so glad Guin set up the special tour for us and that Martin was our guide. He was amazing." Laughing, I added, "Between him and your husband, I've learned all kinds of intriguing bits about the ruins. I can't believe I somehow missed the fact that you and Martin are brother and sister and didn't realize that you grew up here too. "

Morgan gave a wan smile. "Yes, I guess you could say the love of Tintagel runs deep in the family."

I was about to mention running into Dylan when Rhiannon shushed the class. "Okay, ladies, our focus in our last class of the day is forward bends and twists. As you stretch your spine in these asanas, you should experience a calming effect. You may feel tightness in your hamstrings or hips as you hold the poses, but if you feel any pain in your lower back, let me know. We'll either adjust the pose for you or substitute another."

Wendy smiled and whispered. "Leta, if you get any calmer, I may have to wheel you out." Rhiannon gave us both a stern look when I chuckled.

It always seemed counterintuitive to me that our forward bend classes started with positions that stretched our legs. We were doing Supta Padangusthasana —or in English, as Rhiannon explained, Reclining Hand-to-Big-Toe Pose. That meant we were lying on our backs with one leg extended straight overhead with a strap looped over it, both ends held in our hands to stretch the leg.

Groaning softly, as we lowered that same leg out to the side, I wondered why I never could quite get my foot to the floor. I always had to rest it on a block. *And people think yoga is easy.*

Rhiannon continued to talk us through the pose as she hopped up to gather straps, blocks, and a blanket for Caryn, who had arrived a few minutes late and was quietly laying out her mat. I was glad to see Christie move from Lilith to Caryn, almost as though she could tell where she was needed. *Cats can be such a comfort.*

We moved through a series of bends and twists until we got to Shoulderstand, which in most classes is the next to the last pose, followed by Savasana, or corpse pose. The challenge for me and many other yoga students in corpse pose is to lie quietly and clear our minds. It seems simple. You lie on your back, hands by your side. It's that clearing-the-mind thing I find difficult.

Rhiannon instructed us in a soothing tone. "Now is the time to free your mind of negative thoughts. Now is the time to fill your heart with forgiveness, to let go of anger and blame. Strive to forgive yourself and others."

I heard a sob and opened my eyes in time to see Caryn roll over, stand, and run from the room. My heart ached for her.

Eyes closed, I heard the soft patter of Christie's paws and then felt her nuzzle my ear. "Leta, Caryn is so sad."

I sighed as Christie burrowed her silky head in the crook of my neck. *Poor girl. Her pain is still so fresh.*

Cocktail banter that evening focused on our enjoyment of the ruins plus our two yoga sessions. To a person, we agreed we were worn out but in a good way.

Sitting with Belle and Ellie, Wendy and I passed our phones back and forth so our friends could vicariously experience the Tintagel tour. They were both enchanted with the bronze statue, and Belle joked that that was about as close as any of us would get to meeting a medieval knight.

Wendy laughed at her mother. "Aw, Mum, we've got a few nights left. Have you given up on Uther appearing at your cottage?"

Belle's response was classic. "Dear, Uther Pendragon is a king, not a mere knight, and we fully expect to see him before we depart."

When Elaine appeared at our table with Tintagel Trifle for dessert, Wendy and I debated splitting a single serving before we threw up our hands and went for one each. It was easy to decide we deserved it after our exhausting day.

I all but licked my plate clean. "Oh my goodness, that was to die for. What a perfect day."

Cocking her head, Wendy studied at me. "And now, you're ready for bed, right? Think you can keep your eyes open 'til the sun sets?"

As we left the barn, we saw Martin in the parking lot with a bottle of wine and several packages. He gave a jaunty wave as he walked toward the main house.

Looking at Wendy, I winked. "Could something be going on between him and Guin? Maybe love is in the air."

Wendy started humming, and I immediately recognized "A Summer Song" by Chad and Jeremy. "Wow! I haven't heard that song in years." *Just thinking of summer breezes and starry nights makes me wish Dave were here.*

# CHAPTER SIX

I was dead to the world when a tiny paw patted my chin. "Leta," meowed Christie, "you need to get up."

I opened one eye. My room was dark, and I didn't see any light creeping in between the curtains. *What time is it?* I rolled over and touched my phone and saw it was not yet 5:30. "Christie, yoga isn't for hours. Go back to sleep."

My alarm clock licked my chin. "But I want milk . . . now."

It was useless to ignore her, so I swung my legs off the bed and padded to the kitchen muttering, "We never get up this early at home. What's with you?" I opened the fridge door only to discover that yesterday's small pitcher of milk was empty. "Aargh. Can't you wait?" Silly question. Christie was not a patient cat.

My muttering continued as I grabbed my robe. Dickens was awake now, so, trailed by a dog and cat, I crept from my cottage. Except for Vivienne Cottage next door, all the others were dark. *Looks like Caryn's up early too.* I trekked to the barn, where soft lights glowed behind the registration desk and down the hall. I was surprised to find Rhiannon sitting in a comfy chair in the lobby.

With a startled expression, she looked up. "You're out and about early."

"Shhh. I'm trying not to come fully awake, but I think it's useless." I pointed to Christie. "Your cat yogi wants milk, no two ways about it. Why are you up? We don't start until 9, right?"

She held up a notepad. "I woke up thinking about the sequence for this morning's backbends and had an idea about adjusting the flow to accommodate some of the less experienced students. Too bad you're not dressed for yoga. Now that I've worked it out, I think I'll do a short pranayama practice." She chuckled. "Of course, you could do it in your robe."

We walked down the hall to the snack area, where I refilled the small pitcher from the milk bottle in the fridge. "I probably should, but I think I'll opt for a cup of coffee and a shower instead."

Rhiannon made a shooing motion and went on her way. *Maybe I'll throw on some clothes and stretch my legs with Dickens before I take my shower.*

"Dickens, how would you like—" I heard running behind me and turned around.

"Leta, come quick!"

I set the pitcher on the lobby counter and jogged after Rhiannon. She stopped at the door to the studio. The lights were low but bright enough for me to see someone lying in corpse pose near the front of the room.

"It's Caryn," Rhiannon whispered as though she didn't want to disturb her. "I thought maybe she had the same idea as I did for an early pranayama practice, but she's not moving. I spoke to her and lightly patted her cheeks, but she didn't stir."

When Dickens barked, I told him to stay as I walked toward Caryn. Christie had a different idea and darted past us. She reached out a paw to Caryn's cheek, and when she got no response, patted her nose. "Leta, she's not asleep, but she's not awake. Is she hurt?"

By this time, Rhiannon and I were kneeling on either side of Caryn. "Rhiannon, did you check for a pulse?"

"Yes, it's very faint."

I rose, grabbed a blanket, and folded it to place below Caryn's head. From there, I took in the tableau. Both hands lay palm up by her side. It was then I noticed next to her elbow a barely visible pool of vomit—or sick, as my British friends would say—as though she'd raised herself and been ill before lying back down. Her face showed no sign of anguish or pain. Gently smoothing her brow, I realized her skin was clammy. *Clammy skin, shallow breathing, but she looks so calm. What could have caused this?*

Stroking Caryn's arm, Rhiannon asked, "Do we need to call 999?"

I thought quickly. "Yes, and if there's anyone at Knight's Rest with first-aid experience, we need to rouse them. I'll stay here while you make the call."

It seemed an eternity before Rhiannon returned with Gemma in tow. "I called 999, but the nearest A&E is in Truro, about 50 kilometers away, so they're also sending a local GP. Gemma was on her way out for a dawn run, so I grabbed her."

I was so focused on Caryn, I didn't realize the sun had risen. Gemma knelt on the other side of the unconscious girl and touched her brow. "Did you put the blanket beneath her head? Do you think she needs one over her too? I'm trying to think. What causes a weak pulse and clammy skin and makes someone lose consciousness?"

Pointing at the sick, I asked, "Something she ate or drank? But what?"

Gemma nodded. "And what is she doing here? She's dressed in a t-shirt and baggy pants, not exactly yoga clothes."

"Leta," Rhiannon said, "You came over in your nightgown this morning looking for milk. Could Caryn have done the same thing? Made a quick trip for something and been taken ill?"

My mind was hopscotching all over the place. "Could be. I bet these are the clothes she sleeps in. So, why is she in here and not in the dining room?" *What am I missing?* "Oh! Belle's a nurse! Let me go get her."

I took off with Dickens behind me. Christie hadn't budged since she'd taken up her position by Caryn's head. As I ran to Igraine Cottage, I realized Belle would still be sound asleep. She wasn't an early riser, but Ellie would be up.

Lights were burning in the kitchen nook and the sitting room at their cottage, and when I knocked, Ellie came to the door with her finger to her lips. "Shhh. Oh, Leta, good morning."

I quickly explained what I needed and left Ellie to rouse Belle before jogging to the cottage I shared with Wendy. She was sipping tea in the sitting room.

"You look frantic. What's wrong?"

"Let me throw on some clothes while I explain." In no time, I was dressed in shorts and a t-shirt and had relayed the story to Wendy. She said she'd help get Belle moving and be on her way.

Dickens had been peppering me with questions since we left the barn. "Leta, is she sick? Will she be okay? Is she going to the emergency room like you did?" My boy had been there the one time an ambulance had taken me to A&E, as they called it here in the UK.

While he barked, I racked my brain for some reason that would explain Caryn's symptoms but couldn't come up with anything. "I don't know. If we can wake her up, maybe not."

Returning to the barn, I ran into Guin, who motioned me to stop. "Leta, we have an emergency."

"I know, Guin. I was with Rhiannon when she found her. Is there anything about her medical history we need to know? Does she have asthma? Or a heart condition? Anything that would explain what's going on?"

"From what I know, she's a perfectly healthy young lady. Arthur never said otherwise."

I turned as I heard the golf cart and saw Gareth pull up with Wendy, Belle, and Ellie. A black dog followed behind the cart. *That must be Merlin.*

All I could think was that Ellie must have lit a fire under Belle. I'd never known her to move so fast in the morning. The two bustled in, calling to me as they headed to the studio.

When I followed them, I saw something else I'd never seen before—Belle in full-on head nurse mode. Rhiannon and Gemma stood back as she took charge, taking Caryn's pulse, feeling her brow, and calling for a warm compress. Next, she gently explored Caryn's scalp with her fingers.

That surprised me. "Belle, what are you looking for?"

"Checking to see whether there's any swelling. If she fell and hit her head, she might have shrugged it off, only to feel dizzy later. I don't feel anything, though."

When she spotted the sick on the floor, she tsk-tsked and instructed Gemma to roll Caryn onto her side with her top leg bent. A bolster behind her back was the last step. With all that rapidly accomplished, I went in search of something for Belle to sit on. With her arthritis, she couldn't remain standing and stooped over for long.

Gareth grabbed an ottoman and followed me to the yoga studio. Once Belle was comfortable, I asked what she thought.

"I'm inclined to leave her in this position until the doctor gets here. Being on a couch or bed won't make any difference. She doesn't have an injury I can detect or a fever. If anything, she's a bit chilled, though it's not cool in here. If it's not a concussion, my next thought is she ate or drank something toxic. What, I have no idea. The doctor or the paramedics may decide to give her a purgative, though that remedy's not often recommended these days."

"Huh?" I asked.

Wendy answered for her mother. "Something to make her throw up whatever she ingested. Mum, are you saying folks don't use ipecac anymore?"

As far as I was concerned, they were speaking a foreign language. I guess Wendy picked up the lingo growing up with a nurse.

Belle nodded. "Right, dear. Medical professionals have even gone so far as to tell people to throw the stuff away. Times were, a teaspoon of ipecac was the remedy when a child ate something poisonous. Not anymore."

"What else, Belle?" asked Gemma.

"Well, if it's something she ate or drank, it would help to know what it was, and Caryn can't tell us. Gemma, you're probably accustomed to having a team do this for you, but could you scrape up that little pool on the floor so it can be analyzed?"

As Gemma ran down the hall, I glanced at Wendy. "While Gemma's doing that, let's go to Caryn's cottage to see what's on the kitchen counter. Could it be a simple as yogurt gone bad or something?"

Belle shrugged and stroked Christie's back. "I wish I knew."

Christie kept her vigil by Caryn's side, but Dickens followed Wendy and me to Vivienne cottage. Wendy pointed to the door. "Look, it's not closed all the way. Do you think she ran out?"

"That seems likely. I can't think of any other reason she wouldn't close it behind her. Funny—I noticed the light on when I passed by but not the door. I'm probably overthinking the situation, but why don't we do a slow, thorough examination of the cottage so we don't miss anything?"

Wendy's hand flew to her mouth, but not before I caught the corners of her mouth turn up. She cleared her throat. "It's not funny, I know, but you have to admit our reactions are comical. Who else would say something like that? Most people would run in, scan the counter and the fridge and run out, right?"

"Yes, but we've learned the importance of careful observation, haven't we?"

Along with Belle, Wendy and I had a knack for taking in and sorting details. We two were both keen observers, but I was the most adept at getting folks to share their innermost thoughts and concerns. Belle, on the other hand, got all the gossip. "You can't believe what people will tell a little old lady," she liked to say. Wendy was the bold one who more often than not proposed actions that led to breakthroughs. Why I was the one always in hot water was a mystery to me.

In typical gung-ho Wendy fashion, my friend dove in. "Right. And with all the members of the Little Old Ladies' Detective Agency present, we'll figure this out in a flash. Mum's got the nursing angle covered. Ellie can help her, and you and I will get out our magnifying glasses, so to speak. If we can find something to show the paramedics, they can more quickly determine the most effective treatment."

When Gemma had first referred to our original trio—me, Wendy, and Belle—as little old ladies, I wanted to throttle her. Belle was near ninety, but Wendy and I were *not* old! Belle loved the name, though, and when it stuck, I made the best of it. Nowadays, our friends in Astonbury routinely referred to us as the LOLs, and after Ellie joined us on our last adventure, the name seemed even more appropriate.

I closed my eyes and groaned. *Let's hope it's that simple.* "Okay, so the front door's open. Anything else catch your eye outside? I mean, did she get sick here too?"

Dickens barked. "No, but I see rabbit tracks."

Kneeling, I rubbed Dickens's head and studied the ground where he stood. "Why look, Dickens found rabbit tracks."

Wendy smiled. "I saw two near our cottage when I came in last night. Shall I explain to Dickens that rabbits aren't what we're looking for, or will you?"

Thank goodness we had Dickens to help us keep our sense of humor. Beyond his find, neither of us noticed anything else, so we walked inside to the kitchen nook. The cottages were well designed with all the comforts of home tucked into their tiny kitchen areas. An electric kettle sat on the counter, a teapot beside it. Next to it was a jar of honey, a spoon, and a tea strainer with wet tea leaves still in it.

"Looks like she made tea, but where's the teacup?" Wendy asked.

"Not sure. We'll check the sitting room and the bedroom in a sec. Did you notice the cute little tea tins? Arthur gave her those, and we had a cup of the 'K'night blend when I visited with her Saturday night."

Propped between the tins was a small brown packet, with its top folded down. "Hmmm. Looks like more tea. I wonder if she drank this or her usual brew this morning. She told me she was particular about her tea."

Picking it up, I saw two labels affixed to it. The first read *T-T-T for Women* in a fancy script. The second was a typed list of ingredients—nettle leaf, tulsi, and licorice root. I opened it and sniffed before holding it up to Wendy's nose. "Yuck. I can't stand licorice, so I know I couldn't drink this. Is it the same as the wet tea in the strainer?"

Wendy looked back and forth between the bag and the strainer. "I think it is, and look—it has tiny pale purple flecks in it and some seeds. I wonder if that's lavender. I'm an Earl Grey gal, and this doesn't appeal to me at all. Regardless, it must be the last cup of tea she made. So, again, where's the cup?"

I placed the little brown bag where I'd found it, and we wandered into the sitting room. I saw a laptop and stack of papers on the ottoman and a pair of glasses and a yellow sticky note on a side table, but no teacup. "If she was reading, you'd think the teacup would be nearby, wouldn't you?"

In the bedroom, the bedcovers were tossed back and the bed looked slept in, so I concluded that she'd awakened and made herself a cup of tea before dawn. Her phone lay on the bedside table.

Wendy moved into the adjacent bathroom. "Here's a mug on the sink with a tiny puddle in the bottom. I wonder why she brought it in here. Personally, I don't know how she drank it with that licorice taste. Maybe she couldn't stomach it either, but why didn't she just pour it down the kitchen drain?"

Standing in the doorway, I thought for a moment. "Hmm. Let's play it out. You brew a large mug of tea and sit down in the sitting room to read. You sip, you read, you sip some more . . . and you begin to feel nauseated. Would that explain taking the mug to the bathroom and not the kitchen?"

"Maybe. And when she continued to feel ill, she went to the barn in search of something to settle her stomach, maybe a Coke or a ginger ale? But why didn't we find her in the dining area or the snack area? Why was she in the yoga studio?"

"I don't know, but it does seem likely that it was the tea that made her ill."

Wendy hesitated. "Leta, we're all about being thorough, so before we settle on the tea, let's check the refrigerator and the kitchen rubbish. We need to be sure she didn't eat something this morning that could have made her sick. Though goodness knows, upset stomachs don't usually result in losing consciousness."

"You're right, and we should check the bathroom trash too."

Dickens took that as his cue to stick his nose in the painted straw basket next to the sink. "Tissues, cotton balls. That's it, Leta."

A quick check of the kitchen trash was equally fruitless—nothing but some used paper towels. In the fridge, a few unopened bottles of juice sat on the top shelf, and that was that.

We concluded that it had to be the tea if indeed it was something Caryn had ingested that triggered her symptoms. Returning to the barn, we found an elderly gentleman in the studio conferring with Belle and Gemma.

Belle called us over. "Girls, this is Dr. Black. He's done a more thorough examination of Caryn. He's confirmed what I was beginning to think. We already knew her breathing was shallow, but he's also determined her pupils are dilated and not responding to light. He's checked for needle marks to see if she's perhaps a drug user, but there are none."

I stopped short. "A drug user? That never would have occurred to me, though now that you mention it, it would be understandable if she were taking antidepressants or sleeping pills. I didn't think to check for pill bottles in the cottage."

My mention of the cottage got the expected reaction from Gemma. "In the cottage? Is that where you've been? You and your sidekick?"

As usual, Wendy handled Gemma better than I did. "Hey, I'm no sidekick. I'm a full-fledged little old lady, remember? Calm down, we didn't disturb anything, and we're pretty sure the only thing she's had to eat or drink is some tea."

Dr. Black looked at me. "Why would it be understandable for her to be taking pills?"

When I explained her fiancé had died a month ago, he looked thoughtful. "You mean Arthur Knight? I didn't make the connection."

He turned to Gemma. "DI Taylor, I realize you're not here in an official capacity, but may I ask your opinion?"

"Let me guess," Gemma said. "You're wondering whether we should call the local bobby. You're thinking the circumstances may warrant a police presence, right?"

"Exactly. I've been called to too many situations with teens and drugs. I hate to say it, but if her condition deteriorates . . . if she dies, heaven forbid, they'll need as much information as they can get their hands on to rule it a suicide or an accidental overdose."

Gemma nodded. "I agree with you. If it were on my patch, I'd want to be called in as soon as possible."

The doctor looked grim. "Glad that's settled. I'll call the Truro station. Now, the ambulance should be here any moment, and the sooner we can transport this young lady to the hospital along with any samples for testing, the sooner we can determine what to do for her. Can you collect whatever these ladies found in the cottage to add to what you scraped from the floor?"

It beat me how Gemma managed to nod and smile at the doctor and immediately transform her expression into a scowl when she turned to me. *Looks like I've stepped in it again.*

# CHAPTER SEVEN

WHEN THE AMBULANCE HAD come and gone with Guin following behind it, I left my friends in the dining room and took Christie to Iseult Cottage, explaining there'd be no yoga class this morning.

"Leta, will she be okay?" Christie meowed. "She was already sad, and now she won't wake up. What's wrong with her?"

Dickens barked a response. "We don't know what's wrong with her, but we're trying to figure it out."

Christie turned her pink nose up. "What do you mean 'we?' You're no doctor. You didn't even stay by her side."

"At least I found the rabbits. What did you find?"

Sometimes their chatter gave me ideas, but not today. "Enough, you two. I can't think."

I put out food and water for both of them. Christie never did get her milk, but for a change, she didn't complain. As I closed the door behind me, I heard Dickens bark in protest and Christie tell him to hush. They'd had a busy morning, and I was sure they'd soon be snoozing. If Christie was going to get her daily eighteen hours of sleep, she needed to start soon, and it wouldn't be long before Dickens was snoring nearby.

Gemma was standing outside Vivienne Cottage. She'd already collected the wet tea, and I wondered if she was about to inspect the cottage further as a possible crime scene. *Should I offer to help and chance a rude rebuff?* Before I could come to a decision, she called my name.

"Leta, I'm going to check over the cottage one more time. I took the tea leaves to Dr. Black, but I just can't see how a simple cup of tea could have caused such a severe reaction. Do you want to do a second walkthrough with me?"

*Another flip flop. Now she's being nice.* "Sure. By the way, the door was open when we got here."

I took her through how we'd progressed from the kitchen to the sitting room to the bedroom and bath. I pointed to the tea packet and the now-empty strainer. "We didn't see any food items in the kitchen garbage and no food in the fridge, so we're assuming the only thing she had this morning was the tea."

"That seems a reasonable assumption. Did anything seem out of the ordinary as you looked around?"

I walked into the sitting room. "No. We did a quick scan in here, and nothing seemed amiss." Idly picking up the yellow sticky note on the side table, I read aloud, "'C, Love A.' Aww, this must be a note from Arthur that she's kept. He drew a heart with an arrow through it and added XX at the end. And here's her purse on the floor by the couch. I missed that before. Goodness, this thing weighs a ton."

Motioning to me to pass it to her, Gemma dumped the contents on the couch. "There's not much in here—certainly no medications or anything edible. It's these keys that make it so heavy." She held up a big bunch of keys on an oversized round brass keyring. It was so large it reminded me of something a night watchman would carry.

I continued my train of thought from my earlier visit. "We thought it odd the mug was in the bathroom, but then again, we told ourselves, maybe she felt ill and wandered in with it in her hand. We didn't find anything that indicated she'd been sick in there, though."

Gemma looked thoughtful. "Dr. Black wondered if she used drugs, but didn't see any physical signs. Did you find any pills?"

"No, it was only after Belle mentioned it that I thought I should have looked for pill bottles. I took antidepressants when Henry died, and Caryn's doctor might have prescribed some for her too. I suppose those combined with some weird herb in her tea could have caused a strange reaction. As Wendy said, the tea smelled awful. See for yourself."

Gemma sniffed the tea in the small bag and grimaced. "I'd have to agree with you two. It amazes me sometimes what people eat and drink in the name of healthy living. You've made me think, though. Maybe instead of a prescription, she was taking an herbal supplement that interacted with her tea. I mean, how can tea, no matter how it smells, make someone sick—sick enough to pass out?"

I wondered the same thing as I walked into the bedroom. "Well, I guess we should check in here. Since it looks as though she didn't entirely unpack her suitcase, do you want to check the bathroom again while I start in the bedroom?"

She surprised me by agreeing to my suggestion. For the moment, anyway, she was happy to have my help, but I was wary. Experience told me her reaction could change in a heartbeat. Gemma was nothing if not inconsistent in how she dealt with my involvement.

"Um, Gemma, something just occurred to me. Why are we doing this? Doesn't Tintagel have a local police officer?"

Gemma blushed. "No, there's a small station in Bodmin, but the closest station with a detective inspector is Truro. Someone will be here eventually, but it can't hurt to do a preliminary search. I plan to take a page from your playbook and act all innocent when they arrive."

Chuckling, I turned and took in the cards arrayed on the dresser. A brown envelope lay off to the side. I was so focused on tea when I was here earlier, I'd missed them. They were condolence cards, and most included heartfelt notes about Arthur. Mixed in among them were a mini-me Arthur magnet, a metal King Arthur key ring, and a child-size Merlin wizard hat. *Tintagel souvenirs?*

Also on the dresser was a bottle of Chanel No. 5. *A classic. It must be the scent Dickens picked up on when we were here the other night.* The dresser drawers held underwear and an assortment of yoga clothes and shorts, but nothing else.

A book lay on the nightstand, Agatha Christie's *Murder in Mesopotamia*, and the nightstand drawer was empty. That left the closet and the suitcase.

The colorful sundresses hanging in the closet didn't reveal any secrets, but I found a bottle of prescription pills in the suitcase along with a packet of paracetamol. I'd been correct in thinking she might be on antidepressants. She was taking low-dosage Lexapro, certainly not anything that should cause an adverse reaction.

"Gemma, nothing in here but this prescription. Anything new in the bathroom?"

She came into the bedroom. "No, nothing. Let me take a look at the pill bottle."

She opened it and poured the pills into her palm. "Just want to be sure there's nothing else in here. I sometimes jumble my pills together in one bottle when I travel. When it's easy to tell them apart, that is. My blue sinus capsules are easily distinguished from other things. Interesting, she's taking the same meds I took."

*What?*

She plopped on the side of the bed, a funny expression on her face. "Sorry. It's been near the surface since we got here. This brings it all back. No reason you'd know, but I had a fiancé in Oxford. I moved to Astonbury after . . . after he died."

I was speechless. She was right. There was no reason I'd know unless her mother had shared the story with me, and she hadn't. I thought Gemma had transferred from the Thames Valley force to be closer to her parents, not to leave a tragedy behind.

"I'm so sorry. I had no idea. Do you, um, do you want to talk about it?"

"Maybe it's time I did. I think Mark's death is one reason I get so angry with you when you interfere in police matters. Not that he interfered. He was just in the wrong place at the wrong time. If he hadn't been with me, he'd still be alive."

*What on earth?*

She tilted her head and closed her eyes. "We'd been out to dinner, and I was pleasantly tipsy after we'd shared a bottle of wine. Mark had his arm around me, and we were laughing as we walked to the car park. I hardly noticed the man who rushed us, until I felt a burning sensation in my arm and looked down to see I was bleeding. When Mark tried to push him away from me, he took a knife to the stomach. He was gone before the ambulance arrived."

I was stunned.

Gemma gulped. "It turned out our attacker was the father of a girl I'd arrested on drug charges. I had no idea he'd been stalking me until he admitted as much when my colleagues found him and brought him in."

I sat beside her on the bed and put my arm around her. "Gemma, I am so, so sorry. The memories catch you unawares, don't they?"

"Yes. Ever since Guin asked me to speak with Caryn, I haven't been able to put it out of my mind. And seeing her run from class yesterday in tears, I felt for her. Her loss was similarly sudden, and I know how she must feel. It's funny how I go months at a time without coming undone, and then it sneaks up on me. That's one reason I've never asked you any questions about your husband. It's not your fault he died in an accident, but he died as suddenly as Mark did."

This was the second time in minutes she'd alluded to fault. "It sounds as though you hold yourself responsible for what happened."

"The rational part of me says I'm not completely to blame, but the circumstances haunt me. When I replay the scene, I know I should have been more alert. I should have anticipated the father would come after me. As a policewoman, I should know the dangers that can arise from arrests."

"Gemma, Gemma, that's a lot of shoulds. I'm no authority, but I have a hard time seeing it that way. I suspect your boss and colleagues didn't see it that way either. Am I right?"

Another gulp. "Yes, you're right. No one else blames me, and on good days, I know they're right. Today's not a good day, though."

I pulled her in and squeezed her shoulder. "Trust me, I understand. Maybe, if you think we've done what we can here, you can take time for the run you didn't get in this morning. That ought to help you regroup."

Funny, I guess she meant it when she told Guin I was a gifted listener, that I genuinely cared. I was glad she felt she could share her story with me. It explained a lot about her mercurial moods—and our relationship.

She agreed a run was a good idea, and we parted company. Gemma set off toward the lavender fields, as I pulled the door closed to Caryn's cottage and headed to the barn in search of something to eat. My stomach was reminding me I'd been up since before dawn with no food. Approaching the barn, I saw a man emerge from a car and turn to take in his surroundings. He was tall and well-built, with shaggy auburn hair. His sports coat accented his broad shoulders, trim waist, and long legs. *Could he be the local detective inspector?*

I got to the barn door at the same time he did, and he extended his hand. "DI Nancarrow at your service."

"Leta Parker. You must be here about Caryn, and here's Elaine at the front desk. It was my friend Rhiannon who found Caryn this morning in the yoga studio."

Trying not to be obvious in my eavesdropping, I took my time moving toward the dining area. As luck would have it, Elaine called me back before I got far.

"Leta, can you take DI Nancarrow to the studio, please? I'm swamped here trying to rearrange the schedule and answer questions from the other guests."

It was all I could do to keep up with him as he strode down the hall following the arrow that pointed to the yoga studio.

"So, this is where she was lying? Were you here when your friend found her?"

It didn't take long to give him the pertinent facts about discovering Caryn lying motionless and unresponsive. "The unsettling detail is she was lying in corpse pose. And I just realized, if Rhiannon hadn't been up before dawn, Caryn might not have been found for hours. I hope we were soon enough."

He looked thoughtful. "Dr. Black mentioned another detective inspector being here as a guest. Do you know where I might find her?"

"Sure. Gemma's gone out for a run, but she should be back soon. There are several of us here from Astonbury, where she's the local DI."

"Gemma? Not Gemma Taylor, by any chance?"

Raising an eyebrow, I looked at him. "Do you know Gemma?"

His face broke into a grin. "Ah, yes. We attended a leadership program together in December. She's something else."

"That she is. Well, until she gets back, is there anything I can do to help you? My friend Belle is a nurse, and she sat with Caryn until Dr. Black got here. And I checked Caryn's cottage to see if we could figure out what she might have eaten that made her lose consciousness. We were grasping at straws while we waited on the doctor or the ambulance to arrive."

It was his turn to raise an eyebrow, but at least he did it with a smile. "You checked the cottage? That was quick thinking. Any chance you're going to tell me what you found?"

*Why am I blushing?* "Sure. Do you mind coming with me to the dining area? Let me get a bite, and then I'll share all my secrets."

DI Nancarrow sat at a table in the corner, waited for me to collect yogurt and fruit, and made small talk while I wolfed it all down. When I suggested coffee, he nodded, and I returned with two cups.

"Now," he said, "Let's take it from the top. I've heard about tea leaves, but I'd like you to walk me through what else you saw in the cottage."

"If we're going to take it from the top, perhaps we should start with me having tea with Caryn the night we all arrived. That would give you some context."

He looked amused. "Context? Okay, let's hear it."

I suspected I was telling him more than he wanted to hear, but I also felt he needed to know the background. It was a sad tale. I told him about Arthur Knight's tragic death, Caryn's concern it wasn't an accident, and the little bit she'd shared as to why he'd been in Tintagel.

"She seemed in decent spirits at yoga class the first afternoon—not ebullient, but not despondent. I think hearing someone else make the presentation Arthur would have made saddened her. I can't exactly put my finger on it. She seemed . . . indignant. No, that's not the right word. Whatever, it bothered her that Dylan Porter ended his presentation with Arthur's signature line. I could almost hear her thinking, 'How dare he?' That's why I offered to chat with her when the talk concluded."

DI Nancarrow was a good listener, and he didn't interrupt or make light of my ideas the way Gemma often did. He seemed to be taking it all in.

"She told me two interesting things—not that they have anything to do with her condition. One was she thought her fiancé's spur-of-the-moment trip down here was due to a concern about the artifacts arriving from the dig. The other was that she wasn't convinced his death was accidental. Guin, Arthur's sister, wanted Gemma to speak with Caryn about all that, to help her come to grips with it being an accident."

I was taken aback at his response to my long-winded story. "Don't quote me on this, but it could be she's on to something."

*Huh? Did I mishear him?* "Excuse me?"

"I wasn't the investigating officer, but when the original detective suddenly retired, I was asked to review his cases. He'd been hiding his failing health for some time, and our superiors are worried that his work may have suffered. They asked me to start with the files on drug activity, but the Arthur Knight investigation is also of particular concern."

*Gee, I know Wendy says I'm amazing at getting folks to open up to me, but I never expected this.*

As usual, my management experience kicked in. My technique for getting folks to share information was to say as little as possible, to work the pregnant pause, and I did it almost unconsciously. "Seriously?"

He tilted his head and squinted. "Yes, seriously. What else did Caryn share?"

I didn't think the story of their romance was what he was looking for, so I skipped that. "Only that he'd taken a leave of absence from teaching and given up leading the dig to focus on the British Museum exhibit and his writing. Dylan Porter has only recently taken over the Tintagel dig."

"Yes, I'd learned of the on-site change but not the why. That fits with what I've picked up from the local gossip. I get the sense Arthur's leadership was missed. Still, you can't read too much into that. Those kinds of feelings tend to surface whenever a new boss comes on the scene. Unless the old one was despised, of course. And that's not what I hear about Arthur. He was a local legend—the hometown boy made good who also brought renown to the area in the process. It wouldn't be an exaggeration to say he was much loved."

"That's so sad. I recall the newspaper article said something like, 'Cornwall mourns the loss of its native son,' but didn't realize how true it was."

We were both quiet for a moment. *I don't know what he's thinking, but I can't help wondering why he's being so forthcoming with me.*

"Bet you're wondering why I'm telling you all this?"

*If my superpower is listening, then his must be mind-reading!*
"Well, yes, I am," I admitted with a grin.

"Your friend Gemma would never tell you this, but during our training program when she was so worried about her dad being a suspect in a murder, she couldn't stop talking about you."

"In a good way, I take it? Now, that's a surprise."

He chuckled. "Oh, don't get me wrong. I got the impression she frequently wanted to choke you, but she was counting on you to clear her dad and ensure his name was removed from the list of suspects. If that meant you wound up identifying the real killer in the process, then that was fine by her. And, speak of the devil, here she is."

In walked Gemma, straight from her run, towel around her neck. It was only after she downed a large glass of water that she looked around and spied us in the corner of the room. "Jake?"

DI Nancarrow stood. "Gemma, I can't believe it's you."

As he moved to hug her, Gemma held up her hand. "I'm way to sweaty for that."

She smiled and pulled a chair up to the table. "What are you doing here, Jake? I thought you were in Exeter."

"I was, until my promotion to detective inspector. They had a vacancy in Truro, so that's where I am now. It has a bit of an urban feel like Exeter, but with only a quarter of the population."

That comparison brought to mind my shift from living in the suburbs of Atlanta to living in the tiny village of Astonbury. It wasn't a difficult adjustment for me, but I wondered about DI Nancarrow. "Has it been hard to get used to?"

"Not a bit. I grew up in Boscastle, one of the smaller villages just up the coast. You may have heard of it and the famous 2004 flood."

"The only reason I know of it is my husband and I ate lunch there the day we toured Tintagel several years ago. They have quite an exhibit detailing how horrific and sudden it was. When you stand on the bridge overlooking the harbor, you can almost imagine the water roaring down the hillside. You weren't there when it happened, were you?"

"Fortunately, no. I'd gone to university by then. My parents were still there, but they were among the lucky few who suffered no damage."

He smiled at Gemma. "And I hear you've been promoted too. Do you still live behind your parents' inn, or have you moved?"

"Still there. There was talk of my moving to Gloucester, but nothing came of it, and I'm glad."

The two carried on with shop talk, and I stood and started to excuse myself.

Jake held up his hand. "Whoa, wait a minute. I still haven't heard what you observed in the victim's cottage. Can you spare me a few more minutes?"

Gemma snorted. "Oh no, don't tell me Nancy Drew here has you thinking she's figured out how Caryn came to be unconscious."

Glancing sideways at the local DI, I couldn't help myself—I smirked. He went me one better and grinned.

"No, not exactly. But she shared a few bits of information that fit into another investigation."

At that, Gemma looked aghast. "Good grief, Leta. We've only been here two nights. What have you gotten yourself into?"

I stood. "I think I'll let you two put your heads together. After all, Gemma, you've been over to the cottage too, and you can tell the inspector what we found." *Ha! Let her talk her way out of that.*

As I walked away, I heard him ask her what exactly I meant. He sounded more amused than upset. In some ways, his easy-going manner reminded me of Dave's. In our conversations, my boyfriend seemed often to be on the verge of chuckling, a trait that endeared him to me.

# CHAPTER EIGHT

Wondering where Rhiannon had gotten to, I stopped by the front desk to ask Elaine. She pointed me to the family home, explaining Rhiannon was staying in one of the bedrooms there. "I guess most people would expect Aunt Guin to be the one falling apart, but Rhiannon's taking it pretty hard. Aunt Guin says she has a sense Caryn will be okay. She always says she can't explain how she knows, but more often than not her feelings are on target. That's the only reason I'm not in tears. Aunt Guin is so rarely wrong, I could swear she has second sight."

*Interesting take.* No matter Guin's sixth sense or second sight, I'd only ever known Rhiannon to be rock-steady—someone who didn't let things ruffle her. Finding someone lying unconscious in corpse pose would fluster anyone, though. I thought Guin might be a little less composed if she'd been the one to discover Caryn.

I found my friend sitting in a simple cross-legged pose on the soft grass in front of the family home. As I approached, she opened her eyes and smiled. *That's my gal. She looks serene, but that could be a facade.*

"Rhiannon, how are you doing?"

She took a deep breath and exhaled slowly. "Better than I was at dawn. Are there any updates?"

"Not on Caryn, but things are moving along." I told her about the local DI's arrival and the fact that he already knew Gemma. I didn't share what Gemma told me about her Oxford tragedy. It wasn't my place. I wasn't sure how I would handle Wendy—should I tell her or not? She was my best friend in the UK, and we pretty much shared everything. I'd have to ponder that dilemma.

Rhiannon sighed. "Caryn was so troubled, and now this. She can't seem to catch a break. If only I could feel as confident as Guin does that she'll pull through. Guin says trusting her instincts allows her to 'carry on and remain calm,' as we say. I wish I could feel that way too."

I sat on the steps below my friend. "Did you spend much time with her? Since you arrived Friday before the other guests, I suppose it was quiet here."

"Yes, it was like an island oasis on Friday. Guin and I spent a peaceful few hours planning the yoga sessions, and by late afternoon, I was able to relax by the pool. That's where I first met Caryn. If I had to guess, I'd say she'd spent most of the day dwelling on Arthur and what might have been. At least, that's how I read her somber mood. After expressing my sorrow at her loss, I got her to talk about her work at the British Museum. That lightened the atmosphere."

"Did she talk about Arthur's work on the Tintagel exhibit?"

"Oh yes. She described the walls and pottery shards Arthur's team had unearthed. It was similar to what we heard from Martin yesterday, only in more detail. I got an extensive lesson on Phocaean Red Slip Ware. Not red as we think of it, but a maroon shade with almost a tinge of purple. That pieces of it were found here at Tintagel is further evidence that trade with the eastern

Mediterranean was ongoing in the fifth and sixth centuries. Isn't that astonishing? It's also been unearthed in Ireland."

I chuckled at her enthusiastic description. "It never ceases to amaze me how rich the history is in Great Britain. I felt the same way about Greece when I visited. It's funny. In college, I also much preferred my Ancient Civilization courses to those on American history. Did Caryn happen to mention Arthur's concern about the artifacts?"

"Yes, but it was difficult for me to follow her train of thought. She'd wax poetic about Red Slip Ware and then say something like, 'Arthur wanted to check on that,' as though I'd know what she meant."

*Red Slip Ware was more detail than she'd given me.* "Did you get the sense she was merely reminiscing or was there more to it?"

Closing her eyes, Rhiannon looked thoughtful. "I'm not sure, but judging by the number of times she alluded to it, I'd say it was weighing heavily on her mind. Guin might have a better idea."

I nodded and stretched my legs. "Have you two decided whether we're having an afternoon class today?"

"Yes, Guin feels we must, as the guests paid good money for the retreat. Only Morgan has mentioned bowing out, and I think that's because she knows Caryn and is more distressed over the situation than the others."

"You know, I thought Morgan looked pale at the afternoon class yesterday, and I wondered if she was ill. I hope there's not some bug going around."

"Gosh, I sure hope not. It didn't come up when Guin spoke with the other guests, and she was able to be discreet and say as little as possible about Caryn's condition. It was only with Morgan that she felt she had to go into more detail."

"Right. Given what we heard yesterday from Martin, I bet this is another big blow for the girl. First, a man she's known since childhood and then dated dies in an accident, and now his fiancée is taken ill. I wonder how close she and Caryn are."

Rhiannon nodded. "I would imagine fairly close, but I don't know. So, we'll only have seven in class including you and Wendy. I don't see either of you being too distraught to carry on."

"You know us very well. Today was also the day Gareth was going to give any interested parties a tour of the lavender farm. I wonder if he's still planning on that. I know Ellie and Belle were looking forward to it."

Rhiannon nodded. "Oh yes, and I plan to take it. He has two golf carts, and Art will help him ferry us to and fro. I've already alerted him that Belle may need a bit of extra help."

A random thought popped into my head. "Are we going to meet Gareth's wife? I mean, he has one, right?"

My question elicited a chuckle. "Oh yes, he has one, but Merry stays busy with the farm. She's a bit shy and prefers making lotion and honey with lavender and the various herbs she grows. The rest of her time she spends marketing all of it to shops around Cornwall. The woman is a wonder at growing herbs and coming up with different fragrance combinations. Guin handles the yoga and the resort overall, while Gareth runs the farm. He's happy to provide tour services and to mingle at dinners with guests, and Art loves his role as the one bellboy, but Merry is content to stay in the background."

I thought about that dynamic as I walked back to Iseult Cottage. I was shy as a child, so much so my mom worried I wouldn't develop social skills. She marveled at how I wound up facilitating leadership classes and large meetings in my career, and Henry relied on my ability to "work the room" as he called it when we attended parties and awards banquets at his company. *Funny how life works out.*

"Where have you been?" Wendy called from her lounge chair by the pool. "For the past several hours, we've been like two ships passing in the night."

Laughing, I plopped on the chair beside her. "You must have returned to our cottage while I was with Gemma in Vivienne Cottage. What about Belle and Ellie? Where are they?"

"Ellie's reading and Mum is having an early lie-down after getting up at dawn. You know she doesn't often get up before nine. We agreed we'd all meet for lunch before the one p.m. tour with Gareth. By the way, I fed your demanding cat. Dickens is still snoozing, but Christie wanted food."

"Did you fluff it and center it in the bowl until it suited her?"

"Ha! Yes, I did. Amazing how she sits and looks at you as though you're slow on the uptake. And when she meows, I can almost hear her saying, 'you silly woman, can't you get it right?'"

*If she only knew how accurate she was.* As much time as she spent with me and my four-legged companions, I wondered whether she'd one day be able to "talk to the animals" like I did. No one ever had, but I kept thinking someone would eventually.

"You know, I could do with a lie-down myself. That demanding cat, as you've dubbed her, got me up at 5:30. Maybe after this afternoon's yoga class, I can nap. So, tell me, have you seen that dishy Detective Inspector?"

"I sure have, and I must say, he and Gemma look well-acquainted. She introduced him to me before they went into Caryn's cottage together, and when they came out, he put his hand on Gemma's arm. He headed to the barn, and she went to her cottage. Can you remember a time you've ever seen anyone touch Gemma other than her mum or dad? I can't."

Most people wouldn't have picked up on the significance of that interaction, but then, Wendy wasn't most people. Like me, she had an eye for detail and was adept at reading people, and like me, she'd been around Gemma quite a bit. Prickly and standoffish were adjectives that came to mind when I thought of our local DI.

"True. Of course, other than your twin, I don't know that I've ever seen her near an attractive single man. And he's too old for her, in my humble opinion."

"So, you think Peter's attractive? I think he is too, and I can't figure out why no one's snatched him up. I mean, there aren't that many single attractive men in Astonbury. He's even fit, unlike so many men his age with their paunches."

I laughed at Wendy. Peter and she might be twins, but they weren't much alike. He was tall. She was short. She was outgoing, and he was introverted. They were both blonde and blue-eyed, but there the similarities ended.

"He can't help but be fit with his cycling and cricket. I'm thankful he pushed me to start riding again, or I might have one of those paunches you mention."

She removed her sunglasses and squinted in the sunshine or at me, I wasn't sure. "Tell me the truth, Leta, have you ever thought of Peter that way? I mean, as boyfriend material? Not that I don't love Dave to pieces, but he does live across the pond."

I might have choked had I been drinking anything. How could I tell her that Christie regularly opined that she preferred Peter to Dave? I thought it had something to do with Peter's resemblance to Henry—tall, blonde, and slender—not that I took romantic advice from my cat. Dickens, oddly enough, had known from the get-go that Dave was attracted to me and thought both men were fine boyfriend material.

"Well, I wasn't looking for a boyfriend when I first arrived—gosh, it's been a year ago now. And, unbeknownst to you and me, your brother was dating someone at the time. If I hadn't met Dave, cycling with Peter might have led to something more than friendship. It's hard to say. There's no doubt he's an attractive man and one of the few eligible bachelors in Astonbury."

Wendy shrugged. "Isn't that the truth? Beyond Peter, the only one I can name is Toby, and some might consider him ineligible because he's recently divorced. Is it any wonder I fell for Brian—until he showed his true colors, that is?"

Her brother and I were both thankful Wendy figured it out. We thought Detective Chief Inspector Burton's true colors were obvious from the get-go, but neither of us was ever going to say that to her. Their spring vacation to Tintagel put an end to the romance, though he seemed to harbor the misbegotten notion that she might change her mind. If he heard the way she talked about him when they returned from vacation, he'd know better. At least I *thought* he'd know better, but then again, his interpersonal skills were sorely lacking.

"I think you fell for his looks. There's no denying he's a silver fox, as you described him."

"Enough about him. What do you know about this DI Nancarrow? Did he give you the third degree? He told me he'd be back to talk to me later, but I don't know what I can tell him beyond what he's already heard from you."

I gave Wendy a synopsis of my conversation with the DI. For some reason, I now thought of him as Jake, maybe because it rolled off the tongue more easily than his three-syllable last name. When I shared the details of my tea conversation with Caryn, my friend held up her hand in the stop motion.

"Wait a minute. Yesterday when you told me about your chat with Caryn, you only talked about her emotional state. What's this about Arthur being concerned about something? Something amiss with boxes from the dig? That sounds serious."

"Well, yes, it does, and Rhiannon gave me a bit more detail about some red bowl, but let me get back to Jake."

When she tilted her head and mouthed *Jake*, I knew she was amused at me calling him by his first name. All I could do was chuckle and continue. "So, hold on to your hat, Jake tells me he's reviewing the case file about Arthur's alleged accident."

Wendy sat forward in her lounge chair. "What? He doesn't think it was accidental? And Caryn didn't either?" She paused. "Leta, if it wasn't an accident, it had to be murder. And if it was murder, why? Why did someone want him dead?"

Though I'd been thinking along the same lines, I played devil's advocate. "Whoa, wait a minute. Reviewing the file doesn't mean the conclusion will change. Or if it does, they could decide it was death by suicide and not an accident."

"He was engaged. He was starting a new phase in an already successful career. Why would he be suicidal? Nope, it was murder."

I loved her certainty, probably because I felt the same way. "Wendy, if it was murder, then Caryn's instincts were right. She wasn't shy about expressing her concerns to me. I wonder who else she may have shared them with besides maybe Guin and Gareth. Heck, she alluded to them with Rhiannon."

"Forgive me, Leta, I don't know why this phrase from Shakespeare leaps to mind, but it does. 'It must follow, as night follows day,' that someone is worried about what Caryn knows. Even if she doesn't *know*, she has suspicions about why and maybe even who. Take it a step further, and it's possible someone was worried enough to go after Caryn."

Smiling at my friend, I responded, "Now it's your turn to forgive *me* because it's not funny in the circumstances, but why wouldn't a quote from *Hamlet* spring to your mind? You *did* teach English for over thirty years. But, that's quite a leap, isn't it? The police are merely reviewing the circumstances surrounding Arthur's death. They haven't reopened the case. And from that and Caryn's suspicions, whether unfounded or not, you've concluded there's foul play involved?"

"Yes. Think about what Martin said yesterday. Even if he didn't say it outright, I think he wonders about it being an accident. Then Arthur's fiancée mysteriously falls unconscious. Don't you see the connection?"

*Uh-oh.* "Not as clearly as you do."

"It's more likely you're trying *not* to see it! It doesn't matter, though. We're perfectly positioned to piece together the why and the who of both incidents, related or not—Arthur's alleged accident and whatever's going on with Caryn. With Mum, Ellie, you, and me, we'll have it sorted in no time."

*This is a perfect example of what I thought earlier—Wendy is the bold one.* "I was game when we were searching for what Caryn might have eaten or drunk to cause her severe reaction, but now you're leaping to solving a possible murder and maybe more?"

"Who better to read the tea leaves or follow the trail of breadcrumbs? Choose your metaphor. I say the Little Old Ladies are on the case."

*And so it begins.*

# CHAPTER NINE

WENDY REMAINED POOLSIDE, SO I was free to talk to myself as I showered, or talk to Dickens and Christie. *How do I let myself get involved in these things?* Wendy was almost gleeful at the prospect of the Little Old Ladies' Detective Agency taking on another case, and I, as always, was reluctant. *You'd think Belle and Ellie would rein her in.*

As I chose a comfortable red-and-white sundress to wear for the farm tour, I pondered the implications of what we knew so far. If something Caryn ate or drank caused her condition, we were talking about poison. That might be a logical conclusion, but we'd have to identify the toxic substance before we could work our way to who. At least, that was my reasoning. And how could we amateurs figure that out? It seemed to me the substance had to be in the tea, but it wasn't as if the Little Old Ladies could analyze or *read* the tea leaves, as Wendy said.

"Dickens, Christie, what do you think? If it *was* the tea, what are our next steps?"

Dickens stretched and rolled over for a belly rub. "Beats me, Leta."

"Seems like sniffing the tea would tell you something. Have you tried that?" suggested Christie.

Christie's input had merit, except Wendy and I had already done that, and the only smell we could pinpoint was licorice. The label on the little brown bag mentioned licorice root, so that made sense. I recalled the other two ingredients as being nettle leaf and tulsi but had no idea how they should smell. *Who would?*

I didn't have an answer for that as I grabbed my straw hat and opened the door. Hearing yoga was later in the day, Christie was content to stay behind, stretched out in the sunshine coming in the bedroom window.

Dickens trailed after me. "What's for lunch? Will we see Art? How 'bout Merlin?"

My boy could always make me laugh with his rapid-fire questions. I didn't have an answer about the lunch menu, but he barked happily when I confirmed we'd soon see both Art and Merlin.

The Astonbury group had saved me a seat at one of the round tables. Engaged in lively conversation, they didn't miss a beat as I joined them. Dickens went straight to Belle and laid his head in her lap.

Scratching his ears, she looked at me. "And how are you doing after this morning, dear?"

"Pretty well. We were fortunate to have Nurse Davies available. I sure wouldn't have known to turn the patient on her side. Did Dr. Black share any additional thoughts on what might have made Caryn so ill?"

"Nothing beyond being pretty sure it was something she ate or drank, not some germ or virus. So, there's no danger it's catching."

Gemma frowned. "I sure hope they can put a rush on analyzing the samples that we sent with the ambulance. I called the hospital, but there was no update on that. They did tell me she was resting comfortably and her breathing was better, though she's not regained consciousness yet."

On the other side of the table, Ellie and Rhiannon were discussing lavender and its medicinal qualities. Ellie kept lavender oil in the kitchen at the manor house to use on minor burns, and Rhiannon used it to scent the weighted eye bags at her Astonbury yoga studio.

I pictured a lavender gift Henry had given me. "I just love the scent. I had a neck wrap in Atlanta I could heat in the microwave for my achy shoulders, but I lost it in my move. Rhiannon, do you think Merry has anything like that for sale?"

"Merry? Who's Merry?" asked Gemma.

Rhiannon answered. "She's Gareth's wife. He grows the lavender, but she turns it into lotions and honey. She probably produces oils too, but I haven't heard mention of scented neck wraps or pillows. We'll get to meet her today when the tour goes by their cottage."

From a nearby table, Penny from Dartmouth called to us. "You'll want to be sure to take in her herb garden. Did you know she provided the basil for last night's pasta?"

As the self-professed owner of two brown thumbs, I only wished I could grow herbs. "Basil is my favorite, but I have to get my supply from our local farmer's market. Just talking about it makes me hungry for pasta tossed with olive oil, basil, and freshly grated parmesan cheese."

"Herbs, something about herbs," Wendy murmured.

Gemma cocked her head. "What, Wendy?"

"I don't know. Something flew into my brain and out again. That seems to happen to me more and more often these days."

My friend described it just the way I would. "I feel your pain, Wendy. These days, thoughts seem to flit in and out of my head before I can grab them."

Ellie studied her cup of tea. "If, as you mentioned this morning, the bag of tea was labeled *T-T-T*, I'm guessing it's from Tintagel's Tiny Tea Shop. There's a selection of their tea for sale in the lobby. Has anyone contacted them to see if they ever add anything else? Maybe in such small amounts that it's not worth noting on the label? It could be the poor girl had a strong allergic reaction to something, the same way people who are allergic to peanuts can go into anaphylactic shock."

I saw Gemma's mouth open slightly. *Uh-oh, here it comes.*

Next, she rolled her eyes. "No way. Don't you ladies start. DI Nancarrow was called in to investigate, and he doesn't need any help."

"Not even from you?" I asked.

Before she could respond, Belle piped up. "Now, Gemma, you know how helpful we can be, and since we're all four here, why not let us nose around—innocently, of course?"

"Aaargh. You know full well why not. It's a police matter."

Belle and Ellie spoke at the same time. "Yes, dear."

*So much for Belle and Ellie reining in Wendy.*

When we saw Art and Gareth waiting outside with two golf carts, Wendy stopped short. "Oops! Forgot my hat. I'll be right back."

Morgan hadn't appeared for lunch and Caryn was at the hospital, so we were easily able to accommodate everyone in the carts. Belle and Rhiannon climbed in the cart driven by Gareth, followed by the sisters, Penny and Sue. Running up with her sun hat in hand, Wendy clambered in. Ellie, Gemma, and I followed Dickens to Art's cart and were joined by the mother and daughter from Boscastle. I was glad the ladies reintroduced themselves as Lilith and Lily, as I'd forgotten their names.

The daughter wrinkled her nose. "It drives Mum crazy that I decided to go by Lily instead of my given name, but two Liliths is confusing. When I was little, my brothers called me Lilith Junior, and I was never happy with that."

I told her my full name was Aleta, and only my parents had ever called me that. I knew where I stood with them when I heard my full name. Dad used it affectionately. My mother, on the other hand, only called me Aleta when she was scolding me.

Art greeted us. "Ladies, let me introduce Merlin. Shall we let him run behind us with Dickens?"

After we exclaimed over the frisky border collie and took turns petting him, we agreed that was a good plan. Merlin and Dickens barked and frolicked as we waited for Gareth to lead the way in his cart.

Art handed around slender notebooks of laminated pages as reference material. The first page gave a short history of Knight's Rest. Art's grandparents and great-grandparents before them had raised sheep. Some of the men in the family had also fished to supplement the family income.

For over one hundred years, the Knights had relied on sheep for their livelihood. It was Gareth's idea to shift to lavender as their main source of income. As the popularity of lavender products grew in the twenty-first century, Gareth had slowly downsized the flock of sheep and increased the lavender crop. Now, he kept only a handful of sheep, and they were penned up to keep them from eating the cash crop. Merry used the sheep's milk for her soap making.

"Ellie, look at these pictures of soap and lotion. It makes me think of your daughter-in-law Sarah and her products, all made from the sheep at Astonbury Manor. Of course, she takes it a step further with the artisans on the estate also using the wool for sweaters and such."

"Leta, we'll have to purchase some of Merry's products to try for ourselves and take some home to Sarah. She's interested in different varieties and learning from the competition."

Art chimed in. "Mum will be happy to chat about soap and lotion and her herb garden. She's forever trying new things." He pointed to the golf cart ahead of us. "Okay, ladies, we're on our way."

Driving slowly, Art began by explaining the cottages were named for the women who figured in the Arthurian legend—Igraine, Iseult, Vivienne, Guinevere, Morgana, Elaine, and Morgause. He wasn't surprised his passengers had already figured that out. "It's often our male guests who don't get the connection. Usually, they've heard of Guinevere, but that's about it."

He pointed to the large cottage that sat slightly behind and to the right of the barn. "That's the original home my great-grandparents built in the 1800s. When my grandparents had Uncle Arthur, their first child, they enlarged it to include more bedrooms, then an office, and finally a conservatory. Until Dad and Aunt Guin added the cottages, those were the only two structures, the family home and the barn."

Our young driver pointed off in the distance. "That cliff you can barely see is the high point in Tintagel, the clifftop where the ruins are. Is anyone taking the tour this week?"

The corners of Ellie's mouth turned down. "I wish I could, but even with the new bridge, I'm afraid the uneven ground on top would be too treacherous for these old bones. I'm grateful Leta and Wendy brought back lots of photos."

Art chuckled. "Someone in the village once suggested a golf-cart tour, but it's just not feasible. Since he was in the pub when he voiced the idea, the rest of the patrons concluded he'd had a bit too much to drink at the time."

I laughed at the idea of a golf cart bumping over the rocky surface of the cliff and concurred it must have been an alcohol-fueled brainstorm.

Art turned our cart down the gravel drive toward the lavender fields and the cottage farther down. "There were a few rows of lavender at Knight's Rest in my grandparents' day, but the land mostly belonged to the sheep and Merlin's predecessors. Other farmers in the area grew vegetables, but there wasn't much call for lavender back then."

Suddenly, Merlin shot past us, followed by Dickens.

Merlin looked over his shoulder. "Come on, Dickens, keep up. Let's see if we can scare up some rabbits."

Ellie pointed at Dickens. "He's running as fast as his short legs will carry him. He'll be worn out tonight for sure."

Looking over his shoulder, Art commented. "That's how they were yesterday. They ran up and down the rows of lavender, collapsed in a heap, and then started again."

Merlin's mention of rabbits reminded me of Dickens discovering their paw prints. "Art, do you have lots of bunnies?"

He chuckled. "Oh yes. Fortunately, they don't care for lavender or any strong-smelling herbs. I think Mum would take to rabbit hunting if they did. The only herb they won't leave alone is her basil, so she's moved those plants and fenced them off."

Rows and rows of fragrant lavender greeted us, and Art parked about halfway down the field. We climbed from the golf cart and took in the glorious sight of purple stalks waving in the wind. Art walked backward down one of the rows as he explained that the lavender plants grown at Knight's Rest were Lavandin, a variety prized for its strong scent.

Lily buried her face in a plant. "Oh my, I want to gather it all up and pile it in my bedroom. It's that tempting."

I wondered whether Merry had the oil in spray bottles for use on pillows. I'd be in heaven if she did and would have to stock up. That was one thing Sarah didn't have at Astonbury Manor. She specialized in lotion and soap.

Spying Dickens and Merlin resting in the distance, I walked to the end of the row where they lay. There, amidst rocks scattered across from the field of lavender, I saw several clumps of plants with large pale purple blossoms. "I wonder, are these a different variety of lavender?"

Though I didn't expect an answer, Merlin barked. "Dickens asked the same thing. He thought they were lavender plants until he smelled them."

Dickens stood and wandered over. "Merlin's right, Leta. As soon as you take a sniff, you'll know it's not lavender. These things smell awful."

I stuck my nose in the plant and had to agree with Dickens. "Ewww. What an unpleasant odor. I wonder what they are."

Merlin said he didn't know the name, only that Art had told him to stay away from them. "Like he had to tell me that. I know when something's not good for me."

*Interesting. I'll have to ask what they are.* I'd lost sight of my group, so I trotted towards the opposite end of the row. I saw they'd decided to walk to the herb garden and the small stone building in the midst of it. Farther down the hill closer to the cliffside sat a larger cottage—not as large as the one by the barn but bigger than the guest cottages.

Both groups of ladies were chatting with a petite woman wearing a large floppy sunbonnet. I caught a glimpse of a long blonde braid as she turned. *This must be Merry.*

I joined Art and Gareth, who stood off to the side. Gareth leaned down to whisper in my ear. "Go on, Leta, join them. Merry's giving them her herb talk, and she'll soon shift to how she makes the lotion and soap."

Moving closer, I heard Wendy ask about herbs in tea. It was clear Merry was in her element as she spoke of using peppermint, lemon verbena, and various other herbs in her tea blends and lotions. She laughingly admitted she was partial to lavender not only because she lived on a lavender farm but also because of its sweet and fragrant taste and its ability to calm the mind, reduce tension, and even alleviate headaches. "Guin and I agree that the best cure for stress is a yoga class followed by a cup of lavender tea."

I couldn't see Belle, but I recognized her voice. "I noticed the lavender and lemon verbena lotions for sale in the barn, but I didn't see tea. Is lavender tea also available?"

When Merry turned and responded, I realized someone had provided a chair for Belle. "I make various blends for our family and for Guin to serve for guests, but we don't sell it. Instead, we supply lavender to Tintagel's Tiny Tea Shop on Fore Street. You can find several lovely lavender blends there. It's our way to support the local economy. We stick to lotions, soap, sprays, and oils and leave the tea market to them. In turn, they stock our products, and Guin sells a sampler set of theirs."

Art said something to his mum I couldn't hear, but she turned and called me over. "Art tells me you're the owner of Christie."

She held up a crocheted mouse. "I fill these little things with catnip for Archie and I thought your kitty might enjoy it too."

Laughing, I thanked her for the gift and carried it to Ellie and Wendy, who were standing by Belle's seat. "Look at this! Isn't it adorable?" As they passed it around, I added, "Belle, I'm glad to see you're being well taken care of."

"Oh, that young man Art ran inside and had a chair for me before I was out of the golf cart. I told his mum he was a keeper."

A random idea flashed through my brain, and this time I was able to catch it before it disappeared. "Ladies, I wonder what Merry could tell us if she looked at the tea we found in Caryn's cottage."

Wendy had a sly grin on her face. "That was the thought that blew in and out of my brain at lunch, and it suddenly came back to me when I passed Vivienne Cottage on the way to grab my hat."

I made the expected comment about great minds thinking alike, but it was Ellie's image that made us all guffaw. She described our thoughts as colorful butterflies and the four of us running to snatch them from the air with butterfly nets.

When the laughter subsided, Wendy wiped the tears from her eyes. "Well, guess what, ladies? When I snagged that particular idea from the air, I followed through and ducked in Vivienne Cottage for the little brown bag."

I was shocked. "You did what?"

"Just what I said. I scooped up the bag and put it in our cottage."

"You know, taking that bag of tea could be construed as tampering with evidence. Better you than me."

Wendy winked. "Now look, you and I, you and Gemma, and then Gemma and DI Nancarrow have gone over that place.

Gemma gave the wet tea to the paramedics, so what harm can it do for us to have the dry stuff?"

The two senior members of the Little Old Ladies' Detective Agency seemed to be enjoying our exchange. Ellie shrugged. "What's done is done, wouldn't you say, ladies? Now, what's our next step?"

Belle leaned on her cane and stood. "I say we speak to Merry to see if she's willing to help us. Ellie, why don't you and I handle that?"

Wendy and I watched from afar as the two approached Merry. Though we couldn't hear the conversation, we could observe the body language and facial expressions. First, Merry's eyes widened as though in surprise. Then she tilted her head and seemed to be listening attentively as Belle and Ellie spoke. When Merry closed her eyes and nodded, we knew they'd made the sale.

When they returned, Belle gave a thumbs up. "At first she was stunned, but once we explained the delay in the hospital doing the analysis, she was eager to help. We all know the faster we can identify what's in the tea, the more quickly a treatment can be decided on. She said to come back this afternoon and she'd take a look. We agreed you and Wendy would walk down before dinner."

The last stop on our farm tour was beyond the larger family cottage along the cliff edge. Belle and Ellie remained in the golf carts while the rest of us walked closer to the overlook. The view of the ocean was breathtaking, as were the ruins of Tintagel in the distance. Even Dickens and Merlin seemed taken with the vista. Both stood with their noses raised to the wind, their eyes closed as the strong wind blew their ears and fur.

The dogs followed the golf carts as we moved toward the barn but detoured at the lavender fields, probably in hopes of finding bunnies. *My boy is sure to get another good night's sleep after his excursion.* As I climbed from the cart, I stopped to talk to Gareth. "If you're joining us tonight, will you bring my little Dickens back with you, please?"

Gareth grinned. "If they go at it as hard as they did yesterday, I may have to carry him back—after he has dinner, of course."

Wendy and I chatted as we changed into yoga clothes. We agreed that despite the underlying worry about Caryn, we'd enjoyed the farm tour and the glimpses of the castle ruins.

"Christie, are you walking, or shall I carry you to yoga?" When my sassy cat strutted out the front door and toward the barn, I had my answer.

Wendy watched the black tail switch back and forth. "You know, I expect Dickens to understand your hand signals and voice commands, but I thought cats had minds of their own."

"She does, but she likes yoga, and she picked up on the yoga clothes and the mat. As for walking or being carried? Who knows?" That was all true, except there was no doubt Christie had understood my question.

Stopping by the front desk, we asked Elaine if there were any updates from the hospital. She explained that Caryn wasn't out of the woods yet, but was improving. "Aunt Guin called to say she's on her way back since Caryn seems to be holding her own. I think Dad may take her place later."

Once again, Rhiannon was on her own in the studio. If not for the situation with Caryn, Rhiannon would have taught the back bend class this morning and it would be Guin teaching a session on inversions now. I hoped we'd still be able to squeeze that in before the retreat ended. As Rhiannon predicted, there were only seven of us—Gemma, Lily and Lilith, Sue and Penny, and Wendy and me. Today, our props included bolsters and folding chairs in addition to blocks and blankets. When I folded a blanket to sit on, Archie stretched out on top of it.

Christie was quick to set him straight. "Hey, we're supposed to lie on the ladies, not the blankets, you silly thing."

When he made a rude sound almost like a raspberry, Lilith looked up. "Those two are hysterical. Christie meows, and Archie all but sticks his tongue out at her. Now, look at him." He was strutting away, his tail held high.

By now, we were all chuckling, and we laughed even harder when Archie darted out the door. Gemma pointed at Christie. "What on earth did she say to him?"

It took some effort for Rhiannon to settle us down, and she almost lost us again when we moved into cat pose. We stifled giggles as we murmured about Christie doing cat pose. On our hands and knees, we alternately arched our backs and flexed our spines downward while lifting our heads. When she sauntered beneath my stomach, I smiled at her.

I could already feel the stress leaving my body, and as we moved into the more difficult poses, all thoughts of tea, herbs, and sleuthing flew from my mind. *Ohm*.

# CHAPTER TEN

As I rolled my mat, I wiped my brow and glanced at Wendy. "I'm glad you're sweating too. That was a good workout. Puts me in mind of my mom saying, 'Southern girls don't sweat, they glisten,' though I think those girls were sitting on the veranda, sipping iced tea, and fanning themselves."

Wendy chuckled. "Oh goodness. Can you simultaneously glisten and be worn slap out? That's another Southernism that makes me laugh, and I'd say today we're proof you can be both at the same time."

We straggled back to our cottage, followed by Christie and Archie. The grey cat had been waiting at the front desk when we emerged from the studio. Glancing behind us, Wendy chuckled. "He seemed miffed earlier, but look at them. They're becoming quite the duo, aren't they? And they don't look the least bit tired."

"No, they don't. But then again, they weren't doing back-bends. Goodness, those take a lot out of me. Regardless, I predict those two will be conked out in no time. I can't decide what I want to do first—take a dip in the pool, take a shower and a nap, or visit Merry? What do you think?"

"That's a tough one. What say we get the tea and walk to Merry's? After that, we can take a quick swim."

As we tossed our mats in the sitting room, our feline yogis ran to the kitchen. One impatient look from Christie was all it took to remind me to put out fresh water. I watched as they shared the bowl, Archie greedily lapping water with his tongue and Christie daintily dipping her paw in to carry dabs to her mouth. When Christie sashayed toward the bedroom, Archie was right behind her. *My, my, it's as if she meowed, come hither.*

Merry looked up from her workbench and wiped her hands on her apron as we approached. "You've piqued my curiosity, ladies. I can't imagine anything harmful being in tea from Tintagel's Tiny Tea Shop, but I'll take a look. It could be something that's not a problem for most people, something that causes a severe allergic reaction in only a few."

She looked at the label. "Oh, T-T-T for Women is their biggest seller. That's why it's one of the three blends included in the sampler set we sell. The others are their chamomile citron and their lemon lavender blend."

Pulling an earthenware saucer from beneath her work-bench, she poured the loose tea on it and used a pair of long tweezers to separate the ingredients. "These hard brown pieces are the licorice root. Here's the nettle, and this green leaf is the tulsi that gives it a slight mint flavor. Hmmm. I'm curious about these purple bits and the seeds."

She carefully separated the ingredients into small piles. "Because of the color, some might mistake the purple for lavender, but that's not what it is. And none of the three listed ingredients are seeds either. Let me grab some of my dried lavender and my *Big Book of Herbs*, my go-to reference book." Ducking into the small stone building, she soon returned with a well-thumbed book and a pottery jug with a cork stopper. It was labeled *lavender*.

Merry sniffed the jug and handed it to Wendy to do the same. Wendy passed it on to me. "I dry our lavender and then use it in the tea Guin serves. The lavender gives it a mint-like scent, and the flavor is light but on the sweet side, as you've probably noticed."

We agreed it had a pleasant fragrance, almost flower-like, and that we both liked the tea we'd been drinking. Then she asked us to sniff the small pile of purple in the first saucer. Our wrinkled noses told the story.

Wendy spoke up first. "That's a completely different smell, and it's not pleasant at all. I wonder why we didn't notice it before."

"Do you recall smelling licorice? It likely masked this other scent. It requires a 'practiced' nose to pick up distinct scents in a dry blend. Once brewed, though, the subtle smell would have transformed into a strong unpleasant flavor—so pronounced that it would overpower even the licorice. You might not smell it in the wet tea leaves left behind in the strainer, but you would taste it when you sipped your tea."

I made a gagging sound. "For me, licorice would be bad enough. If it tastes anywhere near as bad as that purple stuff smells, why would anybody drink it?"

Merry shrugged. "If you think it's good for you, you might suffer through it. Plenty of people do that with some medicinal blends. Now, let's see if I can figure out what it is. I have a disturbing hunch, but I'd prefer to be certain."

Flipping the pages of the *Big Book of Herbs*, she paused at one and turned the book around to show us. There was a photo of a pretty flowering plant and another of a seedpod, and the heading read "Jimson Weed". "I think this is what it is, and that's not good." She read aloud. "Jimson Weed is part of the deadly nightshade family, and its effects are similar to those of belladonna. Ingesting jimson weed can cause serious illness or death. The effects of the seeds are more potent than that of the flowers or leaves, and they include headache, extreme thirst, dilated pupils, weak pulse, nausea, convulsions, and coma."

Wendy looked at me. "Caryn threw up and had a weak pulse, and she's unconscious. How on earth does jimson weed wind up in a bag of loose tea?"

Merry motioned us to follow her. "I want to show you something." We walked through the lavender field to an outcropping of large rocks. There, among the rocks, were the plants I'd seen earlier—the ones with large pale purple flowers. "This is jimson weed."

"Oh, I saw these today when I followed Merlin and Dickens. It smells awful."

Wendy looked puzzled. "Why on earth did you smell it? What did you think it was?"

I couldn't very well explain to her that Dickens and Merlin pointed it out to me. "Well, it was purple, and I wondered whether it was a different variety of lavender. I admit when you think about it, it doesn't look anything like lavender other than the hint of color."

"That's what's so puzzling," Merry said. "Technically, it's an herb, but anyone who knows herbs would know what it is and would never use it for a tea ingredient. And a novice deciding to pick it and use it for tea would be tantamount to someone pulling any old mushroom from the ground and popping it into their mouth. People should know better. Unfortunately, it's recently become popular with kids looking for a hallucinogen, and that's led to some serious situations."

As we returned to the herb garden, we debated what Merry's discovery meant. I stared at the saucer and the little brown bag of tea. "Merry, does the tea shop prepare its tea blends, or do they order them from somewhere else?"

"Oh yes, they make it themselves. That's why they buy the dried lavender directly from us, and they buy other herbs from local farmers. Only a few of the ingredients are ordered online, things that don't grow in our climate, like kaffir limes."

Wendy asked the obvious next question. "So, if the tea shop mistakenly put jimson weed in the tea, it would be in more than one bag, right?"

Merry looked horrified. "Oh my goodness, yes. We need to alert Guin right away to check through all the tea from Tintagel's Tiny Tea Shop before someone else is harmed. And we need to call the tea shop too, though I can't imagine they would make that kind of mistake. They've been doing this for years."

I was still playing it out in my head. "But if we don't find purple flecks and seeds in the other bags labeled *T-T-T for Women*, that tells us something else."

Speechless, Merry folded her arms across her chest and rocked back and forth. As distressed as she was at the prospect of the tea shop making a horrific life-threatening mistake, the idea that someone purposely put a toxic plant in Caryn's tea seemed almost too much for her.

She looked from me to Wendy before suddenly leaning over the work table. She prodded the bits of jimson weed with her finger. "You know, there's something else odd about this. The jimson weed isn't dried like the nettle, tulsi, and licorice root."

I could almost see the wheels turning in Wendy's head. "And that means . . . it wasn't prepped properly?"

Nodding slowly, Merry responded, "Yes. If a person mistook it for something else, gathered it, and dried it in a batch, you'd expect it to be dried like the other herbs. And it would make sense to find it in more than one packet of tea. That's almost preferable to the alternative."

Merry nibbled her lower lip. "But it's not dried. If someone had a spur-of-the-moment idea to try the pretty purple plant in tea, they might have picked a bouquet of jimson weed, torn it in bits, and immediately mixed it with the tea ingredients. Just as you might sprinkle fresh basil on a salad."

She paused. "Except how would it wind up in a packet of tea from the tea shop? I can't make sense of it."

I tried to process what she was telling me. "So, if someone like Caryn unknowingly wanted to try the pretty plant in tea, she'd sprinkle it in the teapot with the loose tea. There'd be no reason to add it to the little bag. And yet, in the bag is where we found it, in the bag and the wet tea in the strainer. Hell's bells, when you put it all together, it can only mean one thing."

Wendy threw up her hands. "Leta, isn't that exactly what I tried to tell you earlier? If we find jimson weed is present in Caryn's little bag but not in the others, it means someone is out to get her, someone dosed her tea. Either way, we need to get to the barn and start checking the tea right away."

"Wait," said Merry. "Here comes Gareth. He needs to hear this, and he can help us check."

Her tall blond husband had a welcoming smile on his face. "Hello, ladies. What brings you back to the herb garden?"

Merry pointed to Wendy and me. "Gareth, it's awful. You have to hear this."

I could tell he didn't know what to think as the three of us talked over each other. Still, he managed to get the gist of what we were trying to tell him. Oddly enough, he didn't seem disbelieving.

He pointed to the golf cart. "Let's go. We've got to move fast in case all the tea is tainted."

As we piled in the cart, he added, "Would you be surprised if I told you the thought of poison entered my mind when I heard Caryn was taken ill? Don't ask me to explain why. It's just that between Arthur's death and Caryn's worries, I was beginning to second-guess everything. Her being unconscious brought it all to a head, at least for me."

*Not good, not good.* "Okay, let's take care of the tea displayed in the reception area first. After that, we can take stock of what we know. And I think we should check every single little bag of tea, not just T-T-T for Women. What if all the blends are tainted with jimson weed?"

Gareth accelerated up the hill to the barn, and we all tumbled out before he came to a complete stop. Ellie was chatting with Guin at the counter when we ran in.

They both turned and seemed to realize at the same moment that something was up. Looking perplexed, Guin spoke to her brother. "Gareth, what's wrong?"

While he explained what we needed to do, Merry went to the shelves on the wall to collect the boxes of tea. There were only ten boxes, and we quickly divvied them up and started checking through them.

The fastest way to determine if there were purple bits buried in the blends was to dump the contents of the individual bags one by one—all of them, not just the blend for women. I took two boxes to a table by the front door and made fast work of emptying the three bags in each. No purple bits, no seeds.

Wendy called from one end of the counter, "No jimson weed here."

Merry and Gareth looked up from the other end of the counter where they'd taken their boxes. They shook their heads.

Gareth was the first to speak. "Guin, have you sold any sampler boxes to the other guests since the retreat started? We'll need to check those."

"Oh my goodness. No, except for what I've just sold Ellie."

That's when Ellie cleared her throat and held up a box of tea. "I guess you need to check this one too. I just had Guin add it to my tab."

I blanched and ran to grab the box from her hand. When I opened it, I gasped. "Here we go, three little bags—the women's blend, chamomile blend, and lavender." I quickly poured the tea on the counter. No jimson weed.

We breathed a collective sigh of relief before Guin said what we had to all be thinking. "So, everyone else should be safe."

Merry asked, "Except, if the bag of tea didn't come from here, where did it come from? How did Caryn wind up with one bag of tea? Elaine and Caryn hiked and drove to Truro last week. Did the two go to the village since she's been here?"

Guin shook her head. "No. She refused to go to Tintagel. She said it would be too painful, and I understand that. And Merry, you know how particular she is about her tea. She brought her tins with her, the ones Arthur gave her."

I played back the scene in Caryn's cottage when Wendy and I got there. "I saw those when I had tea with her Saturday night. How did she get this one bag?"

Wendy ran her hand through her hair. "I think the answer's obvious. Someone wanted her to have it. Someone planted poisoned tea in her cottage."

My mouth dropped open. "Omigosh! We've got to call the hospital now. We've got to let them know what triggered her condition so they can give her an antidote, assuming there is one."

When we all started talking at once, Guin took charge and rang the hospital. Wendy ran out the door yelling she was going to our cottage to google jimson weed, and I ran for Gemma. *For once, there's no way she can scoff at our ideas.*

# CHAPTER ELEVEN

I POUNDED ON THE door to Guinevere Cottage. "Gemma, come quick."

When she came yawning to the door, I grabbed her and dragged her to Iseult Cottage, attempting to explain what was going on as we walked. Amazingly, she got the essence of the tale. Even more amazingly, she didn't pooh-pooh what I told her.

The door to the cottage was open, and we rushed in. "Wendy, I've got Gemma. Tell us what you've found out about jimson weed."

Wendy stood at the kitchen counter, phone in hand. "It's toxic all right. Per the internet, the treatment is different depending on the patient's symptoms. Could be they've already used a purgative like magnesium sulfate unless they held off because they weren't sure what she'd ingested. I don't think they would have given her Valium because she wasn't having convulsions. You can't believe all the information about the people who've fallen victim to the plant throughout history, but none of that will help with taking care of Caryn."

Gemma was looking from me to Wendy and back. "Is someone calling the hospital?"

I nodded. "Yes, Guin called as we ran out the door. I suspect they don't need our help in determining how to treat her."

"Right. Well, it's time to call Jake—umm—DI Nancarrow. He was waiting to hear the results of the analysis on the tea, but you've pretty much confirmed his suspicions. And he'll be looking even harder at the Arthur Knight case after this. Blast, I can't believe I just said that to you two."

I tilted my head and grinned. "Actually, he already told me about reviewing the file on that case."

"He told *you*? Why would he do that? He knows better than to share that kind of information with a . . . a civilian!"

If anything, I grinned more broadly. "It seems you spoke highly of me when you two were in your leadership class together. If I didn't know better, I'd think you valued what the Little Old Ladies bring to the table."

Gemma rubbed her eyes. "I can't believe this is happening. Who knew you two would ever meet? I never would have sung your praises if I thought it would get back to you, and you know why? Because you get in enough trouble as it is, without any encouragement. There's no telling what you'll get up to now."

By now, Wendy was cackling. "This is priceless. You mean to say you think our 'interference' is helpful? Not that we don't know it is. I just never thought I'd hear you say it."

"Okay, look. I might as well come clean. I said some of this to Leta this morning, but not all of it. Goodness, was it only this morning? Seems like days ago."

By this time, we were all sitting at the kitchen table. Wendy opened the cupboard and pulled out a bottle of wine. "I always come prepared."

Laughing, I found wine glasses as Gemma continued. "Wendy, the first time you two and your mum trampled over a crime scene, I was ready to shoot the three of you. But, when it was all said and done, you ladies ferreted out a scheme I never could have imagined. A literary crime, for goodness' sake. In Astonbury!"

I raised my glass. "In the second instance, no trampling was involved, nor anything literary, but we managed to identify the killer."

"Yes, Leta, but you almost got yourself killed. That's what I was alluding to this morning. You unearth information that winds up cracking the case, but not without putting yourself in harm's way. And given what happened in Oxford, it worries me no end."

Wendy reached over and put her hand on Gemma's where it rested on the table. "Aw, Gemma, I had no idea our involvement brought that up for you. I'm sorry."

Dumbfounded, I asked, "Um, Gemma, does that mean that Wendy knows about . . . what you told me this morning?"

Gemma explained that when she first moved to Astonbury, she took a leave of absence to recover from her physical and emotional wounds. The physical one healed fairly quickly, but not the others. Her parents Libby and Gavin consoled her as best they could, and Libby confided in her two best friends in Astonbury, Belle and Ellie. As far as Gemma could tell, those two and Wendy were the only locals who knew the story. "And that's the way I chose to keep it until my emotions bubbled up this morning."

*That's one less thing I need to worry about. Wendy knows, and so do Belle and Ellie.* "I'm glad you had your mother and father. I don't know how I would have made it through Henry's death without my family."

Wendy squeezed Gemma's hand. "We know you're a very private person, Gemma. That's why Mum and I never breathed a word, even to Peter. I hope you know your story is safe with us."

When Gemma nodded in acknowledgment, Wendy changed the subject. "Now, let's return to the present. Do I hear you saying that you welcome our involvement as long as we try to be more careful? Well, mostly it's Leta who needs to be more careful. No one's come after me yet."

"Not quite. The word 'welcome' is a stretch, but there's no denying you somehow manage to uncover information neither Constable James nor I seem able to. And I don't mean to say you stumble across it. I think part of it is you don't speak to people in an official capacity, and they're more likely to open up to you two. And goodness knows Belle is right about what people will tell a little old lady."

I laughed. "Yes, the senior member of the Little Old Ladies' Detective Agency is quite proud of her success. She loves that bag I gave her, the one that says, 'Your first mistake was thinking I was just a little old lady.' And she likes the business cards I had printed as a joke."

Gemma smiled. "Yes, Belle is amazing. Still, Leta, you're the one who's most adept at getting villagers and visitors alike to reveal their deepest darkest secrets. I mean, look at what happened today. We were searching Vivienne Cottage and before I knew it, I'd told you about Mark. As I said, that's not something many people know."

"You give me too much credit. The feelings you tamped down surfaced because of Caryn's loss."

Wendy corrected me. "Maybe, but I keep telling you, Leta, you're an intuitive listener. People sense your genuine interest in what they have to say, and I think that's a big part of it."

I sensed Gemma was about done with the praise-fest. "All right, I'm going to say one more thing, and then we need to get down to business. Both of you, for whatever reason, ask questions that make me see things in a new light—that give me a fresh perspective. Maybe it's because we're so different, but whatever it is, it works."

*Will wonders never cease?* I never dreamed I'd hear anything like this from Gemma.

Wendy poured more wine. "Okay, then, what are our next steps?"

Closing her eyes and shaking her head, Gemma sighed. "I can tell that reining you two in is going to be a challenge. I don't see there being any next steps for you, but I know better than to think you'll stop now. Why you didn't come to me about questioning Merry is beyond me."

She got her answer from Wendy. "You don't know why? Come on, Gemma. You either would have suggested we were crazy or were meddling little old ladies or something equally insulting. We know better than to involve you when we want a quick result."

Suddenly, Gemma's eyes opened wide. "And how did you get in the cottage to get the teabag, Wendy? Jake and I asked Elaine to be sure it was locked."

"All I can tell you is it wasn't locked when I got there."

Gemma pushed her chair back. "Enough. I'll check with Elaine after I call Jake. He'll want to interview Merry and quite likely everyone on the premises to find out what they saw or heard. It could be someone knows how Caryn came by the single packet of tea. They could have seen something they thought nothing of at the time. Do you think you two can stay out of trouble at least through dinner?"

I cracked up. "Baby steps. We can manage baby steps."

When Gemma left, we collapsed in the sitting room. It was hard to believe what had transpired since dawn, or pre-dawn for me. *So much for a dip in the pool or a nap.*

Wendy must have been thinking along the same lines. "Leta, let's just jump in the pool in our yoga clothes. Who cares? That will revive us, and then we can take quick showers before cocktails at the barn."

I raced to the door. "Sold."

Wendy did a graceful dive and I jumped in. I wasn't a great swimmer and my dives were clumsy at best, so I was much more of a 'throw my hands in the air and leap' kind of gal. It may have been summer in Cornwall, but the water was still chilly. When I surfaced, I spied Dickens and Merlin running toward the pool.

"Leta, Leta, can I jump in too?"

I was trying to fend off my dog when Merlin hit the water. "Well, I guess you can."

Wendy pulled herself up to sit on the side of the pool. "Too bad we don't have a ball for them to chase. Oh, to be a dog. Look at those two."

Dickens paddled over to me and licked my face. "Can we get a pool at our house, pretty please? And can Merlin come home with us?"

Laughing, I glanced at Wendy. "I think he wants me to get a pool. Sorry, boy, no pools."

"What about Merlin? Can he visit?"

Wendy reached to rub his head. "What'd he say then? Does he want a water slide too?"

Her comment made it easy to joke about Dickens talking. "Nah, he wants Merlin to come home with us."

"Right. I'm sure Christie'd have something to say about that. Now, Archie, on the other hand . . . she might go for him."

We talked about how the princess seemed to be two-timing Watson as we relaxed for a few minutes. I emerged from the pool followed by Dickens, who shook all over both me and Wendy.

While we ladies hit the shower, he and Merlin sprawled beside the pool.

It was a warm evening, and I chose black Bermuda shorts with a hip-length lemon-yellow top. A black scarf with bright patches of primary colors completed the ensemble.

Wendy's turquoise jumpsuit set off her blonde hair and blue eyes, and the beaded necklace was a perfect accessory. I could tell my fellow fashionista was studying my outfit. "What? No red or purple? I don't think I've ever seen you in yellow, but I like it."

I laughed. "I do, on occasion, branch out to yellow or pale pink, but yes, red and purple are my favorites. Let me feed Christie, and I'll be ready to go."

I set out a dish of dry food and a saucer with a dab of wet food. Whether the princess would deign to touch either remained to be seen.

Dickens tried to bolt in the door when I opened it, but I held him off. "Uh-uh. Christie won't get a chance to turn her nose up at her food if I let you in, and you know it. One swipe of your tongue, and it'll be gone. You'll get your dinner later."

Only Penny and Sue were in the dining room when we arrived. After we poured ourselves splashes of sauvignon blanc, we joined them and described how much we'd enjoyed our visit to Dartmouth the previous year. We both expressed our envy at their living on the River Dart.

When Belle and Ellie joined us, Belle asked about the Naval College. It was some place we didn't get a chance to visit on our previous trip, and she was eager to see it, especially because it was where Queen Elizabeth met Prince Philip. Penny said it was worth the trip, and Sue suggested we also take in Coleton Fishacre, a home built in the 1920s. They thought we'd enjoy its Arts and Crafts architecture and Art Deco and Jazz Age furnishings.

Rhiannon and Guin arrived a few minutes after seven, and both Gemma and Morgan were still missing. I wasn't concerned about Gemma, but I wondered about Morgan. I hadn't seen her since the day before. *This double whammy must have hit her hard.*

Guin picked up a glass and tapped a knife against it to get our attention. "Ladies, I'd like to thank you for your patience today about the changes in the class schedule, and I wanted to let you know that Caryn has regained consciousness."

A few people clapped and commented "thank goodness" and "I'm so glad." Though only a select few knew how serious the situation was, all were relieved their fellow yogi was better. Lily asked whether Caryn would be back, but Guin didn't have an answer.

She got our attention one more time to provide an update about the class schedule. "As we were unable to get to our inversions class today, we'll hold that session in the morning. Midday Tuesday was intentionally left free for shopping, touring neighboring villages, or simply relaxing by the pool. Then we'll have another restorative class in the late afternoon." The news about Caryn lifted the cloud hanging over Knight's Rest, and the dinner conversation was considerably lighter than it had been at lunch. We all agreed the afternoon class was a good one but had taken a lot out of us. There were plenty of comments about sleeping well that night.

I sat with Rhiannon, Belle, and Guin for dinner. The first question out of Belle's mouth was about Caryn's treatment and whether learning about the jimson weed had been a help.

Guin nodded vigorously. "Oh yes, with that knowledge, they knew to give her an infusion of something called physostigmine—I think I have that right. They told me it's an antidote for belladonna poisoning too. The two plants are in the same family.

Believe it or not, there have been several cases of teenagers using jimson weed as a drug. That's why the hospital knew how to treat it."

Belle shook her head in disbelief. "What's that line from the Tom Hanks movie? 'Stupid is as stupid does.' Some things never change. If it's not some new synthetic drug, it's a plant that's been around for hundreds of years."

Looking around the room, I noted how the makeup of the group had changed. There were no special guests like Dylan Porter and Martin Pascoe. Gareth had joined us for dinner Saturday and Sunday evenings, but he was taking his turn sitting with Caryn tonight.

*So, where are the other two yogis?* "I wonder where Gemma's gotten to . . . and Morgan."

Rhiannon's eyes twinkled. "Gemma ran by the desk to say she was meeting DI Nancarrow for dinner in the village. Wouldn't it be lovely if it was more than a business meeting?"

"I suspect it's work-related, but it could be the start of something more. He's a likable guy."

"And not bad-looking, either," Guin said.

Rhiannon looked thoughtful. "And Morgan? She didn't join us on the farm tour today, nor did she make the afternoon session. Is she all right?"

Guin twitched her nose. *She makes me think of Elizabeth Montgomery in* Bewitched *when she does that*. "I haven't spoken to her since I returned from the hospital. She'll be relieved to hear Caryn's regained consciousness. If I don't see her in the next little while, I'll ring her to give her the news."

"How close are Morgan and Caryn?" I asked. "When Martin told us yesterday that Morgan dated Arthur in school, I wondered. I mean, I suppose it's not the same as trying to be friendly with an ex-wife, but still."

"I don't think that ancient relationship got in the way, especially since Caryn and Morgan aren't together all that often. Morgan's mostly in Cardiff or lately here in Tintagel with Dylan, and Caryn stays busy with the museum in London."

"What about the men?" asked Belle. "Were there any hard feelings between them when Morgan and Dylan got serious?"

Guin laughed. "Goodness me, I don't think so. Dylan and Arthur were thick as thieves as students and then professors at Cardiff. I think the relationship with Morgan had well and truly ended before Dylan met her, and I think those two are much better suited for each other."

I smiled. "Yes. Martin mentioned that Morgan fell hard for Dylan. Isn't it funny what makes two people fall head over heels in love?"

Belle patted me on the shoulder. "Much like you and Dave, and I'd say you two are very well-suited."

My cheeks felt hot, and I knew I was blushing. "And just think, I was sure it was Wendy he was attracted to the night we met him. It goes to show my instincts aren't always right."

The conversation turned to how Morgan had met Dylan here at Knight's Rest one summer when Arthur brought him home. Along with Martin and Guin, they'd all palled around together here at the farm and in the village.

Guin said she knew right away Morgan had fallen for Dylan. "When I said the Arthur and Morgan relationship was over, I meant more on Arthur's part than hers. My sense is she was still carrying a torch for my brother, but that was probably more a product of it being slim pickings around here than it was a deep love for Arthur. That changed almost as soon as she laid eyes on Dylan."

"It would be the same in Astonbury," Belle said. "Villagers are thrown together and relationships shift over time. You mentioned Martin. Is that the man who brought the model Saturday night?"

"Yes, it is. It must be hard to keep the connections straight. Martin is Morgan's older brother. He and Arthur are the same age, and I'm next in line. Mum had Arthur and me only twelve months apart—Irish twins, you know. And Morgan was the youngest of the four of us by only a few months. Then came Gareth a few years later. And there you have it—the Tintagel connection. With Dylan and Arthur both getting degrees from Cardiff and going on to become professors there, they formed a strong bond too."

She laughed. "We used to tease Dylan and then Caryn that they'd never be official members of the clan since they weren't raised here."

I wondered again whether there was more than a longstanding friendship between Guin and Martin, but I didn't ask. My day was starting to catch up with me. "Ladies, I can hardly keep my eyes open. I think I'll skip dessert and head back to the cottage."

Belle smiled. "I'm sure I can stay awake long enough for dessert."

When I stopped by Wendy's table to tell her where I was going, she said goodnight to her companions and followed me. "I'm exhausted too, Leta, and I can't think of anything better than crawling into bed with *The Mists of Avalon*. I'm getting a kick out of re-reading it, especially because it focuses on the women our cottages are named for."

Dickens met us halfway and escorted us down the path. Passing Vivienne Cottage, I saw a light glowing in the sitting room. "I think Jake and Gemma may have neglected to turn off the lights when they left today. I'll run and turn 'em off."

I pushed the door open and started into the sitting room. "Um, Wendy, come here."

Something was off. The room wasn't in disarray, but it looked different to me. Wendy peered over my shoulder. "Uh-oh. Something's not right."

"It looks that way to you too? It's not just me? Maybe Gemma and DI Nancarrow disturbed things when they looked it over."

"I don't think so. They consider it a possible crime scene, so they wouldn't do that. No, I think someone else has been here, though it's certainly not obvious like the scene we stumbled on last year when we found Alice's cottage ransacked. Remember when you discovered Tigger scared half to death beneath the bed and Mum and I took him home with us? This is nothing like that, thank goodness, but it puts me in mind of that day."

She was right, though there were some things I preferred not to remember, like Dickens and I finding a dead body. My sister Anna liked to tease me that I was a master at blocking truly awful things from my mind. She, on the other hand, could recall every detail of horrific sibling arguments, breakups with boyfriends, and work drama. Fortunately for me, I didn't figure in many of those memories.

Barking, Dickens pushed past us both. "Maybe we'll find another cat."

I straightened my shoulders. "What a coincidence that Gemma referenced that scene earlier. She's not here, though, so don't you think we should look around—before we call her?"

Wendy didn't wait for an answer. Instead, she gave me a gentle push and followed me into the sitting room. She stood with her hands on her hips. "It's the pillows. The ones from the couch are usually by the arms, and now they're kind of tossed in the middle. And the ones from the armchairs are on the floor. Why?"

"I'm not sure. Could it be as simple as, Elaine cleaned the cottage and meant to put the pillows back after plumping them?"

My friend moved down the hall to the bedroom. "Except Gemma and Jake asked her to lock it up. Would she have cleaned it after hearing that? And come to think of it, she only empties our trash and makes our beds. She doesn't straighten."

I looked over Wendy's shoulder into the bedroom. It looked much like the sitting room, with the pillows lying in the middle of the bed rather than by the headboard. *What is it about pillows?* The brown envelope I'd seen earlier on the dresser was also on the bed. I couldn't be positive, but I thought the drawers had been opened and not completely shut.

"You know, Wendy, I doubt anybody else would notice that things are slightly off. Whoever was here was careful and yet not. Now, what were they looking for? Because they had to be looking for something."

"What indeed? If we're right and it's Caryn's comments that led to someone poisoning her, maybe this person was looking for some indication of what Caryn knew. You said before you wondered how many people she'd shared her thoughts with. What if she said something to the wrong person? A person who had something to do with Arthur's death?"

I stood staring at the brown envelope. I had to agree Wendy was probably on the right track. "You may have been right all along. Without realizing it, Caryn has stirred up a hornet's nest, though I don't have the impression she has any concrete evidence about what happened to Arthur. She seems to have only vague suspicions."

Wendy picked up on my train of thought. "Right. She was nowhere near here when he died, but her remarks about him dropping everything for a sudden trip to Tintagel . . ."

"But Wendy, what did the intruder think they'd find? A nice neat list of what Caryn knew and who she was prepared to point a finger at? It's not as though she said, 'Arthur left me a note explaining exactly what was worrying him.' It's not like the movies when a letter arrives after the victim dies, a letter giving the game away."

A glance in the bathroom revealed nothing amiss. The jars of face cream and body lotion appeared undisturbed. It was the same in the small kitchen. The tea tins stood on the counter near the teapot. Only the bag of tea was gone, and it was Wendy who'd removed that.

"Leta, maybe the poisoner came back to retrieve the tea because it's the only evidence Caryn was poisoned. If that's what they were after, they were too late." She continued to think aloud. "But who would look for tea on the couch or the bed? Nope, that doesn't make sense."

I returned to the sitting room and stared at the couch and ottoman. "I see her glasses on the side table, but you know what I don't see? The stack of papers that were on the ottoman when we were here. And the laptop. It makes sense someone would take them, but then why look in the bedroom? They were in plain sight. Were they looking for those things and something more?"

Turning in a circle, Wendy looked puzzled. "When I ran in to get the bag of tea, I didn't look in here. The papers and the laptop could already have been gone. Oh, for goodness' sake, I don't know what to think."

"Well, we'd best call Gemma to tell her we *stumbled* across another crime scene. And since the word is she was having dinner with the local DI, we may be able to get them both."

With the phone on speaker, we listened to it ring several times, and I pictured Gemma fumbling with a purse, an unfamiliar image for me. She picked up with a familiar answer, though. "DI Taylor."

I hadn't gotten too far into my explanation of seeing the light on and what we'd discovered before I got a familiar response too.

"You *what*? And how did you get in this time, if the door was locked? Please tell me you two didn't disturb anything!"

I heard Jake in the background, and I could tell Gemma was covering the phone, but I could still make out his words. "Whoa, wait a minute. Let's hear what they've seen. How 'bout letting me talk to her?"

Loud and clear, I heard Gemma respond, "Fine!"

Jake took over. "I take it you and your partner have stepped in it again. Did you find a cat this time too?"

*I think I detect a sense of humor.* "Now that you mention it, that would be par for the course. The Little Old Ladies' Detective Agency has found two so far, but none tonight."

"Well, that's good. As you can imagine, there's steam coming out of Gemma's ears, so let me cut to the chase. First, how did you get in? And don't try telling me the door was unlocked."

"But it *was* unlocked. You can't blame that on us."

He said something to Gemma about keys at Knight's Rest before coming back to us. "Okay, point taken. Now, based on what I've heard about you two, I'm sure you didn't stop in the entryway and turn around and walk out. Am I right?"

Wendy piped up. "We thought about it, but we knew we could do a superficial check without disturbing anything unless you plan to check for footprints. Whoever came in didn't conduct an obvious search, but things are enough off-kilter that we can tell an intruder was here."

We made short work of detailing what we'd observed in our walkthrough, with Jake asking only a few clarifying questions. He was quite polite and not at all dismissive, a welcome change from the response we'd come to expect from Gemma.

"So, DI Nancarrow," I said, "the only things missing as far as we can tell are the papers and the laptop from the ottoman. Oh!

And the phone. I didn't see Caryn's phone. Any chance you took it all away with you?"

Now, I was sure he was chuckling. "Gemma was right about you two. You're incredibly observant. Yes, I have every one of those things. Haven't had time to go through them yet, but they're all safe and sound. Do you super sleuths think that's what the intruder was after?"

Wendy and I explained our working theory that Caryn had shared her doubts and suspicions with the wrong person.

I didn't know how he would take this next thought. "We don't know that she knew anything concrete, but if Arthur's death had something to do with his sudden trip to Tintagel, well . . . then—"

Wendy interrupted me. "If it wasn't an accident, then Caryn's nonstop comments about her doubts meant the killer had to stop her talking. That would explain the jimson weed. First, whoever it is, they poisoned the tea, and then they went in search of any evidence Caryn might have. How are we doing?"

Gemma must have heard most of the back-and-forth, because she interjected, "I hate to say it, Jake, but they may be on to something. Especially given what you've seen in the Arthur Knight case file."

Jake came back on the line. "All right, ladies, here's what we need you to do. Can you get a key from the front desk and lock the door to Caryn's cottage? I realize the horse is already out of the barn, but please do it anyway."

Dickens nudged my leg. "I didn't see any horses in the barn."

I smiled at Dickens's comment as Jake continued. "And then, Gemma and I will see you at your cottage first thing in the morning to discuss this in more detail. And, oh, try not to alarm any of the other guests. Just get the key and lock up, okay?"

I felt as though I'd entered an alternate universe. First, Gemma agreed with our theory without insulting me, and now, DI Nancarrow planned to share what he knew. My only experience with the constabulary had been Gemma, who was prickly at best, and her downright bullying boss, Detective Chief Inspector Burton.

The lobby was empty when Wendy and I got to the barn, so I pulled the cottage key from the cubby behind the front desk. "Hell's bells, Wendy. There are two keys to every cottage, and they're kept in these cubbies. Our cubby is empty because we each have a key, but Caryn only used one. That means the other key for Vivienne Cottage has been here the whole time."

"You mean Elaine may have locked up after the morning commotion, and then someone took the key to go back in? Or maybe she didn't get around to locking up until after I dropped by to get the bag of tea, and that's how I was able to go in earlier."

"Uh-huh. Elaine replaces the key after she locks up, whenever that was, and then someone removes it and spirits it back to the cubby after visiting the cottage. The cubbies are a lovely old-fashioned touch, but not too awfully secure."

We agreed we'd solved the mystery of the cottage going from locked to unlocked, though it was too late to do much good. Returning to the cottage, Wendy switched off the lamp on the end table and pocketed the key. "Whether the horse is out of the barn or the train has left the station, what's done is done. I say our next step is to map out who was where when. Maybe that analysis will point us toward the person who took the key, but not tonight. I'm going to bed with my book."

Dickens and I found Christie curled in a ball on my pillow. As I washed up and changed into my gown, he barked off and on. "When do we look for the horse? Maybe tomorrow? Can Merlin go with us?" He was always confused with our idioms, and I chuckled as I recalled similar comments he made about phrases like "pulling my leg" and "butter me up."

Who knew what tomorrow would bring? I had visions of an old Western where the sheriff pins a star on a newly deputized shopkeeper or two. *That's it. Instead of the Little Old Ladies, we'll be the Knight's Rest Posse.*

# CHAPTER TWELVE

Tuesday morning when Jake and Gemma knocked on our door, we were ready for them. Wendy and I'd already drunk one pot of coffee and had another waiting for the *official* detectives.

Dickens greeted our guests by rolling over. "How 'bout a belly rub?"

Gemma seemed to be in business mode, but Jake obliged with a laugh. "Hello, boy. What's your name?"

As I was making introductions, Christie put in an appearance. She hesitated and then wrapped herself around Jake's ankles. "Who is this one? Is he Gemma's boyfriend?"

*So she senses it too.* Unable to answer her question directly, I introduced her instead. When we were seated at the kitchen table with coffee, my opinionated cat made herself at home in Jake's lap—a sign she approved of him, at least for the moment.

Wendy held up the two keys to Iseult Cottage. "First, we've determined how Vivienne Cottage came to be unlocked. Cottage keys are kept in the cubbies behind the front desk. Leta and I have our two, but since Caryn was the only occupant next door, the second key was still in the cubby. That system works well when a front desk is manned 'round the clock, but that's not the case here."

Jake's eyes widened. "So, when there's no one out front, anybody can grab a key? Not good, not good at all."

Gemma nodded. "It seems like inviting trouble, but I guess they've never had any problems before. Anything else before we get down to business?"

"Only that Wendy and I thought we'd start with mapping out who was where when to see whether we could identify likely suspects for the intrusion. If we can, that should lead to who poisoned the tea."

Our two detective inspectors looked at each other. One smiled and the other rolled her eyes. "What did I tell you, Jake? They already have a plan."

"And fortunately for us, Gemma, it fits with ours. Ladies, my partner here tells me there's no way to keep you from following the breadcrumbs, so we agreed the safest and most helpful assignment for you two would be just what you described."

I gave him my best Southern belle smile. "That sounds fine as far as it goes, but mapping everyone's whereabouts is only the beginning. From there, we'll chat with the guests and the family and see what we can learn."

Gemma looked ready to explode until Jake put his hand on her arm. She muttered something about us being impossible to deal with but allowed Jake to take the lead.

"Now, ladies, think about it. I'll be speaking with the same people, so why double up? Plus you're talking about someone who, at the very least, set out to do serious harm to Caryn, and maybe even intended to kill her. Can't you see how dangerous your inquiries would be?"

This time, he couldn't keep Gemma from erupting. "Here we go again. You never see the danger. You're like bloodhounds with your noses to the ground, and you don't stop until someone else gets hurt." She pointed at me. "And it's always you, Leta. You never fail to put yourself in dangerous situations."

It was Wendy's turn to get fired up. "Oh come on, Gemma. We're in a contained environment, and we'll stick together. It's pretty unlikely anyone would go after both of us at once. How stupid would that be? As for doubling up, Jake—um, I mean DI Nancarrow—Gemma will tell you that folks often tell us things they don't share with the police."

Jake looked at us. "Ladies, would you give us a moment, please?"

This was new territory for us. Wendy and I walked outside, leaving Gemma and Jake in the kitchen. Dickens followed us, but Christie wasn't giving up her comfy spot in Jake's lap. Though we listened intently, even with the cottage door open, we couldn't make out the conversation.

When Gemma came to the door, she looked less than pleased. "Tuppence, Agatha, we need you in here."

Jake laughed. "I must say, I like the nicknames. Now, I know you're well-aware of how woefully understaffed the constabulary is, and here in Cornwall, our problem is exacerbated by how far-flung our police stations are. Taking that into consideration, we have a one-time deal for you two *amateur* sleuths—strong emphasis on amateur."

This was intriguing. I was sure the word "deal" never would have come out of Gemma's mouth. "Okay, we're listening."

"We two, the *official* detectives, will focus on the Arthur Knight case and enlist the Little Old Ladies' Detective Agency to dig into the circumstances surrounding the poisoned tea and the search of Caryn's cottage. How does that sound?"

Wendy cocked her head and studied him. "And we'll share information back and forth?"

Gemma glared. "No! You'll share information with us, and you'll follow our lead. You will *not*, I repeat *not*, get involved in investigating Arthur Knight's death."

My feisty friend wasn't backing down. "Now, wait a minute. The two have to be connected. No one decided to randomly go after Caryn. It's what she knows or thinks she knows about Arthur's death that made her a target."

I could tell Gemma was close to exploding. "Wendy, we're not complete idiots. We know that! But there's no way we'll allow you to investigate anything to do directly with the death of Arthur Knight. It's entirely too risky. Can you spell dangerous? Too dangerous!"

This was a fascinating dynamic, and I thought Jake must have had to twist Gemma's arm nearly off to get her this far. This was also a more typical reaction from Gemma. I sighed. "Okay, we'll make it work."

When Wendy's mouth popped open, I gently placed my foot on hers beneath the table. I knew she was surprised I'd caved so easily, but she seemed to get the unspoken message to leave it be.

Stunned into silence, Wendy and I remained at the table, as Jake and Gemma went next door to check out the scene of the latest crime. I could tell Wendy wanted an explanation as to why I'd hushed her up, but I cut her off at the pass. "Wendy, I need a little time to process what we just witnessed between Jake and Gemma, and I need food before I can do much more."

"Me too. Why don't I run to the dining room to grab fruit and yogurt so we can have an uninterrupted powwow? That way, maybe we can make sense of what we heard, and you can tell me why you gave in. They were awfully agreeable—well, at least DI Nancarrow was, and I'm not sure I'm buying it."

I agreed that was a good plan, and off she went. Dickens had followed the official detectives out the door, and I was left with Christie.

Looking up from her dab of wet food, she meowed. "Yup, definitely something going on between that Jake bloke and Gemma. I think they like each other. They had their heads together laughing and whispering while you and Wendy were outside."

"Laughing? Gemma was laughing?"

She pointed a dainty paw at her dish. "I'll be happy to tell you about it, but isn't there something you need to do?" *So demanding*, I thought as I fluffed her food and centered it on the saucer.

After two licks, she sat back and looked at me. "I can't remember every word, but I think they were talking about a game. Gemma asked Jake how she was doing. Doing what, I wondered? But when he said her acting skills were impressive, I got a hint, I think. Isn't acting what they do on TV?"

My sassy cat was an observant little thing, and she spent long hours in my lap as I watched movies on Amazon Prime and BritBox. Who knew she absorbed my running monologue on the plots and acting?

"Yes. What else did they say about acting?"

"I didn't hear that word again, but Gemma used the word *bamboozle* like they had you and Wendy *bamboozled*. What does that mean?"

*Maybe Wendy was on to something.* "It means to fool someone. Keep going. What else did you hear?"

Christie made me wait while she finished her dab of food. "Something about a hook, a line, and a sinker. That's why I kept thinking they were playing some kind of game."

*Oh for goodness' sake! They played us. But to what end?*

By the time Wendy returned with food, I had moved from shock to fuming to disbelief. "Okay, Agatha, I've got a new set of stages for you—shock, fuming, disbelief, and action."

My friend looked at me as though I'd lost my mind. "What on earth are you going on about?"

"You walked out the door saying you didn't buy how agreeable our two detectives were, and I sat here and thought about that. I replayed the two scenes in my head, and that's exactly what they were—scenes in a one-act play. I think Jake is Gemma's acting coach."

Wendy looked confused. "Huh?"

Trying hard not to let on that Christie had enlightened me, I replayed what had transpired in our cottage. "For starters, I think we're benefitting from the relationship that's developing between the two. I firmly believe Gemma's learning from how Jake handles us, as in, you get more flies with honey, and I suspect that's his natural demeanor, not an act. But I also think they concocted this scheme, probably at Jake's instigation, to keep us safely occupied and out of the way."

Christie meowed. "Tell her what I heard, Leta."

"Wendy, they set out to bamboozle us, and we fell for it. But I'm convinced they *know* we'll bring valuable clues to the table, and they're happy to let us do it. We can work that to our advantage. One reason I didn't rise to the bait at the end was my sense that something was off. I couldn't put my finger on it, but Gemma almost looked as though she were having fun yelling at us."

Tilting her head, Wendy nodded. "Right. We're accustomed to her going off at us, but her anger is genuine. It was weird this time—a bit over-the-top."

Dickens wandered in and went straight to Christie's bowl. I could tell he was disappointed there wasn't a trace of food left, and I went to the cupboard to pull his dry food out.

"Wendy, were Gemma and Jake still next door when you came back?"

Dickens answered before Wendy could. "They're locking the door now."

I bolted out the door with Dickens on my heels and caught them as they walked toward the barn. "DI Nancarrow, one question. Any chance you have those papers with you, the ones from Caryn's cottage?"

In typical fashion, Gemma rolled her eyes. I sensed hesitation on Jake's part, but I was willing to bet he knew what was coming.

"No, they're back in Truro. Why?"

"Here's my thinking. Gemma will tell you we're pretty darned good at studying documents and seeing connections if there are any, and we can't very well get into trouble sitting around reading. What if we take a look? We may not find anything. They may simply be notes on the exhibit she's working on, but unless you've got some expert from the British Museum waiting in the wings to tell you what the notes mean, what have you got to lose? We'll be happy to pick them up from the Truro police station. Will that work?"

I could tell Gemma was trying to come up with a rebuttal, but she knew I was right. It wouldn't be the first time we little old ladies figured something out through the simple act of reading.

Gemma puffed her cheeks out and Jake looked sideways at her before answering. "Okay, Leta, I give. Here's my card. Call me when you think you can be there. If I can't meet you, I'll have copies in an envelope waiting for you. Is it all right with you if I go back to work now? Or is there something else I can do for you this morning?"

I gave him my best curtsy and simpered. "No sir. Thank you, sir."

I sashayed in the door to Iseult Cottage. "Guess what I did."

Wendy arched her eyebrows. "From the look on your face, I'd say it's something you're proud of."

"I remembered the papers in Caryn's sitting room earlier, but the thought blew through my brain and I lost it. For some reason, it reappeared and I managed to snag it with my butterfly net before it escaped!" We laughed at the image as we had when Ellie first came up with it.

When I explained the concession I'd gotten from Jake, Wendy grinned. "I wish we had them right now, Leta, but yoga comes first. I guess the upside is we may be able to learn a thing or two about who was where when, while we're in class—and oh yes, we get to do headstands too!"

I cracked up. "I *do* love headstands and shoulder stands. Let's enjoy ourselves *and* while we're at it, make it a point to chat up the others—Lilith and Lily, the Dartmouth sisters, Guin, Elaine, and Morgan, too, if she puts in an appearance. She seems to be taking Caryn's situation pretty hard."

Both Rhiannon and Guin were in the studio today, and I knew why. Having two instructors provide hands-on assistance with headstands and handstands would allow us to refine these more difficult poses. It had taken me years to do a headstand in the middle of a room, without a wall to rest my heels on when I wobbled. As for handstands, I'd yet to be successful going up unassisted. Even with Rhiannon helping me by catching my legs as I threw them in the air, I could only briefly stay up.

I thought my arms weren't strong enough to support me. Rhiannon said it was my mind getting in my way, not my arms. Whatever it was, Wendy had somehow mastered the pose, while it remained my nemesis.

These thoughts rolled through my mind as I noted that everyone had made it to class—other than Caryn, of course, who was still in the hospital. Wendy and I strategically positioned ourselves to be able to talk to different people. She unrolled her mat beside Morgan, who to me, still looked wan, almost unwell. I found a spot with the Dartmouth sisters.

Penny whispered, "I considered ducking this class, as I'm rotten at both head and handstands."

Leaning closer, Sue agreed with her sister. "That she is. At least I've gotten decent at doing a headstand against the wall and can even go up on my own now. Maybe one day, I'll make it to the center of the room."

Archie wandered over to climb into Penny's lap and lick her bare ankles. "My Guin can help you."

The sisters laughed, and I noticed Christie had taken up the same position in Morgan's lap. *Maybe a bit of cat love will cure whatever ails her.*

Except for my continued inability to do a decent handstand, I enjoyed the class. Headstand, shoulder stand, and legs up the wall were my three favorite poses, and all were included today. Christie joined me for corpse pose, and I smiled at her purring.

Penny reached to pet my girl and ask what I was doing the rest of the day. She and Sue were debating whether to shop or relax by the pool. "I started reading *The Dalai Lama's Cat* last night, and I'm eager to continue, but I don't want to miss the shops."

"Oh, I adored that book and often think I should reread it, but that saying, 'So many books, so little time,' is too true."

Sue blinked. "What if we do a bit of both? A quick trip to the village for a few shops, maybe the Post Office and lunch, and then several hours by the pool? Would you like to join us, Leta?"

*What a perfect opportunity to do a bit of sleuthing*, I thought. "As long as it doesn't include hitting the tacky tourist shops, I'm in. What time does the bus depart?"

We agreed to meet in thirty minutes in front of the barn. I spied Wendy in conversation with Morgan and wandered that way. "Ladies, I'm headed to the village with Penny and Sue. What's on your agenda today?"

"For sure, not the village. I didn't feel well yesterday, but today I'm up for a walk and then a swim. Maybe I can find Merlin and take him with me around the farm before stretching out by the pool."

Wendy asked if she wanted company, since she too had no interest in shopping. I hid a smile, as I knew my friend was a shopping fiend, but today her Agatha Raisin persona was in charge. The two settled on meeting in twenty minutes, and I suggested to Wendy that she take Dickens along too.

As she and I walked to our cottage, we congratulated ourselves on a plan taking shape. "Wendy, I bet you can find out what Guin meant when she told Rhiannon that Morgan was having a hard time. It could be that whatever was already going on with her explains her reaction to Caryn being rushed to the hospital, but I don't know."

"Right. Something prompted Guin to offer Morgan complimentary lodging, and I'm going to find out what it was—if not from Morgan, maybe from Guin. You know I've learned that whole 'ask open-ended questions' technique from you."

Another thought struck me. "Wendy, we said we needed to map who was where when. Do you realize we didn't see Morgan all day yesterday and she wasn't at dinner last night either? That means she had the 'opportunity' to search Caryn's cottage."

Wendy pursed her lips. "True, so where was she? Moping in her cottage? Maybe Penny or Sue at least caught sight of her.

Pinning down her whereabouts is a start, but we've got all the other guests plus the Knight family to check out. And who knows who else wanders in and out of this place? Who makes deliveries, that sort of thing?"

"That makes me think of Dylan Porter, Martin Pascoe, and their co-worker Colin, who were all here Saturday night. We've got our work cut out for us."

Trailing behind us, Christie made a good point. "At least you don't have to investigate Gemma or Rhiannon or Ellie and Belle."

I repeated her comment to Wendy as though it were my brilliant observation and suggested we get our hands on a flipchart pad or at least a big piece of paper and some tape. In the spirit of Maisie Dobbs, the character in Jacqueline Winspear's novels, we hoped to have enough information by this evening to map out everyone's whereabouts, though I suspected we'd still have gaps. Maisie used the backs of pieces of wallpaper to map her findings. Flipcharts didn't exist in the 1920s and 30s. If we worked hard, we might even have a start on means and motive.

We had just enough time to change into clothes appropriate for our separate outings. With a few minutes to spare, I jogged to Belle and Ellie's cottage to bring them up to speed.

With a list of bullet points in my head, I quickly rattled off the latest. "So that's where we stand. Wendy and I are off to surreptitiously interview Penny, Sue, and Morgan, and we may have some work for the four of us either later tonight or tomorrow."

True to form, they were champing at the bit to get involved. I'd hardly spoken to Ellie since the flurry of activity over the boxes of tea, and when she offered an idea, I knew she'd been thinking about it ever since. "Leta, all this hubbub over tea makes me want to know what Elaine may have seen the past few days. She's in and out of the barn and she sees folks coming and going." Ellie may have only recently become an official LOL, but she was a natural.

"Good thinking, Ellie, and what about Art? He was there for Dylan's lecture, and he and his sister set up the buffet and clear the tables each night in addition to the light housekeeping for the cottages, so he may have noticed something."

When I left, the two senior members of the Little Old Ladies' Detective Agency were brainstorming a plan of attack. *If only I could give Dickens and Christie assignments too, we'd crack the case in no time.*

# CHAPTER THIRTEEN

THE DARTMOUTH SISTERS, AS I thought of Penny and Sue, were waiting by their car, dressed in comfy-looking skorts and sneakers. I'd chosen a black sundress and a straw hat trimmed in black ribbon. It was not yet eleven, but it was already uncomfortably warm.

I hadn't spent much time with the sisters, and it was fun learning a bit more about them. Both were married but took lots of trips together without their husbands. They were in their forties, Penny being the eldest by two years, and both were teachers. Sue taught English, and Penny taught math.

"Leta, it's funny to hear you say you don't do numbers. That's what Sue tells me all the time. Amazing that we can be sisters and have that striking difference. We're very much alike in other ways—our love of reading, chocolate, and cats, for starters."

Sue laughed. "And our addiction to chocolate explains our tendency to be on the plump side."

As I answered their questions about my accent and how I wound up in the UK, they expressed their astonishment about my move.

Penny looked at her sister. "Goodness, I can't imagine having the temerity to move across the pond. I must say I'm impressed. Tell me, has it turned out as you hoped?"

"It's turned out to be beyond my wildest dreams. I've made new friends, gotten involved in village life, and learned to relax . . . well, as much as someone like me can. And Dickens and Christie love it too."

They were an inquisitive pair and wanted to know what hoops I jumped through to get my four-legged companions from Atlanta to the Cotswolds and how well they'd settled in. That led to a description of the donkeys, day-to-day life in Astonbury, and finally to the advent of the Little Old Ladies' Detective Agency.

"Seriously?" asked Sue. "Belle thinks she's Miss Marple?" They chuckled and imagined how they might form a similar group in Dartmouth. "With Agatha Christie's summer home just up the River Dart, we're perfectly positioned for a bit of intrigue, don't you think?"

That last question came up as we were debating where to have lunch. When I innocently let drop that the Malthouse was the place Dylan and Martin frequented, my new friends immediately wanted to eat there. *That worked like a charm,* I thought.

The first thing on my lunch agenda was to find out what the sisters knew about Morgan and Caryn and what they might have seen since we'd been at Knight's Rest. I debated telling them what had made Caryn ill but then decided what the heck. When I explained about the tea, they were suitably shocked but also knew I was playing detective and were eager to help.

"Just like Rosemary and Thyme," cried Penny. "I'll be Rosemary, and Sue can be Thyme, though no one ever mistook us for gardeners. It's our husbands who spend time digging in the dirt." It took me a minute to recall the BBC series about the two gardening sleuths. *These two are naturals.*

I couldn't help myself. "Look at this. After that comment, we have to share an appetizer—rosemary and thyme-infused baked camembert with breadsticks."

Waiting on our dish, we sipped our pints. I discovered the sisters had eaten breakfast with Caryn on Sunday but hadn't learned much about her. They knew about Arthur Knight's death but not that Caryn was his fiancée.

Sue's smile faded. "That is immeasurably sad. Now I understand why she seemed so distant that first night. When we heard she'd been taken to hospital, we thought she was coming down with something and that's why she was so quiet."

Her sister squinted. "I bet you want us to think about what else we've seen, and the first thing that pops to mind is Caryn at the front desk after the King Arthur lecture. She handed what might have been postcards to Elaine, and they chatted for a moment. I remember thinking to myself, 'Who sends postcards anymore?' It seems most people nowadays post things on Facebook and that's it."

"Good eye, Penny—I mean Rosemary. What else stands out for you? It could be anything. Sometimes we observe things and don't realize their significance."

Sue interjected. "We figured out you and Wendy and Rhiannon all knew each other when you introduced yourselves the first day as hailing from Astonbury. It was more subtle, but we also picked up on something between Caryn and Morgan—something about the looks they exchanged. Maybe it's only that they both seem so sad, or perhaps it was some kind of tension."

Once again, Penny squinted, a sign she was thinking. "I guess Morgan must have known Arthur Knight too, since her husband worked with him. Is that why she's so sad? I wouldn't think his death would affect her to the same degree, though."

I told them I'd puzzled over the same thing until I learned Morgan had grown up with Arthur and briefly dated him. "And then there's Guin. She's Arthur's sister, but she seems to be bearing up well. She has such a calm demeanor or aura, I guess you'd say. Nothing seems to get to her."

"Except business issues, I think," said Sue. "I heard her on the phone this morning before class chastising someone about a late delivery. Even then she was stern, not rude or angry. Wish I could be more that way with my students. There are some days I want to rip their heads off, don't you know?"

As a former English teacher, I sympathized with her. Patience was not one of my strong points. It was timely that our main courses arrived then, as I thought they'd told me most of what they'd observed. I asked them to come to me if they recalled anything else, and we dug into our meals.

While we ate fish and chips, I focused on the pub and its employees. Based on his manner, I assumed the man behind the bar was either the owner or the manager, and I judged him to be around my age. The young girl who served us lunch looked enough like him that they had to be related, maybe a daughter or a niece. In a small village like this, more people were related than not.

When she stopped by our table to clear the dishes, I told her Martin Pascoe had told me about the Malthouse. "I'm glad he did. Lunch was delicious."

She beamed. "Martin! He and Dad went to school together. He's a regular."

"So I gathered. I guess that means you knew Arthur Knight too. So sad about his accident."

"Yes, it was. Shocked the whole village. He'd been here only the night before. He and Martin and Dylan—like old times, Dad said. That cute new guy Colin and a few of the others from the dig joined 'em."

*Sounds like a boys' night out.* "Did they ever get to the bottom of what he was doing at Merlin's Cave so late? We're staying at Knight's Rest this week, and the family seems to be holding up, but I imagine knowing what happened would help."

The young girl scoffed. "Well, the police asked how much they drank as if that would make him do something stupid like go in the water at high tide. Dad says when they were younger, those three could drink him under the table, but they've settled down. Heck, Dylan left after only one round. Said he had work to do at the office. Oh! And he suggested Arthur stop by if he saw the lights still on. Martin and Arthur and the others stayed 'til just past dark, but had maybe two more rounds at most. No shots or anything."

When she left with our dishes, Penny stared at me. "Were you playing detective? Which Agatha Christie character are you?" When I told her I was Tuppence, she cracked up.

Her sister commented she preferred the first Tommy and Tuppence mini-series from the '80s, the one with Francesca Annis. "But, Leta, that makes me wonder. As our resident Tuppence, did you see Martin at Knight's Rest Sunday night?"

"Yes, Wendy and I saw him right after dinner. It looked as though he was going to visit Guin at the main house."

"Ah, but did you see him later, after dark?"

"After dark? I was tucked in bed with my book by then. Was he leaving?"

Penny seemed proud of herself. "Yes, he was leaving, but from Morgan's cottage. I remember being curious because he hugged her as he left, and we know she's married to Dylan."

I realized they didn't know the two were siblings. "I think there's an innocent explanation for the hug. Martin is Morgan's brother."

Sue winked at her sister. "I guess if we're going to be Rosemary and Thyme, we're going to have to brush up on our snooping skills. Do we get a demerit for that mistake, Leta?"

"Well, the Little Old Ladies' Detective Agency tries to cut their trainees some slack. On a serious note, every little bit of information helps."

We made it back to Knight's Rest in time for me to relax on the couch. Neither Wendy nor Dickens were anywhere to be seen, but Christie was lying on her back on the couch, paws extended. Joining her there, I played a few rounds of Words with Friends. I'd gotten behind on my games, and my sister Anna had nudged me. When I messaged her she didn't understand how busy I was taking yoga class, lying by the pool, and touring the local sites, her response was a smiley face with its tongue sticking out.

When Christie crawled in my lap, I set my tablet aside, laid my head back, and closed my eyes. Her purring was the perfect accompaniment to a short nap.

"We're home," Wendy called as she walked in the door with Dickens. "Oh, were you squeezing in a nap? Sorry."

"It's okay. I know I need to change for class. You can't have been walking this whole time. Where've you been?"

"Wearing myself out, that's where—all in the name of gathering clues. Dickens and I took a nice long walk with Morgan and Merlin, and then as I was on my way to change for a swim, Lily grabbed me."

"Lily? Did she want to talk to you?"

"She wanted someone to walk part of the Coast Trail with her, and she said her mum told her no way. I persuaded her I had to have a cup of tea with a scone before I could move another inch.

I tell you, Leta, those lavender scones Guin serves every morning are scrumptious, maybe better than anything on Toby's menu."

"You're not going to tell him that, are you?"

"Nah, probably not. Anyway, I've picked up a few bits of information, but nothing earth-shattering enough to keep me from a quick shower."

We agreed we'd save our reports for a debrief with Belle and Ellie after yoga class. While Wendy showered, I rang our senior partners to tell them the plan.

Ellie answered the phone and assured me they'd be ready. "Leta, dear, you gave us the perfect task. We'll have it all organized in time for your arrival, and we'll make a pot of tea too."

Another restorative class was on the agenda for the afternoon. While it was true I'd learned to relax after moving to the Cotswolds, daily restorative sessions weren't my cup of tea. I much preferred the active classes, and there were too many thoughts tumbling through my head today for me to follow the instruction to clear my brain.

I wondered whether Christie and Archie sensed I was a lost cause, as neither of them paid me a visit. They meandered from person to person, snubbing only me, and the person they spent the most time with was Morgan. *Their kitty intuition tells them where they're needed.*

As we rolled up our mats, Guin called to Wendy. "Meet me at the front desk. I found a flipchart and markers squirreled away in a closet, left over from the last business group we hosted."

We dropped our mats by Iseult Cottage and tended to Archie and Christie. Those two had developed a routine—a sip of water, maybe a treat, and then a cuddle.

Prancing by the door, Dickens barked. "I had a good nap. What's next? The pool? Another walk?"

Wendy glanced at him. "I hope he doesn't think he's going for a third walk. If that's the case, it's your turn." It always amused me when Wendy seemed to know what Dickens was saying. *Maybe someday*, I thought.

With our flipchart pad and markers, we knocked on the door to Igraine Cottage. Dickens may have wanted a walk, but he was quick to settle for a visit with Belle and Ellie. They were sure to provide plenty of belly rubs.

Ellie poured tea, Wendy ferried it to the sitting room, and I tore off a sheet of the flipchart paper to hang on the wall. The pages were like large Post-It notes with adhesive on the back.

Belle sipped her tea. "Ladies, I suggest you share your findings first and then allow Ellie and me to be the cherry-on-top."

That comment amused me. "Now I'm intrigued. If you've solved the case, I'd love to hear it."

Smiling, they glanced at each other and shook their heads, explaining they'd collected only a tiny bit of information but thought one thing might be significant.

Wendy threw up her hands. "Okay then, I'll go first. I've discovered why poor Morgan is so sad and pale. Yes, she's sad about Arthur Knight, as they were childhood friends and sweethearts in school, but she's mourning a more personal loss. Only two months ago, she suffered her third miscarriage. She and Dylan have been trying to have a child for over ten years now, and she's had not only numerous cycles of artificial insemination but also been through her third and final in vitro fertilization treatment. They're pretty much out of options."

I was stunned. "Oh my goodness. They must have desperately wanted a child to go through all that. Doesn't it take a heavy toll on a woman's body?"

Belle explained. "Oh yes. Consider the increasing sense of loss that comes with years of trying unsuccessfully to get pregnant.

Then add the drugs and hormones used to treat infertility, all of which can cause anxiety, sleep loss, mood swings, and depression. So, a woman is already in a fragile emotional state without the IVF treatment resulting in a miscarriage."

"Yes, I worked with a woman at the bank who had IVF twice. The second one was successful, but they had to wait several years between attempts because it cost so much. How on earth did Dylan and Morgan manage to do it on a professor's salary?"

Wendy looked at me. "That's right. I forget it's not covered by most insurance companies in the States, but here, the treatments are provided at no cost by the NHS—you know, the National Health Service."

"Well, I guess it's good they didn't have the additional burden of going broke during all that, but it's still awful. So that explains how fragile she is and why she's been MIA off and on this week."

Belle patted her daughter on the knee. "Did you learn anything else of significance, dear?"

"I'm not sure how significant it is, but the poor girl had to give up her bakery business in Cardiff as a result of her second miscarriage. She'd started to turn a monthly profit after two years of losses, and then she was put on bed rest. You can't run a demanding small business like a bakery from your bed. Two months of bed rest and a late-term miscarriage put paid to that dream."

I shuddered. "She loses her business, her chance of having a baby, and her childhood sweetheart. I'm amazed she's been able to cope at all. I wonder how her husband is handling the situation. It won't have affected him physically, but emotionally? It has to be hard on him too."

"That reminds me of something else she mentioned," Wendy said. "As women do, we shifted to speaking of men in general, and she commented that with each miscarriage, Dylan coped by throwing himself into his work, that he never wanted to talk about it. He's affectionate and caring, but not verbal. To make matters worse, since Arthur's death, he's grown more distant and distracted. It's hard on her not being able to mourn either loss by talking about it."

"Goodness, Wendy, she must have seen you as a gift from above, someone she could talk things through with."

"I think she did, Leta. Now, as for Lily, I enjoyed getting to know her better. At least there were no heartbreaking stories to hear. She's a lively girl. Goes on weekly rambles in Boscastle with her friends and didn't want to miss an opportunity for one here. She's pursuing a computer science degree at Oxford and will return for Michaelmas term in October. My, how the world has changed. That degree program didn't exist when I was there. Anyway, we had a wide-ranging conversation that hopscotched hither, thither, and yon."

Ellie nodded. "Yes, I have the impression she's a sharp girl. Did she observe anything the last few days that could be helpful to us?"

"Two things, one more interesting than the other, I think. Leta, you know we saw Martin Sunday night headed to Guin's cottage? Well, Lily didn't see him but saw another man. She wasn't sure who it was, but it couldn't have been Martin because this one was tall, and she wondered if it might have been Gareth. He knocked on Caryn's door after dark."

Ellie put her hand to her chin. "Could it have been Dylan on his way to see his wife?"

Wendy looked thoughtful. "I suppose. Whoever it was, she only saw him knock on Caryn's door and speak with her briefly. She wasn't looking after that."

I sat up straight. "Well, if it was Gareth, he may have been checking on her since she didn't make it to dinner. If it was

Dylan, then the place was swarming with men Sunday night. The one intriguing fact Penny and Sue shared was seeing Martin leave Morgan's cottage Sunday night and hug her goodbye. I could tell they were disappointed when I explained the two were siblings. They were ready to dub it an illicit romance." When I quoted the question the sisters asked about demerits, we all had a good chuckle.

Belle thought Dylan visiting Caryn was surprising. "I got the impression from her reaction to Dylan's talk that she's put out with him."

Thinking back on my chat with Caryn, I thought that wasn't exactly it. "I think, right or wrong, it's more that she blames Dylan for Arthur being down here in the first place. Arthur mentioned a concern about the artifacts coming into the museum and that seemed to be the impetus for his sudden trip. Because Dylan leads the dig, she sees him as ultimately responsible for Arthur being at Tintagel, and I'm pretty sure she blames Martin equally. It may not be rational, but I can see how she'd feel that way."

Ellie nodded. "I can see that. So if it was Dylan, he might have been attempting to smooth things over, or he could have been concerned about her state of mind. Given what happened to the girl, we shouldn't rule out it being something more sinister."

Wendy agreed. "As Mum likes to remind us, we shouldn't rule out anything or anyone. Anyway, Lily mentioned one more thing, and it jibes with what you heard from Caryn. She noticed Dylan trying to speak with Caryn Saturday night and Caryn jerking away. So, it does seem there was tension between them."

When Belle looked my way, I knew it was my turn. "I must say I enjoyed getting to know Penny and Sue better. I didn't realize they were both teachers. I suggested lunch at the Malthouse because Martin told us Sunday it's where he, Arthur, and Dylan hung out. The sisters got into the spirit of sleuthing when I told them about the Little Old Ladies' Detective Agency. They decided they'd be Rosemary and Thyme and were eager to share what they'd observed. Too funny!"

Ellie laughed. "I loved that show, especially for its marvelous tips on different plants I could try in the gardens at Astonbury Manor."

"Well, we all know gardening tips would do me no good. Now, back to what I gleaned over lunch. The sisters may not have had anything revealing to share, but the barmaid was a fount of information."

Looking from our senior partners to me, Wendy chuckled. "Leta and I get some of our best intel from pubs."

"That's right, even without a pint in hand! I mentioned to the barmaid that Martin told us about the pub, and she said that he, Arthur, Colin, and Dylan were there the night before the accident along with a few other folks working on the dig. She thought it ridiculous the police wanted to know how much Arthur had to drink. According to her, Dylan left after one round, Martin and Arthur were next after nursing a second one, and Colin and the younger crowd stayed a good bit longer. Dylan was headed to the office and suggested Arthur stop by. I guess if we were privy to the case file, we'd know whether Arthur did or not. If he did, Dylan may have been the last person to see him alive."

Wendy's eyes widened. "You realize the office is on the way to Merlin's Cave, right? Still doesn't explain what he was doing there, but it could place him nearby."

"Yes, I was thinking that. The steps that wind down to the shore are at the bottom of the hill. That's all I have to report." I turned to Belle and Ellie. "Ladies, the floor is all yours."

Ellie laughed. "Since we had our first chair yoga session today, we had the perfect opportunity to chat with Guin. Of course, we were the only two students, and Guin fussed over us and made us feel quite special. Belle and I enjoyed it so much, we plan to ask Rhiannon to do some private sessions for us at the manor house. We didn't think to take Christie with us, but we got a taste of cat yoga with Archie. I bet we could get Watson and Christie to team up in Astonbury."

"I'm sure Christie will be happy to train Watson," I said. "Can't you just see her?"

Belle rolled her eyes. "Moving right along, I told Guin I'd love to hear more about how Caryn was doing and invited her to sit with us over a cuppa in the dining room. She was happy to oblige."

The update on Caryn's progress included the news she might be able to return to Knight's Rest on Wednesday. Guin felt comfortable about Caryn continuing her recovery here, since Belle would be nearby and available through Saturday.

As they chatted with Guin, it was Ellie who introduced the search of Caryn's cottage by telling her Wendy and I were concerned about someone breaking into the cottage next door to us.

Belle chortled. "Right, more likely you two would have tackled the intruder if you'd seen him or her. But that entrée allowed us to inquire about security and who had access to the property. Guin was quite clear it must be an outsider, maybe a delivery person, not anyone in her family and certainly not any of the guests—until she ticked off who was in and out Monday, that is."

I nodded. "I bet once she thought of the locals who came and went, she didn't want to point a finger at any of them either. Am I right? And let's not forget we had a doctor, an ambulance crew, and DI Nancarrow here too."

"Guin mentioned Dylan brought takeaway to Morgan Monday evening. He and Martin are worried about her depression, and they all but trip over each other popping in to check on her. Guin thinks they're overdoing the hovering bit."

"So," said Ellie, "narrowing down who could have searched the cottage is no small task. It could have happened any time between Gemma leaving the cottage and you two seeing the light on after dinner. All kinds of people had an opportunity to sneak in."

Wendy looked at me. "Unless we find a witness to someone entering the cottage during the right timeframe, this whole idea of who was where when isn't going to get us anywhere. We need to identify a motive."

That notion made me choke on my tea. "Okay, Agatha, where do we start? We always consider the four Ls—lust, love, lucre, and loathing. Have we seen or heard anything that points to one of those? This may be the point when P. D. James's list fails us, or maybe it's that we don't know enough about our victim to consider what the motive could be. The only possibility we've come up with is Caryn was targeted because she questioned Arthur's death being an accident."

Sticking our her tongue, Wendy made her case. "Now, Tuppence, I think there's another possibility. What if her poisoning has to do with all the noise she's making about artifacts? Caryn made no bones about Arthur being concerned about them coming to the British Museum, and she pretty much said that to anyone who would listen. Maybe Arthur was worried about more than shoddy packing. What if something more sinister is going on, maybe *missing* artifacts? I'm grasping at straws, but something tells me we need to think outside the box."

Closing my eyes, I thought of all the mystery books I'd read. "Are we talking about smuggling? Do you think there's a black market for relics? That items are being siphoned off and sold to collectors instead of making it to the museum?"

Now, Belle looked excited. "Ooh, I love that idea! It could be a wealthy collector, someone like J. Paul Getty, who paid whatever it took so he could sit and admire his finds. There must be billionaire collectors like him nowadays."

Wendy got into the spirit of brainstorming. "What about drugs? On all those BBC mysteries, drugs are smuggled in shipments of statues and artwork and even cheap trinkets."

Ellie held up her hand. "Ladies, ladies. If something is going on with the artifacts, we don't need to know what it is. Let's start with the simple idea of something being amiss. Who would that point a finger at? Who would be alarmed at there being whispers about the artifacts? I think that's a short list."

Right off the bat, I could think of only two people. "If we take that approach, the two names that leap to mind are Dylan and Martin, right? And then there's the freckle-faced Colin. He mentioned working at the warehouse sometimes, and that's where the artifacts are packed."

Nodding, Belle added, "Maybe Morgan too, since we're talking about her husband and brother. She'd be protective of them. That's four possibilities, and beyond that, all the workers at the dig, whose names we don't know."

Wendy leapt to her feet. "We should share this artifact theory with Gemma and DI Nancarrow. I wonder how much digging they've done into what could be amiss with the pottery shards and whatever else is being shipped out."

I rolled my tight shoulders and realized the calming effects of yoga were rapidly disappearing. "I don't know, Wendy. We're bouncing all over the place. I feel like we should focus on Caryn for the next little while and when we think we've exhausted that avenue, go to Jake with our findings. Maybe, just maybe, he'll let us in on what he's discovered about Arthur's death. What I wouldn't give to see the case file."

"Good idea," said Belle. Let's get back on track with the few remaining things we uncovered, in case there's anything helpful in those observations."

When Wendy plopped down with a grumble, I sensed she was impatient and wanted to call DI Nancarrow right that moment, but she acquiesced. "Okay, Mum, let's hear what else you ladies discovered, and then let's get cracking on the Arthur angle."

Ellie patted her on the knee. "It won't take long. We also found an opportunity to speak with Elaine and Art. Elaine adores Caryn and rattled off all the things they've done together since Caryn arrived. The one detail that interested us was Caryn coming to the barn late Saturday night. Elaine had finished cleaning and readying the dining room for Sunday morning breakfast and was headed to the front door when she found Caryn behind the front desk. She knows Caryn as an early-to-bed girl, but there she was in her pajamas close to midnight loading paper into the printer."

Belle added. "Caryn explained she'd stumbled across one of Arthur's last emails and she wanted to check on something. The two chatted as the printer spewed page after page, and Elaine said it was a thick stack. When she asked whether Caryn planned to read it all before turning in, Caryn showed her the title page."

I prompted. "And?"

"Elaine teased her that she was sure to be sound asleep in minutes if that's what she was reading. It was something like Evolution and Archaeology—Elaine couldn't recall exactly. Is it any wonder? Sounds dry as dust."

Wendy agreed. "Better than a sleeping pill. Didn't you also say you spoke with Art?"

It was Ellie's turn to chuckle. "Yes, he gave us chapter and verse on garden deliveries and the time he spent with the dogs, but nothing we see as useful."

As the founder of the Little Old Ladies' Detective Agency, I felt a need to take control, if only briefly. "That's a wrap, then, and I have a proposal. Let's allow the facts to percolate, so to speak, while we do cocktails and dinner with the group, all the time keeping our ears to the ground. There's no telling what else someone may let drop."

Dickens interrupted me with a bark. "Will they drop food? I can take care of that."

I rubbed his head. "I think Dickens wants to help. Let's put him in charge of sniffing out clues. What do you think?"

"That's all well and good," Wendy interjected, "But when do we ring DI Nancarrow?"

"I was getting to that before my dog so rudely interrupted me. Let's plan our approach to Jake before we ring him. We need to choose our words carefully so he'll consider not only our artifact idea but also share his findings on the Arthur Knight case. Hopefully, Gemma will be at dinner tonight. We can try greasing the skids with her by sharing our intel, but, and this is vital, I don't want to ask her permission for anything. This is Jake's case, and he's much easier to deal with. Plus, if Gemma's here, we can ring him without her sitting next to him voicing objections. Sound like a plan?"

After poking fun at me for calling the local DI by his first name, Belle and Ellie quickly agreed, but it took Wendy a moment. "Okay, okay. Let's shower and then map out what we'll say to Jake or DI Nancarrow or however you decide to refer to him. You can't seem to keep that straight. Is it his good looks that are keeping you off balance?" She laughed. "Should Dave be worried?"

"Only if Jake likes women twenty years his senior. His easy-going manner puts me in mind of a younger Dave. On the other hand, those broad shoulders . . . hmmm." *Definitely time to call Dave.*

# CHAPTER FOURTEEN

NO NEW DETAILS WERE discovered over dinner, and in unspoken agreement, Wendy and I skipped dessert and strolled to our cottage.

Dickens trotted behind us, barking intermittently. "I was a super snagger tonight, Leta. Snagged some fries and a chunk of biscuit. Got a belly rub from Belle, too."

I had to explain my burst of laughter to Wendy somehow. "I was thinking about Ellie and her butterfly nets. What do you say we collect our thoughts and map out what we know about everyone we've met at Knight's Rest? We may not have a complete picture of whereabouts, but we've learned a few things about a small group of people."

"I like that idea. Maybe that approach will lead to a list of potential suspects. If nothing else, it should make for good talking points to use with Jake—or DI Nancarrow."

Opening the door, I was greeted by Archie and Christie. I didn't realize we'd left them locked in, but the princess was quick to let me know. "It's about time you got here. We're going for a moonlight stroll." The sun hadn't set yet, but I didn't argue with her.

"Not too far, please. I'll be waiting for you."

Wendy expressed her surprise at how well-behaved Christie was, and she was right to an extent. My girl had been good about sticking close by, but I figured that was because she liked the attention she was getting as a yoga star, not because she was particularly obedient. It didn't hurt that Archie stayed glued to her side.

Wendy poured the wine, and I hung the flipchart paper in the sitting room. Setting my glass down, I grabbed a marker. "I don't think we need to consider Penny, Sue, Lily, and Lilith. What do you think?"

"There you go again. Our resident Miss Marple would chastise you for that leap, but I agree we can save them for later. After all, we don't have any evidence they knew Caryn before Saturday, so unless one of them has a Jekyll & Hyde personality, I can't see it."

"Let's start with Caryn in the center, and add Martin, Dylan, Morgan, Guin, and Gareth in a circle around her. Art and Elaine can wait 'til later too."

As I wrote, Wendy sipped her wine. "It occurs to me we don't know very much about Caryn, other than her connection to Arthur. Are we missing the boat by not learning more about her?"

*She has a point,* I thought. "Except for Alice, we barely knew any of the victims in our murder inquiries. We filled in the gaps as we spoke with family, friends, enemies, and witnesses—many of whom were suspects. Do you remember what we discovered when we traveled to Dartmouth in October to learn about that victim? Let's capture the little we know and hope a more complete portrait of Caryn will emerge."

I listed *British Museum* and *Arthur's fiancée* beneath Caryn and moved on to Martin. Wendy called out details while

I wrote—*Lifelong friend to Arthur, Works with Dylan and Arthur, Morgan's brother, Drinks with Arthur night before the accident, Visited Guin and Morgan Sunday night, Friend or more to Guin.*

I added *Supposed to meet Arthur at Merlin's Cave in the morning.* "I feel sorry for him. He was so sad about Arthur. Did that seem genuine to you?"

Wendy nodded. "That's the spirit. Question everything. I think it was Hugh Laurie as Dr. House who said, 'It's a basic truth of the human condition that everybody lies.' And Mark Twain also said something to that effect, as in, we pretty much lie all the time. So, the answer to your question is maybe."

Her references made me laugh. "Ha! Less than helpful, Wendy. I wonder what it says about the two of us that we readily quote TV stars in the same breath as literary giants?"

"It says we're well-rounded *and* well-read!"

"I'll take that explanation. Now, if our local DI has Arthur's phone, he may have proof of the scheduled meeting via texts or voicemails. Unless, of course, the two men set it up over drinks. Enough on Martin. What about Dylan?"

Folding her legs beneath her in the chair, Wendy spouted another list. "Archaeologist and scholar, School and work friend to Arthur, Married to Morgan, New book coming out, Took over Arthur's role at the dig, Made presentation Saturday, Tense moment with Caryn Saturday, <u>May</u> have knocked on Caryn's door Sunday night."

I studied the list. "I think there's more." I wrote, *Likes to think at Merlin's Cave, Left pub early after drinks, Asked Arthur to drop by office, Brings dinner to Morgan Monday.* "Can you think of anything else?"

"Not yet. Go back to Martin and add that line about thinking at Merlin's Cave, and then I think we should add Colin. We know very little about him, but he was here Sunday."

"Good catch. We don't want to forget anyone. We know he's a photographer and he's new to the area. What else?"

Wendy tilted her head and spoke as I wrote. "*He's from London, and he was at the pub with Dylan, Arthur, and Martin. That's a short list.*" She chuckled. "And I think he and Rhiannon would be cute together—two tall blondes."

Laughing, I added those observations beneath his name. "Too bad we don't know anything about his whereabouts Sunday and Monday, except he was at the dig and kindly took our picture."

I moved on to Morgan and drew a line beneath her name. I wrote, *Arthur's teen love, Married to Dylan, Something between her and Caryn(?), Martin's sister.*"

Rubbing Dickens's belly, Wendy looked thoughtful. "I know we have to suspect everyone, but I have a hard time seeing her poisoning Caryn's tea."

Wendy and I seemed to switch off playing devil's advocate. "I do too, but remember the adage not to rule anyone out. If it helps, we're just jotting down what we know about her, and it's sad as all get out."

"Goodness, Leta, where did that Southernism come from? I haven't heard that expression since I left Charlotte."

I chuckled. "I don't know. Sometimes, they just pop out from the far corners of my brain. I could add that she's pretty as a peach since she has that flawless complexion and strawberry-blonde hair."

Wendy grinned. "Next you'll say, 'Bless her heart,' but in this case, it won't be a dig, it will be sincere. You might as well carry on writing while I recap what we know. *Martin's younger sister, Owned a bakery but had to close it, Three miscarriages, One in*

*June, Missed the farm tour and the Tintagel tour, Missed Monday afternoon class and dinner."*

Standing back, I studied the list. "Wow. Looking at the list for Morgan, I realize she was MIA most of Monday, meaning she had the opportunity to search Vivienne Cottage."

Tilting her head, Wendy agreed. "I can't argue with that, but I don't see a motive."

"We haven't begun to touch on motive for anyone yet. Funny, I read a comment on motive in my Lord Peter Wimsey book last night. I am so glad Jill Paton Walsh resumed the Dorothy Sayers series. I adored the books Sayers wrote in the 20s and 30s, and I think Walsh's later books are just as good."

"And what wisdom does Lord Peter share on motives, Tuppence?"

"He says motives are a distraction, that once you know the how, you know who. But in this case, the how doesn't seem to be getting us any closer to the culprit."

Wendy laughed. "I can see him with his monocle, but no one says we have to follow the advice of a debonair fictional detective."

"True. Let's proceed with our list. Guess we need to talk about Guin. I find it interesting that she asked Gemma to help Caryn accept Arthur's death as an accident and now, after the attack on Caryn, I haven't heard her say word one about doubts. Does she still believe Arthur's death was an accident? Gareth said he began to question everything as soon as Caryn took ill."

"But, Leta, she's Arthur's sister. You're not suggesting she had a hand in his death, are you?"

"Why not? The word fratricide wouldn't exist if it had never happened."

"And the word nerd strikes again. Are we going to reference Medea and her brother from Greek mythology or Cain and Abel from the Bible? Or better yet, Shakespeare's *Hamlet*?"

I shushed my friend. "Hey, just sayin' it *happens*. And, If we're thinking outside the box, it fits." I held up my hand, palm out. "But wait a minute, that idea takes me to Guin's connection to Martin, whatever it is. If he's involved in any of this, would she protect him? What is it they say? Still waters run deep."

Wendy closed her eyes. "I see her as the calm, unruffled head of the family, but if Arthur's concern about Tintagel relics was in some way a threat to Martin . . . Like Medea, would Guin kill her brother to protect her lover, if that's what he is?"

I gaped at her. "Wow! You just wove a full-fledged tale of betrayal from one tiny thread. I'm not ready to go that far, but it's worth keeping in the back of our minds."

She hopped up. "This is why we need to know the details of the supposed accident. It could still be an accident, but one where another person was present, one that grew out of an argument. Maybe tempers flared there on the shore and Arthur wound up in the water. His death may have been unintentional."

"I get all the legal definitions confused, but could it be something like manslaughter because it wasn't premeditated?"

"What they call it doesn't matter—what matters is someone may be lying to cover up Arthur accidentally hitting his head on a boulder. Good grief. We're really going down a rabbit hole now." She paused. "Leta, are you listening to me?"

I shook myself. "I am, but my mind took a slightly different tack, as in whose temper may have flared? Guin's, Martin's, Dylan's, Colin's? Who may have been there when Arthur died? And, for goodness' sake, we have to persuade Jake—or DI Nancarrow or the dishy DI —to put his cards on the table."

"Point taken. We haven't made our list for Guin yet. Ready?"

Once again, I wrote on the flipchart sheet as Wendy ticked off what we knew. *Sister to Arthur & Gareth, Aunt to Art & Elaine, Manages yoga & resort business, Martin's friend or lover, Concerned about Caryn's emotional state, Went to hospital with Caryn, Confident Caryn would be okay, At hospital during farm tour, Easy access to cottages, Concerned about Morgan (generous invitation), Accepts Arthur's death as accidental, Liked/trusted by Rhiannon.*

Wendy frowned. "I wonder why she was so sure Caryn would be okay. I know Rhiannon says Guin trusting her instincts allows her to 'stay calm and carry on,' so to speak, but wouldn't you expect her to be just the teensiest bit distressed?"

"Yes, her calm surprised me. Call me a skeptic, but I don't buy this second sight thing her niece mentioned. Going back to our earlier discussion, we could look at her demeanor another way. If she doctored the tea, she might know enough about herbs to be reasonably certain of the outcome."

"Whoa. See, this is what's so good about talking things out. I never would have gotten there. So, the logical next question is, if it were Guin, did she intend for Caryn to wind up seriously ill or dead, to put it bluntly?"

I sighed. "Hmm. Is she as knowledgeable as her sister-in-law about herbs? That's what I'm wondering. If so, she might know what constitutes a fatal dose of jimson weed, and she may have used the seeds to shut Caryn up, not to kill her. Maybe it's Guin's misfortune that you and I are around. Would anyone else have taken the tea to Merry? Sure, the hospital would have eventually completed the analysis, but after how long? Veddy, veddy interesting."

Shaking her head, Wendy smiled. "You and your *Laugh-In* references. You do sound remarkably like Arte Johnson when you say that."

I drew a line beneath Gareth's name. "Enough. Let's move on before we get stuck. We've got one more adult family member to consider. What do we know about Gareth?"

"He's a likable sort. He's also easygoing and calm but in a different way from his sister. And, for the record, I can't see him hurting his brother."

"Right, but as you keep saying, let's capture what we know. Ready?" Again, I wrote as she dictated. *Merry's husband, Father to Elaine and Art, Youngest Knight sibling, Manages the farm, Provides tours, Access to cottages, May have visited Caryn Sunday night.*

Dickens barked, "He likes dogs. Merlin says he's a good guy."

Laughing, I added likes dogs to the list. "What else?"

"I think that's it. Besides, we need to determine our approach to DI Nancarrow and call him—before you turn into a pumpkin, as you're fond of saying."

My friend was right. I could almost feel my brain shutting down in anticipation of crawling into bed. And I hadn't yet called my boyfriend to say goodnight. I hung a second piece of paper on the wall. "Do we have any conclusions to share? I think we at least have to tell him who had the opportunity to search the cottage and who didn't. Who could have planted the teabag or given it to Caryn is more difficult, I think."

Wendy hopped up to take a turn with the marker. "Okay, the list of people who were here at the right time to sneak into the cottage is pretty clear—as long as we leave off guests other than Morgan. It includes Guin, Gareth, Morgan, Dylan, Elaine, and Art—if we must—and even Merry. I say we make an executive decision to exclude Gareth's family and be done with it."

"I can go with that. Let's take a stab at the tea scenario too. The people on that list would be Guin, Gareth, Morgan, Martin, and maybe Dylan. So, Dylan is an unknown for the tea timing, and Martin wasn't here when the search could have occurred. Oh fiddle-dee-dee, this isn't very useful, is it?"

Hands on her hips, Wendy exuded confidence. "No, but we did lots of legwork and can keep nosing around tomorrow. At least it's a start. If we drive to Truro to look at the paperwork from the cottage and the laptop, we may gain clarity about motive and be able to narrow the list. Easy peasy. Our talking points are that we've identified these people for the two events at Vivienne Cottage—the poisoning and the search—and dare I say, we want to see the Arthur Knight case file? To help clarify what we're thinking about the attack on Caryn."

I heard Christie meowing at the door but couldn't make out what she was saying. As I got up to let her in, I handed my phone to Wendy and suggested she call the dishy DI.

The meows grew more plaintive as I approached the door. "Hello, I'm home. Where are you, Leta?"

When I opened the door, I expected Christie to dash in. Instead, she sat and gave me the evil eye. "Took your time, didn't you? What if I were in danger? What if a fox had been after me?"

I picked her up and hugged her. "Well, if you're that worried about being in the great outdoors, perhaps you should become an indoor kitty. What do you think?"

Wriggling out of my arms, she ignored my question and ran to the kitchen. I took the hint and put a dab of wet food in her bowl and went through the ritual of fluffing it until she ate it all. The silent treatment continued as she stood, tail straight up in the air, and stalked to the bedroom. *Uppity little thing!*

Wendy called, "Leta, we have an appointment in the morning. I made another executive decision, this one about breakfast. We'll eat early and hit the road before yoga. Are you okay with missing the meditation class?"

She already knew my answer to that, as we both preferred the classes we thought constituted exercise. "You know I am. If I had to choose one to miss, that would be it. Rhiannon will be so disappointed in us. Never mind that. Did you tell him about our artifact idea and our need to know more about the Arthur Knight case?"

"I didn't mention any of that because he's meeting us at the Truro station in the morning. I say we take our flipchart pages to show him and then request the case file. With the information laid out in front of him, how can he refuse?"

"I guess we'll see. You know, this will be the first time we've worked at a police station. Dare I say this should be veddy, veddy interesting?" With that, I said goodnight.

Dickens followed me to the bedroom, where we found Christie lying on the bed. I realized I hadn't given her the catnip mouse and pulled it from my bag. "Here you go, princess. See what you think."

She'd never been much into toys, so I wasn't sure how she'd react. I watched as she touched it tentatively with a paw before snagging its tail and pulling it closer. She sniffed it and seemed to consider what to do next. "What is this thing, Leta?"

"A gift. Do you like it?"

Her response was to do that funny cat wiggle and pounce on it. She rubbed her face on it and gave a throaty purr, a sound I hadn't heard from her before.

Dickens put his nose on the bed to watch. "What's that sound, Leta? Is she sick?"

"I think she's happy. Look at her."

We both watched as Christie cuddled the yarn mouse and settled into her usual purring sound until suddenly she bit the little thing and gave a loud meow. "I like it."

Laughing, I made short work of changing into my nightgown and joining her on the bed. With Dickens stretched out on the rug and Christie lying by my side, I was ready to end my day with a call to Dave. As I dialed his number, I realized I hadn't spoken to him since Sunday night. We had exchanged a few texts Monday, but I didn't elaborate on the events of the day. He knew Caryn was ill and was in the hospital and that I took a tour of the lavender farm, nothing beyond that.

His cheerful greeting was just what I needed. "Hello, Tuppence. I'm picturing you all tucked up in bed. Am I right?"

"Of course you are. I'm plum wo' out, and I've got lots to tell you." I knew he'd get a kick out of my Southernism. What he'd think about my activities remained to be seen. During his April visit, we had our first argument, and it was over what he saw as my risky sleuthing undertakings. I couldn't disagree he had good reason to worry about me, especially after my dangerous encounter at Astonbury Manor.

Trying to articulate to him how I felt about what Gemma called *my snooping* led me to examine why I kept winding up involved in police cases. When I retired early, I imagined myself reading good books, writing my columns, and sipping tea. What I hadn't counted on was a sense that something was missing. I thought I missed Henry, and I did, but it was more than that. I'd lost the sense of purpose my career gave me.

The good news was that two of the traits that made me successful in the corporate world were easily transferrable to everyday life—attention to detail and listening. Folks found me easy to talk to, and I found listening fulfilling. It was a win-win, especially when it came to ferreting out clues that solved a case.

Thankfully, Dave understood, though he didn't worry about me any less. Instead, he armed me with personal protective gear and became a willing partner in solving the murder of a new friend. After that episode, he saw how easy it was to get involved and how addictive sniffing out clues could be. Time would tell how long his newfound appreciation would last.

After I painted him a picture of Christie's antics with the catnip mouse, I brought him up to date on the happenings at Knight's Rest. "I'm happy to report that Caryn is on the mend and that Wendy was instrumental in figuring out what caused the symptoms." I explained the jimson weed discovery to him, and he was suitably impressed with our quick thinking.

"You've made me curious. I'll have to google that one. If teenagers in England are using it as a hallucinogen, I imagine it's going on here too, and it sounds plenty dangerous."

He was all ears when I told him mine and Wendy's suspicions a romance could be in the offing for Gemma. "The dishy DI? That's a good one. Honestly, Leta, you and Wendy have such a way with words, I think you two should write a book. A mystery with a bit of romance tossed in. The main character could be a female DI like Gemma, flaws and all. What do you think?"

*So far, so good, I* thought. *No undue concerns.* "Oh, I can't wait to tell Wendy. We could have a Constable James character, and our DI could have a love interest in a nearby village. Heck, we could use the Tintagel investigations as the basis for the plot."

"Investigations, plural? I assume the dishy DI is trying to get to the bottom of who poisoned the tea, but is there more?" He groaned. "Don't tell me something else has happened."

I spilled it all, everything we knew about Arthur Knight's alleged accident, the search of the cottage, the suspects, and the relationships. He listened patiently and asked good questions. "Archaeology, artifacts, Arthurian legend—this has all the makings of a fascinating literary mystery. It reminds me of that book we like, *The Lost Book of the Grail.* I wonder what you'll find in Caryn's papers."

"Probably not anything as significant as the location of the Holy Grail, but hopefully something that helps DI Nancarrow get to the bottom of the Arthur Knight case and by extension the attack on Caryn, if the two events are indeed related."

Dave chuckled. "And, Leta, you and Wendy plan to apply your investigative powers *only* to the papers and the laptop. At the police station, right? I shouldn't worry that you're taking your oversized magnifying glasses anywhere else?"

"If those papers are as revealing as the ones we studied in our last case, we'll be able to give DI Nancarrow everything he needs to narrow the suspect list. Who knows? I may be calling you to research something like I did last time."

*He wasn't buying it.* "Don't think you're fooling me. You didn't answer the question. Just promise to check in with me so I know where you are and that you're safe. Okay?"

"Yes, Tommy. Wendy and I will be careful, and I'll call you at all appropriate times. Seriously, I don't see us wandering the streets of Tintagel in search of clues. We'll be fine." *Phew. Dodged that bullet.*

# CHAPTER FIFTEEN

HOW WONDERFUL TO WAKE up to the aroma of freshly brewed coffee. I stretched and rolled and discovered I was alone in the bedroom. *Wendy must be tending to my fussy cat, and I bet Dickens is out searching for rabbits.*

When I wandered into the kitchen, Wendy handed me a mug of coffee. "I've taken care of our four-legged friends, and I've been thinking. Why don't we see whether Mum and Ellie would like to accompany us to Truro?"

I yawned and propped my hip against the counter. "Are we allowed to wake your mum this early? I know she'll be disappointed if we don't at least ask, but I'm not brave enough to disturb her before nine. On the other hand, she was a huge help last time we needed to peruse papers. She and Ellie both. Remember, you were jealous that we handled the case without you?"

"Don't remind me. As it turned out, I would have enjoyed myself much more with you three than with my traveling companion here in Cornwall. Oh well, live and learn. I'll run to Igraine Cottage and ask Ellie. She can decide whether to rouse Mum."

She ran out and Dickens ran in. "Leta, I saw two bunnies by the barn. Where are we going today? Is Wendy taking me for a walk?"

Christie was bathing herself in a sunspot on the floor. "I don't know about you, Dickens, but I'm going to yoga. Leta, when we get home, can we go to yoga every day?"

"Only if Rhiannon decides to take you in as a boarder. Twice a week is plenty for me."

The princess appeared to be considering that option. "Nah, I'd miss the donkeys, and I wouldn't see Watson."

I looked at Dickens. "Did you hear that? She didn't mention us. So, Christie, you'd miss Martha and Dylan and Watson? No one else?"

Dickens walked over to his feline sister, rolled her over with his head, and licked her face. "Come on, you know you'd miss me."

Leaving them to hash things out, I took a quick shower and was ready for the day when Wendy returned. "Okay, all settled. Mum is fired up about taking a trip to Truro and promises to be ready to roll by nine. Her only request is that we're back in time for her afternoon nap. You know how she loves her naps."

"Heck, I love my naps too. Snoozing whenever the mood strikes is one of the many joys of retirement. I can't tell you how many times I was in a three p.m. meeting wishing I could crawl in a corner and doze."

Wendy and I strolled to breakfast with Christie in the backpack and Dickens at our heels. Rhiannon was in the yoga studio with Archie, so I explained the situation and handed her the backpack. As I predicted, she teased us about missing meditation, suggesting we'd been looking for an excuse the whole time.

Surprisingly, Christie wasn't at all disturbed at being left in the studio with Rhiannon. When we let her out of the backpack, the two cats rolled and chased each other. *Guess they're limbering up for class.*

With all four members of the Little Old Ladies' Detective Agency in my taxi, I didn't have room for Dickens to ride safely. He peered in the back seat and tried to climb between Wendy and Ellie, but I knew his safety harness wouldn't stretch to the middle.

When I explained I couldn't very well ask one of the ladies to sit in the middle, he took it in stride. "Okay, I'll hang out with Merlin today. Will you bring me a surprise? Please?"

The drive to Truro was a scenic one. With dahlias and wild fuchsias in bloom, the landscape was dotted with splashes of bright yellow, purple, deep orange, and magenta. I pulled over twice for Ellie to snap pictures to show to her gardener. On the drive, Wendy and I used the time to bring our senior partners up to speed on the details we mapped out the night before.

We must be an unusual sight, I thought, as we trooped into the Truro Police Station carrying our flipchart pad. When we approached the constable at the front desk, he quickly ushered us back, grinning all the while.

When Jake caught sight of us, his expression echoed that of the constable. "Ah, the Little Old Ladies' Detective Agency is out in full force this morning. Welcome."

He exclaimed over Belle and executed an exaggerated bow to Ellie when we introduced her as the Dowager Countess of Stow. Hearing that Belle fancied herself a modern-day Miss Marple, he asked about Ellie's persona. "So, we have Tuppence, Agatha, and Miss Marple, but the dowager countess doesn't have a stage name? You ladies will have to work on that."

He set us up in a small conference room with the laptop and papers. "These are copies of what we found in Caryn's cottage, so feel free to scribble notes if you like and help yourself to the whiteboard. I'll be tied up on a call for the next little while. Things are beginning to heat up on the drug case I'm working on." Leaving us with pens, pencils, and highlighters, he told us to take our time. *It sure would be nice if he'd rub off on Gemma.*

As the member of the team who was most adept with a computer, I scanned the names of the file folders on Caryn's desktop. "You know, ladies, I feel a bit funny looking at her computer. It's not like studying a murder victim's personal information. This feels more intrusive, as though I'm violating Caryn's privacy."

Wendy looked up from separating the papers. "Let's see what these printouts tell us while you limit your reading to folders that look to be about exhibits and museum matters—things that aren't of a personal nature. I feel a little bit the same way about these papers, but so far it's nothing but articles. We may have to overcome our qualms if we don't come up with anything useful with this approach."

She continued flipping through the stack. "This is interesting. A quick glance tells me we have a mixture of scholarly articles and a handful of emails between Arthur and his publisher. It sounds harsh, but since Arthur's dead, I don't feel bad about looking at his correspondence."

Belle held out her hand. "Wendy, why not let Ellie and me start with those? Didn't you say you wanted to review the Arthur Knight case file too? With Leta on the laptop and you with the file, we'll use our time more efficiently."

"Yes, Mum, except I don't have the file yet. Guess it's time for me to tackle that topic with DI Nancarrow."

We laughed as she stood and straightened her shoulders. At a height of five feet, she didn't present an imposing physical figure, but she radiated command. She picked up the flipchart pages we'd brought and strode to the door. *I bet her students hopped to when they saw her like this.*

"Do you want backup?" I asked.

"Nope, I've got this. Be back in a jiffy."

The rest of us went to work on our assigned tasks. Belle and Ellie murmured between themselves as they shuffled papers into piles. Caryn's computer files were well-organized, and the titles made it easy to ascertain the contents without opening every one. I hesitated to open the folder labeled *Arthur* for fear it was personal, but when I clicked on it, I was relieved to see it contained two folders—"Book" and "Tintagel Exhibit". *Hmm. Maybe she helped him with both.*

Because Caryn had spoken so readily about artifacts, I opened the Tintagel folder first. It was populated with subfolders about displays, lighting, signs, brochures, and more. The one that seemed most pertinent for my purposes was labeled *Archaeology*. Sure enough, it was filled with files on the history of the dig and finds cataloged by type like structures, pottery, and bones. I wondered where to start. *What might give me a clue as to Arthur's concerns?*

I was puzzling over that when Ellie cleared her throat. "We've separated the pile into two categories—emails and what we're calling research. I'm going to study the emails more closely, but as Wendy mentioned, most are between Arthur and his publisher. I've found only one exception, an email from him to Caryn. They're all dated during the week preceding Arthur's trip to Tintagel, and, interestingly, they're not about *his* book. The publisher asked for his help with a manuscript from another author."

"Hmmm. That seems odd."

"Perhaps not, when you read the explanation she offered. The editor assigned to the book was suddenly unavailable due to a death in the family, and the publisher was short-handed and at her wits' end. She didn't know where to start with vague comments like 'need to check' and hoped Arthur could help. In her email, she referred to the book as A&A and wanted Arthur's opinion about certain passages."

I leaned forward. "Are there attachments to the emails? Are they printed out too?"

"Yes, dear, with highlights plus Arthur's comments. Isn't it amazing what people can do on a computer in this day and age? Belle and I would've sat with paper copies and scribbled our notes with a pencil. Instead, it's all printed neatly, even the comments."

"I wonder what it was about that correspondence that made Caryn print it out?"

"Can't tell yet, but I hope it will become clear. Now, Belle has the stack we've dubbed research."

Belle held up a sheet of paper. "Someone has scribbled notes and used a pink highlighter throughout these pages. If this is what Caryn printed late Saturday night, they must be her notes. All I can tell you so far is the subject matter is archaeologists—in particular, a handful who studied and led digs in Great Britain. Several taught at the University of Edinburgh; others at Oxford and Cambridge. All were associated with significant digs at locations like Stonehenge or sites in Scotland and Northern Ireland, and all were prolific in publishing scholarly papers and books in the 30s and 40s. I must say their bibliographies are a bit overwhelming. As Ellie said about the emails, hopefully I'll find something in all this that will explain Caryn's interest."

I nodded. "I'd like to think it's something beyond her work at the museum, something that will give us insight into what happened to her—and Arthur. It had to be the laptop or those papers or both that the intruder was searching for Monday. Surely, something in all this will explain why."

As I returned to searching the laptop, I wondered where Agatha had gotten to. *Is being gone for twenty minutes a good or a bad sign?*

When Wendy returned ten minutes later with a thick file and a smile on her face, I had my answer. "I see you were successful. Did it require your entire repertoire of stern school teacher looks to convince him? Or did you play the damsel in distress card?"

"A damsel in despair, perhaps. As in, 'Oh woe is me. How can we find out who's responsible for the dastardly deed of poisoning poor Caryn without understanding what happened to her beau?' I was unfolding the list of suspects when he stopped me and handed me the file. I'm to fetch him when we're done in here."

Belle gave her daughter an affectionate look. "I recall the woe-is-me technique from your school years, though I only fell for it in my weaker moments."

Wendy winked. "Now, Mum, don't give away all my secrets."

We resumed our separate tasks. Though I dug deep into the Tintagel folder on the laptop, I couldn't find anything that gave me a clue as to Arthur's concerns. I suspected whatever it was, it grew from something he saw in the boxes arriving from Cornwall, not from any documentation.

Still trying not to dive into personal folders, I shifted to the folder labeled "*Book*," more out of curiosity than because I felt it was relevant. An hour passed with me engrossed in *Tales of Tintagel*, Wendy scribbling pages of notes, and Ellie and Belle

whispering and occasionally laughing. I took their joviality as
an encouraging sign.

Once again, the dowager countess cleared her throat. "May
Belle and I share our findings? We think they're quite significant."

Seeing our nods, she began. "The email attachments are
intriguing, so much so that I'd like to read the final version of
the book these excerpts come from. It appears to be another
book about King Arthur and his connection to archaeological finds at Stonehenge and Glastonbury, or perhaps it's a
larger work on British archaeology with only a chapter on
Arthurian legend. I could make out the gist of the comments
but was still puzzled. Let me show you."

Wendy and I went to stand behind Ellie as she laid out the
pages and pointed. "See here, this paragraph is highlighted
and the comment to the side says *maybe CV*. About a dozen
comments mention *cult-hist, CV, or CHA*. But look, everywhere you see the abbreviation *CV*, Caryn has also highlighted it in pink. We know it was her because she used pink on
the pages Belle reviewed."

Belle chimed in. "Of course, cha-cha came to mind for
*CHA*. What nonsense! And the only thing we could think
of for *CV* was curriculum vitae, but that didn't make sense.
A CV includes a person's education and work experience.
When we asked ourselves what a *CV* could have to do with
this material, we had no clue."

Now it was her turn to showcase her detective work.
"While Ellie was studying the emails and excerpts, I read the
articles with the pink highlights. It wasn't until we cross-referenced the stacks that we began to make sense of what we
had."

*I think they're waiting for a drumroll!* Belle looked smug. "Would you ladies believe that *CHA* stands for cultural-historical archaeology?"

I'm sure my dismay was evident. "I guess I'd believe anything at this point. Do I even want to know what that is?"

"Not required, but knowing that *CV* stands for Clifford Vere is something you'll want to remember."

Smiling, Wendy tilted her head. "And why is that important, Mum? I can tell you're dying to tell us."

"Clifford Vere was renowned during those twenty years and long after as a proponent of cultural-historical archaeology, but his work was viewed less and less favorably when processual archaeology gathered steam in later years."

I groaned. "Please tell me I don't need to know what that is either."

Belle's eyes twinkled. "Again, not required. Let me lay out how all this connects."

It was Wendy's turn to groan. "Why am I thinking, 'Listen my children, and you shall hear of the midnight ride of Paul Revere'?"

At least she made me laugh. "Could it be because you're a retired English teacher?"

The schoolteacher's mum cleared her throat. "All right, ladies, don't spoil my fun. When Arthur noted *CV* throughout the attachment from his publisher, we think he was indicating the passages referenced the works of Clifford Vere. There were pages of research on several other archaeologists from that period, but none had the right initials."

I made an intuitive leap. "You think that's what the editor meant when he said he needed to check? Maybe it sounded familiar to him?"

Ellie held up her hand. "I think that's a strong possibility. I wouldn't expect the publisher to have a clue, since she hadn't read the entire manuscript. That's the editor's job, but when it fell in her lap, she had no choice but to scan it. She was complimentary of the overall thrust of the book and the clarity of the writing but was concerned about the editor's notes. Did he need to check because it reminded him of something else? Being a publisher of nonfiction works on archaeology likely means she's fairly well-read on the subject, but not as knowledgeable as a scholar like Arthur."

As Wendy and I sat in rapt silence, Belle explained further. "If we hadn't cross-referenced the two stacks, we wouldn't have seen it."

Pointing to the emails, Ellie elaborated. "When I reread the emails dated two days before Arthur left for Tintagel, it hit me. The first was from his publisher thanking him for his help. The two must have had a phone conversation in between emails because, in this one, she said she was dismayed that Arthur thought some of the material was almost verbatim from another source. She worried it was intentional and not simply a footnoting error."

Wendy's mouth dropped open. "So it was more than a passing reference to Clifford Vere's work. It was whole chunks from his articles?"

Belle nodded. "Based on Arthur's quick review, yes. And she wrote, 'I plan to speak with *him* right away. Unless he has a plausible explanation, I will have no choice but to revoke his contract. I can't keep someone as a client who is this careless with source material, no matter how obscure. How would I trust him going forward?' Arthur responds that before she acts precipitously, he needs time to do more fact-checking. We can't tell whether or not she responded, as there's no copy of a reply. Perhaps it was another phone call."

Belle paused. "The final email was a request from Arthur to Caryn asking if she could give him a hand by locating a few publications about cultural-historical archaeology, especially any by Clifford Vere. He didn't mention why he wanted it. My sense is he wanted to be doubly sure his conclusion was on target before the publisher leveled an accusation against the author of this book."

I closed my eyes in concentration. "Ellie, let me get this straight. You've concluded *CV* in Arthur's notes means Clifford Vere? As in, he was telling his publisher that's where the passages came from?"

While I was trying to make sense of what Ellie and Belle had shared, Wendy had a different question. "But, wait, I'm stuck on how Caryn had Arthur's emails in the first place. Sure, she'd have the ones Arthur sent her, but how did she have access to the correspondence between him and his publisher?"

Ellie had a ready answer. "Oh, that's easy. When Nigel was alive, we each had access to the other's account. That way, in a pinch, we could check calendars or look something up. Did you do that with Henry, Leta?"

"Oh yes. He was forever forwarding me bills or messages about our health insurance and forgetting to send all the information I needed. Knowing his passwords meant I could check his computer and find the related emails or files in a snap. As the banker in the family, it would have been maddening to have to wait for him to remember to send me those things."

"But, but," asked Wendy, "Caryn and Arthur weren't married. Do single people do that?"

I laughed. "I don't know, Wendy. For us, it was a matter of convenience, and it certainly helped me when Henry died because I was able to get to everything I needed to close out accounts and such. I bet you're thinking of the TV mysteries where spouses find out about affairs and lies because they suddenly come across an email or read a text."

She laughed at me. "Of course I am. How did you know?"

Belle looked at her daughter. "Now that we've settled that issue, where do we stand, ladies?"

I stopped laughing and thought for a moment. "Okay, I can follow your logic, but I'm confused about several things. First, why did Caryn print all this out?"

Ellie stood and picked up a whiteboard marker. "Leta, let's see if we can map out a timeline. First, I think all of these papers were printed at the same time—Saturday night when Elaine saw Caryn at the front desk." Ellie wrote Saturday night. Beneath that she noted *C prints materials*.

I thought back to when Henry died and how my brain worked or didn't. "She may soon be able to tell us why, but in the meantime, a few possibilities come to mind. It's been six weeks since Arthur's death, and she hasn't accepted it was an accident. If she's grasping at straws, she may have gone back over his most recent emails looking for some other explanation."

Wendy perked up. "And you know what? If she's anything like you and me, she quickly handled Arthur's request for articles and then forgot all about it until she looked at the emails again. Then she wondered why Arthur wanted the Clifford Vere material. She may have followed this trail of breadcrumbs much like we're doing."

Ellie stared at the whiteboard. "Think about it. She goes to yoga, cocktails, dinner, and the Tintagel talk. Then she has tea with you, Leta. Maybe she didn't revisit the emails until after you left. Who knows why she chose that moment? But she sees the correspondence between Arthur and his publisher and is curious, maybe it triggers a memory for her. So she prints it all out."

I nodded. "On Sunday, she goes to yoga class but stays behind when we tour Tintagel. I bet that's when she studied the material. Oh my goodness! The book—is the book Dylan's?"

Wendy looked blank before her mouth dropped open. "A&A . . . *Archaeology and Arthur.* The book coming out later this year—the book with questionable material is Dylan's?"

Ellie looked crestfallen. "I can't believe I didn't remember that. And to think I wanted to read it."

Smiling, Belle touched her friend on the arm. "It's your butterfly net. It must have a large hole in it. That's the only way the name of the book could have escaped. And to think mine has a similar defect. We must have gotten a bad batch."

I couldn't help grinning as another thought flew into my brain. "Dang! We'd better get all new nets, because I just remembered something else from Saturday evening with Caryn. Arthur's publisher called her before she left for Knight's Rest and was looking for the most up-to-date version of *Tales of Tintagel.* I found a draft on Caryn's laptop along with a glowing foreword written by Dylan Porter. Skimming the book and seeing those touching words had to trigger happy memories and feelings. And then she reads the emails and, like us, connects them to Dylan's book. What an emotional roller coaster. That explains her abruptly leaving yoga class in the afternoon."

When I noticed Belle's puzzled looked, I explained. "It was a session of forward bends, and near the end, Rhiannon asked us to open our hearts, to strive to forgive and let go of blame. If Caryn spent the day reading Arthur's exchange with his publisher about what could be in Dylan's book, she had to be conflicted. She already blamed Dylan for Arthur's sudden trip to Tintagel, and now she wondered if there was more to the trip than his concern over artifacts. But he's Arthur's friend. He wrote a glowing foreword for Arthur's book and paid tribute to him at the Saturday talk. Caryn had to be in turmoil."

Belle rolled her eyes. "I thought yoga was supposed to make you feel good. Oh well, regardless of why she left class Sunday, let's pick up with the timeline. She wasn't at dinner Sunday night, and the next morning, Rhiannon found her unconscious in the yoga studio."

Ellie continued the timeline. Beneath Sunday, she wrote Caryn's activities but left space between them. "What we don't know is who Caryn spoke with on Sunday beyond any yoga students. Did she leave her cottage? Did she tell anyone about her discovery? Did she contact the publisher and query her?"

Once again, Wendy scrunched her mouth. "Did she call Dylan and confront him?"

I rubbed my eyes. "We *think* it could be Dylan's book, but we don't know for sure. Caryn *thinks* Arthur traveled to Tintagel about the artifacts, but maybe wonders whether he had a more pressing reason. And, who knows, even if the subject of the emails is *Archaeology and Arthur*, Arthur's additional fact-checking may have revealed that Dylan referenced Vere's work in a way that wasn't concerning. Or he was simply careless with the footnotes. Caryn *did* say he was known to be absent-minded."

Pushing back her chair, Wendy stood. "It's time to fetch DI Nancarrow and compare his conclusions with my notes from the files and what we're hypothesizing."

As she ran from the room, I looked at the two senior members of the Little Old Ladies' Detective Agency. "Is this where we voice our usual refrain—the game's afoot?"

# CHAPTER SIXTEEN

WENDY WAS OUT OF breath when she came in the door. "Whoa! DI Nancarrow's on his way and he says he has news."

When he strode in, he had a serious expression on his face. "Ladies, we've had a major break in our drug case, and I'm on my way to make an arrest. As for the situation with Caryn, Gemma's following a lead on that at the moment."

My jaw dropped. "Oh! Great for you on the drug case. I know that's important, but you know we're most interested in what you know about Caryn. We have some ideas as to who had the opportunity to plant the poison, and we're beginning to think this has something to do with a book . . . "

Jake grinned. "Now I've lost my wager with Gemma. She warned me you ladies tend to see literary crimes everywhere you turn, but I bet her you wouldn't do that here in Cornwall. Tell you what, I'll give you a few minutes to entertain me with your book theory, but you'll have to be brief, as I'm headed to Tintagel."

Wendy took the bull by the horns and provided a succinct recap of our findings. It amazed me how well she could boil it down to a paragraph or two. "All we have to do is ask Caryn if we're right about whose book is referenced in these emails. If our conclusion is correct and it's Dylan's, then we think it's likely Arthur's sudden trip was triggered by the book, not by whatever concerns he had about the artifacts. And it follows that he confronted Dylan."

Jake arched his eyebrow. "And you think Dylan killed him over a problem in his book? Why wouldn't the man just fix it instead? Why kill his friend and colleague?"

He had us there until Ellie spoke up. "Perhaps it had something to do with his advance, assuming he had one. The publisher mentioned she'd no longer be able to trust him. If he knowingly lifted the material, he'd have no credible explanation to give her. Even if he offered to rewrite it, she probably would have rejected his proposal."

Looking at his watch, Jake held up his hand in the stop gesture. He was cordial but direct. "Lady Stow, forgive me, but this book idea is a bridge too far for me. I appreciate the work you ladies have put into this, but we're following leads that point in a different direction."

He told us to take our time wrapping up and said goodbye. I could tell from looking around the room that none of us were convinced. We gathered our notes and flipchart pages, and Wendy returned the case file to the constable at the front desk. As I turned off the laptop, I wondered whether it could be returned to Caryn. *And where's her phone?*

I rang the dishy DI. "Hi, Leta here. Since Caryn's coming back today, may I deliver the laptop to her, and is her phone somewhere I can grab it too?"

He paused. "Hmm. Don't see why not. I'll ring the constable to bring it to you now. By the way, when I rang Gemma just now to tell her I'd lost our wager, she said I should remind you your work was done. I don't need to do that, do I?"

*Exactly what I'd expect from Gemma.* "Why, bless your heart. Of course you don't."

Wendy looked up when she heard that expression. "Uh-oh. What just happened?"

"Oh, I fended off a polite admonishment for us to return to our tea and crumpets. I'm not ready to do that yet. Are you?"

One by one, my partners shook their heads. We thought it was time to consider next steps but that we needed food to jumpstart our brains.

Wendy tilted her head. "Gee, don't you think we should visit the Malthouse? After all, you're the only one who's been there, and I'm sure the rest of us need to get a feel for where the Three Musketeers hung out. What say you, Tuppence?"

I threw back my head and laughed. "I say one for all and all for one. Let's go."

It was another beautiful drive filled with lively conversation. We agreed we would enjoy our lunch at the pub and perhaps visit the Post Office for a tour. With Gemma focused on the poisoning while Jake pursued his drug case, we knew we had to tread more carefully as we continued our line of inquiry, and we planned to do just that later in the day. If Caryn was up to it, Wendy and I wanted to speak with her next.

That settled, Wendy shared the information she'd gleaned from the case file. "We already know from your visit to the Malthouse that the police interviewed the barmaid and the man ager. They also spoke with the group that drank with Arthur that night—Dylan, Martin, and Colin among them. They all confirmed that Arthur drank only two rounds. Dylan left before anyone else, and next were Arthur and Martin. Colin and the younger crowd hung around until near closing."

I nodded. "Exactly what the barmaid told me."

"And, Leta, as Martin told us that day at the Beach Café, the notes from his interview indicate he was to meet with Arthur the next day at Merlin's Cave."

Belle was riding shotgun and looked over her shoulder at Wendy. "How many people did they interview?"

"In addition to the crew that drank with Arthur at the pub, not that many—Guin, Gareth, Art, Elaine, and Caryn."

Glancing in the rearview mirror, I caught Wendy's eye. "So, tell us what the police learned from interviewing Dylan."

"He confirmed that Arthur called him from London to say he was coming down and wanted to get together. He said he didn't know why his friend wanted to meet, but it wasn't unusual for him to visit for no particular reason."

"Perhaps," Ellie said, "Arthur wanted to catch Dylan off-guard."

I was momentarily distracted by a large lorry trying to over-take my taxi. "Good grief! That was too close for comfort. Now, what was I thinking before we were almost run off the road? Oh, right. Did Dylan say whether Arthur made it to the office that night?"

"Nothing in his interview about that, though he said they met earlier in the day. Let me look at my notes from the bar-maid interview." She rifled through her papers before finding the right spot. "Funny, there's no mention in her interview about what she said to you—that Dylan suggested Arthur stop by the office. I wonder whether it slipped her mind at the time or whether the investigating officer failed to make note of it."

She flipped the pages again. "And according to my notes about the interview with Dylan, he says the last time he saw Arthur was at the pub."

Belle held up her hand. "It may not matter, but I'm curious as to how Arthur got to the village. Didn't he come down on the train?"

"Mum, he keeps—um, kept—a motorbike at Knight's Rest. The police found it parked near the Beach Café. They got the information about the bike from Guin. Speaking of Guin, I didn't see anything of note in the interview with her. She said Arthur walked the farm with Gareth before sitting down to tea with her. He was excited about his progress on his book and said it was close to complete. He joked with her that he could always find more to tweak and add, and needed to hit send and be done with it so he could focus all his attention on the museum exhibit."

Again, I caught Wendy's eye. "Did he mention the artifacts to her? Did she sense he had anything on his mind?"

"Funny, in the interviews, the only local to mention the artifacts is Gareth, and then, as we would expect, it comes up with Caryn. Initially, a London detective spoke with her, but she later visited the Truro station to tell them her concerns about Arthur's death being labeled an accident. Not surprisingly, the notes in the case file make it clear the original DI in charge thought she was overwrought and pretty much discounted her questions."

I was searching for a parking spot near the Malthouse when Ellie asked, "And I guess there's no mention of a book other than Arthur's, right?"

"Correct. I want to look more closely at my notes when we return to Knight's Rest but for now, that's the gist. I'm looking forward to chatting with Caryn next."

We'd missed the lunch crowd and there were plenty of tables available. Choosing a sunny table near the door, we seated Belle and Ellie facing the window.

As I approached the bar with our drink orders, the barmaid greeted me. "You're with a different crowd today. Are you ladies interested in lunch or only starters?"

I laughed and told her we were ravenous, and she promised to go over the specials when she brought our drinks. We were sipping ciders when Dylan Porter walked in and went straight to the bar. *Oh! This could be an opportunity, but for what?*

Before I could react, Ellie beat me to it. She pushed back her chair, approached Dylan, and extended her hand. "Good afternoon. I'm Ellie Coates. I met you at Knight's Rest Saturday evening."

He seemed distracted as he shook her hand and looked as though he were having difficulty placing her. "Oh, yes. You're quite the King Arthur fan, and you recently read T.H. White's book, right?"

She responded with light chatter about other books on the subject, both fiction and nonfiction, before inquiring about his book. "I was intrigued by your mention of a book coming out. What's the name of it again? I want to be sure to get it as soon as it's available."

"*Archaeology and Arthur.* Your question is timely, as I spoke with my publisher this morning, and she's sending out advance review copies today. My box arrived yesterday, and the publication date is set for October."

Ellie smiled. "Lovely. I'll want to purchase a copy for myself to read right away and then purchase a dozen or so more for holiday gifts. I'll check with my local bookseller as soon as I return to Astonbury. Will you be doing a book tour? I love to give autographed copies."

"It's nice to meet an eager reader. There's a book tour planned, but I don't yet know the dates and locations." He tilted his head. "What would you say to an advance review copy now? We may tweak the cover art or change a few words here and there, but it's essentially in its final form. As for autographed copies, I'm sure we can work that out later."

"Oh! I've heard that term but I've never had an early version. Could I get one from you before I go home and have you sign it? Then, of course, I'll purchase a final copy when they're available."

The two put their heads together and I assumed they were working out how she could get the book. As they exchanged cards, I heard her mention her grandson Sam studying archaeology at Cambridge. That was news to me. I couldn't make out all her words nor hear Dylan's response, but I could see he looked rattled by her comments.

"Oh my goodness," whispered Belle when Ellie returned to the table. "That was bold and brilliant."

Wendy must have observed the same thing I did. "But Ellie, what did you say at the last to fluster him so? He looked . . . what's the word . . . ?"

"Discomfited?" I suggested.

She stuck her tongue out at me. "It's marvelous to have my own personal word nerd on hand. That captures it perfectly."

Ellie batted her eyes. "What? I merely engaged the man in conversation about his book."

Belle hadn't seen the body language, as she was facing the windows. "What did I miss? Did you say something to distress him?"

The dowager countess turned serious. "Yes, I believe I touched a nerve. I thought it was a long shot, and it was certainly a white lie, but I told him Sam was studying Archaeology at Cambridge and would want a copy. It wasn't until I said Sam would want to know whether Clifford Vere was referenced in the book that the man looked ill at ease."

Wendy winked at me. "This should be interesting, Leta. Ellie's gone and set the cat among the pigeons."

"I'll say. And while we're using cat clichés, should we also ask whether she's let the cat out of the bag? He's got to think we know something, and I'm not sure whether that's a good or a bad thing."

My petite friend grinned. "Of course it's a good thing. If he thinks we're on to him, he may do something to give himself away."

*Uh-huh.* "Or something to stop us from nosing around. I think we need to be extra careful with our snooping from here on out."

Wendy shushed us by tapping her knife against her glass. "Inappropriate conversation, don't you think? Shall we finish our food and talk more in the car?"

I knew what she was trying to tell us. Though we'd been speaking in hushed tones, we didn't want to chance our conversation being overheard. We couldn't risk anything more getting back to Dylan.

We were eager to hear what else had transpired between Ellie and Dylan, so we skipped the Post Office tour and headed to Knight's Rest. We had barely settled in the car and fastened our seatbelts before Ellie began her recap.

"I must admit I had no idea what I was going to say until I opened my mouth. I just knew it was an opportunity not to be missed. I told myself I would have approached him before we had our suspicions and kept thinking, 'act natural, Ellie.' So that's what I did. I asked about his book. But I would never have mentioned the whole archaeology thing without our conversation in Truro."

Wendy glanced at her. "And boy did that ever pay off! An offer of an advance copy? Who would've thought it? Not to mention a tell-tale sign that we're on the right track."

Belle spoke up. "Except it would appear the publisher's mind was put at ease, wouldn't it? If, in fact, this is the book from the emails. We need to find out for sure before we waste any more time on this angle. But, Ellie, what better way than to get a copy of the book? I repeat, brilliant."

I caught Ellie's eye. "And how exactly are you getting your copy? We're sure not letting you meet with him by yourself. Is he delivering it or what?"

"That remains to be seen. He said if he came to see Morgan this evening, he could bring it then. If not, we'd work out something else."

"There's so much we don't know," exclaimed Wendy. "What does Caryn remember about drinking the tea? I hope she's recovered enough from her close call to be able to enlighten us. More than that, I say we point-blank invite her to help solve both cases."

In the parking lot by the barn, Art was unloading supplies from the golf cart. "Good afternoon. Have you been shopping today?"

I figured what the heck and told him we'd been playing detective but didn't go into too much detail. He didn't seem surprised. "Mum told me you ladies are something else. Isn't one of you nicknamed Tuppence?"

Belle spoke up. "That's what we call Leta, and I'm Miss Marple. We could use a Hercule Poirot if you're game."

Laughing, he wiped his brow before lifting another box from the golf cart. "Maybe after I finish my chores. Do I get a mustache?" He started toward the barn but called over his shoulder to Belle, offering to take her to Igraine Cottage if she could wait a few minutes.

I followed him in and found Christie and Archie lolling on top of the reception desk as Elaine worked behind it. "Hi, Leta. Come to get the yoga cats? I think Christie knew you were gone this morning. I picked her up after yoga to take her to your cottage, but she squirmed out of my arms and jumped on the desk. Archie was right behind her, and they haven't budged."

Christie stretched and meowed. "Do you know they keep treats on the shelf beneath the desk? All I have to do is stretch and meow, and Elaine gives me one. She's much better at that than you are." As if to demonstrate, she meowed again, and sure enough, Elaine handed her a treat.

"Elaine, has she been pestering you? You know she can be a demanding little thing."

With a smile, Elaine rubbed Christie's head and gave Archie a treat. "No more so than our Archie, except he's not as talkative as Christie. He headbutts me when he wants something."

I asked after Caryn and learned Gareth had gone to pick her up. Maybe Wendy and I could get her to sit by the pool before the afternoon yoga session. And we could offer to bring her dinner if she preferred not to go to the dining room this evening.

Grabbing Christie's backpack from Elaine, I wandered outside. I wasn't sure whether Christie would follow, but she did,

with Archie right behind her. Belle and Ellie were chatting with
Art about his uncle.

Art's face lit up as he described Arthur. "He was amazing.
He may have been a professor, but he didn't have his nose in a
book all the time. Dad says he did when he was younger, but
grew out of it. When he visited, we hiked and rode the coast
on his motorbike. It was so cool when he took me to the ruins
when they were closed to visitors. I can hear him now describing
the history of some rock or wall. And he took me to see the
helicopter lower the bronze statue of King Arthur! I was the only
kid in my class who got to do that."

Belle smiled. "And you're named for him, right?"

"Yes, and I want to be an adventurer like him. Martin jokes
about wanting to be Indiana Jones, but I think Uncle Arthur
really was. I wish he had stayed here in charge of the dig instead
of going off to London."

His smile faded. "I still can't believe he went to Merlin's Cave
at high tide. He was forever warning me to be careful about that,
about the ruins, about the cliffs here. It just wasn't like him."

Belle was working her magic again. Her secret weapon seemed
to be her sweet grandmotherly smile.

As she braced on her cane and stood, she touched Art on the
arm and told him his uncle sounded like someone she would
have liked and murmured something about having wonderful
memories. Art helped her and Ellie into the golf cart and offered
me a ride too. I declined and walked the short distance with two
cats trailing behind me.

In Iseult Cottage, Dickens was stretched out on the cool tile
floor in the kitchen and barely budged when I walked in. *Must
have spent the morning chasing rabbits with Merlin.* The cat
couple, as I was beginning to think of them, ran to my bedroom
and were soon snuggled together on my pillow. It seemed I had

only myself to take care of, so I changed into my red swimsuit, grabbed my floppy sunhat, and stretched out by the pool. *A spell in the sun will clear my head.*

Eyes closed, I raised my phone to my ear when it chimed, and I heard Dave's voice. "Leta, I thought I'd try you before I headed to the gym. Are you back from the police station safe and sound?"

"Yes, I am, and I even survived lunch at the Malthouse. It's Ellie you should worry about today. I'm behaving myself."

As I explained what we'd learned this morning, plus Ellie's move at the pub, it was difficult to tell whether he was impressed or horrified at her speaking with Dylan. "It sounds to me like the little old ladies should stick together until this case is solved. So, what's next?"

"A dip in the pool, yoga, maybe a chat with Caryn . . ." Hearing voices, I stopped. It was Wendy talking to Guin in front of the barn. I couldn't understand what was being said, but I could tell Guin was upset. Wendy gave her a quick hug and headed my way. *Uh-oh. I wonder what's up.* "Oops. I've got to run, but I'll call you later."

When Wendy plopped on the lounge chair beside me, I held my hands up in the what-gives gesture. "What was that about? I haven't seen Guin even mildly disturbed since we got here."

"Well, she is now, and much more than mildly. She's livid with Gemma. When Gareth went to the hospital to pick up Caryn, Gemma *interrogated* him—Guin's word, not mine."

*Gareth?* "Huh? About what?"

"Okay, so by now this is third- or fourth-hand, but Caryn recalled that Gareth knocked on her door Sunday night. He said he'd come to be sure she was okay, since she missed dinner. That's pretty innocent, but he handed her a brown envelope, said it was propped outside the door, and Caryn says the tea was in it."

"Gareth gave her the tea? How can that be?"

"Well, Gareth maintains what he told Caryn was true. It was propped outside the door when he got there. He picked it up and handed it to her."

"Hell's bells! And Gemma thinks Gareth is the person who dosed the tea? That he set out to poison his brother's fiancée? How'd we miss that?"

Wendy jumped to her feet. "I don't think we did. I think Gemma's way off base. So now there's even more reason for us to get to the bottom of this whole thing. Sure, we mentioned fratricide in reference to Guin—which I know was pretty far-fetched—but there's no way I can see it in Gareth—he didn't kill his brother.  And, if he didn't kill Arthur, there'd be no reason for him to go after Caryn."

Closing my eyes, I thought of the many mysteries I read and watched. "I know I keep saying motive isn't important, but what if there's some kind of inheritance at stake in the Knight family? What if we've missed some vital clue?"

"Well, we've seen everything the police have, except for the financial information they gathered. That might shed some light, but I don't see us getting that out of DI Nancarrow. There was something else in the case file, though. Now, what was it?"

I thought back on all the information she'd shared with us. "Was there a phone dump in the file? I mean from Arthur's phone. You haven't mentioned one."

Her face lit up. "Yes! That's it. And the odd thing is that it was only requested two weeks ago. I took copious notes from it, but you know how you can jot notes and barely absorb what you're seeing or hearing? That's pretty much what happened by the time I found it in the file. Let's hope my notes make sense now."

*So much for relaxing in the sun.*

# CHAPTER SEVENTEEN

I SWUNG MY LEGS off the lounge and followed my friend to our cottage. It was already three, and we had afternoon yoga at four. By mutual agreement, we changed into our yoga clothes and sat down at the kitchen table. Dickens moved beneath the table and positioned himself where I could rub his belly with my foot.

Wendy studied her notes. "It was fortunate someone labeled the phone numbers on the printout so I could make out who they belonged to. There are calls and texts between Arthur and a handful of people we know—Dylan, Caryn, Martin, Guin, Gareth—plus a name I don't recognize, Belinda."

Since we had no way to check who she was, and there were no texts between Gareth and his brother, we started with the texts to and from Martin. They were about Arthur's trip, a desire to visit the Tintagel warehouse and office, having drinks at the pub, and the final one about meeting at Merlin's Cave. In response to Martin's questions about why the warehouse, Arthur responded, "To check on packing."

"Wendy, the text about meeting at Merlin's Cave lines up with what Martin told us and what he said in his interview, right?"

"Yes, that they planned to meet in the morning."

I grabbed a sheet of paper and started jotting notes. "Let's keep looking at the other calls and see where we land."

Wendy murmured as she read and occasionally told me to add to the list. "Look at this last text to Belinda, whoever she is. 'I was off-base. All good with the book.' What does that mean?"

"It must be the publisher. Caryn referred to her as she. Where are those emails between the publisher and Arthur?" When we located them, the email address was *Bprince*, and the signature read 'Regards, B.'

Wendy's mouth dropped open. "Was Arthur texting about Dylan's book? Was he saying it was all aboveboard?" She groaned. "Was Caryn right all along that Arthur came down here about artifacts, and we've gotten off track thinking it was an issue about Dylan's book that triggered the sudden trip? If Caryn mentioned her idea about artifacts to you, wouldn't she have also mentioned the book?"

I was having difficulty setting aside the book scenario. I pointed to the time of the last text—10:30 at night. "What if it wasn't Arthur who sent the text? What did you read in the coroner's report, vague as it was? He estimates Arthur died between ten p.m. and two a.m.?"

"Yes, and to make matters worse, he could tell Arthur drowned because of the water in his lungs, but his body was so battered by the rocks that he couldn't say whether he was conscious or unconscious when he went in the water. What are you thinking, Leta?"

A picture began to emerge. "What if Dylan asks Arthur to drop by the office as if it's no big deal? Arthur is glad to do that because it fits with his plan to speak with him about the Clifford Vere material in the book. By now, Arthur has compared what the publisher sent him with the articles Caryn found and maybe has no doubt the material was copied word-for-word. He confronts Dylan. What is Dylan's response?"

"It seems to me there are two things he could have said. 'No, you're wrong' or 'Yes, but it was an oversight.' But neither response would have led to Arthur's death, would it?"

"It would if Arthur pushed him to correct it, and Dylan said he couldn't. What if that material was more central to the book than we know *and* it wasn't an oversight on Dylan's part? What if the bulk of the book was stolen from Vere? There's no way Dylan could have rewritten it to his editor's satisfaction. He would have forfeited his advance, and there's no way she would have trusted him again."

Wendy grimaced. "That's an awful lot of what-ifs. And besides, in Dylan's interview, he said he and Arthur met earlier in the day. Wouldn't they have discussed the book then?"

"Only if Dylan was telling the truth about when they last saw each other. He would never have admitted they met at night because it would have placed him under suspicion."

It was Wendy's turn to play devil's advocate. "I don't know. I think we should look closely at the Martin and Arthur texts too. What if it's back to the artifacts?"

I thought it was more likely about the book but motioned Wendy to continue.

She gave it a shot. "Maybe Arthur's concern started with worrying about shoddy packing and evolved into him imagining the worst—theft, a black market for medieval artifacts, or something else. What if Arthur lays it out for Martin in front of the pub after drinks?"

"And what? Unless Martin's involved in something nefarious, he'd laugh it off, wouldn't he?"

Wendy looked at me. "Maybe you've hit the nail on the head. What if Martin *is* involved in something sinister? Maybe my wild idea is right and there's drug smuggling going on. He could be working for some drug kingpin and have no choice but to stop Arthur's meddling."

"Wendy, listen to yourself. We've gone from a vague something-about-artifacts to Martin working for a drug gang. That sounds like a BBC crime drama."

She closed her eyes and frowned. "And what would Gemma call the book scenario? Another one of our literary crime fantasies? I'm not sure either one holds water. And to add another cliché, maybe we've gotten wrapped around the axle again."

Dickens nudged my leg. "I don't know what an axle is, but I'll take some water, please." *No complex plots for my boy, just a simple request.*

"And this is where I say, 'Later Gator,' and we head to yoga. We haven't gotten any closer to clearing Gareth, but Rhiannon will have our heads if we miss another class." Besides, it was standing poses again, a class I always enjoyed. We each grabbed our mats and a cat.

When I opened the door, Gareth had his hand up ready to knock. "Leta, just the person I want to see. I've settled Caryn in her cottage. Would you mind checking on her when you come back after your class?"

I was praying he hadn't heard our conversation, and Wendy and I assured him we'd look after her. That gave us a ready excuse to drop in on her and pick her brain as to what she remembered about the emails and articles and the Sunday visit from Gareth.

With two squirming cats in our arms, we entered the yoga studio and found spots for our mats. Christie was indignant as I let her loose. "Really, Leta, I could have gotten here on my own. Unlike you, I would never miss a class." *Right. After two months of yoga, she thinks she's more of a yogi than I am.*

Rhiannon put us through our paces, and in no time, my head was clear of any thoughts of murder and mayhem. As sometimes happened, my knee twinged as I moved into the standing poses, and Rhiannon noticed I was favoring it. She brought me an extra block and helped me adjust my poses to avoid aggravating it.

I focused fully on perfecting my poses without hurting myself, and by the time class was over, my legs were trembling from the exertion. I sighed as I put my blocks and blankets away. "Great workout, Rhiannon."

She beckoned me over, and Wendy joined me as I walked to the front of the room. "First, Leta, you need to ice your knee. Second, you two, tell me what's going on. I know you must be in the thick of it."

As the Dartmouth sisters and Lily and Lilith had left the room, I suggested we three sit. "I guess Guin told you some of the goings-on."

Rhiannon nodded. "Yes. Can things get any worse? First Caryn is poisoned. Then Gareth is questioned about it. What next? So much for a peaceful yoga retreat."

We explained what we knew as to why Gemma thought Gareth was the poisoner, but we didn't share our suspicions about Dylan and his book. Wendy and I were in agreement about not pointing any fingers until we dug deeper.

Leaving Rhiannon to straighten the props in the studio, Wendy and I stopped by the snack area to pick up fruit for Caryn and ice for me. Christie and Archie trailed behind us, stopping occasionally to flop and roll on the pathway warmed by the sun.

I waved as we approached the pool. "Hello, Caryn. How are you feeling?"

Shading her eyes with her hand, she squinted at us. "Improving every minute. I hear I owe you two a huge thank you for figuring out what made me sick. You and Merry, that is. It was fast thinking to have Merry take a look."

We brushed her comments aside, and Wendy showed her the fruit. "Are you up for a fruit plate? I can prepare a tray and be back in a jiffy. And Leta, give me the ice and I'll put it in a towel for your knee."

"Oh yes. My appetite came back in full force this morning, but the hospital food didn't appeal. Thank you."

While we waited for Wendy, Caryn explained Gemma had told her about Belle staying by her side and how we'd all swung into action to help. "I know I was in good hands."

We passed the time in small talk. She inquired about my limp and I explained that I never knew what would trigger my knee to act up. "Sometimes, I can trace it to overdoing it on my bike. Other times, I swear all I do is stand up from the couch and it tweaks, as I call it."

Wendy returned with a tray and handed me the towel-wrapped ice. "Archie and Christie are on your bed again, Leta, and Dickens is sprawled out in the kitchen. He must have worn himself out this morning with Merlin."

"The heat gets to my boy. He may be small for a Great Pyrenees, but his size doesn't matter when it comes to the temperatures. Though he much prefers the cold to this weather, I suspect he'll be ready to romp after dinner when it cools off."

Before she sat, Wendy passed the fruit to Caryn. "Will you join us in the barn for dinner or would you like us to bring you a plate? We're happy to do that."

"I think I'll take you up on your offer. Maybe we can visit while I eat. How would that be?"

*This is working out well.* "Sounds like a plan. Now, I'm off for a quick shower."

Wendy and I walked to dinner with Belle and Ellie and updated them on how Caryn was doing. Only Rhiannon and Gemma were in the dining room when we arrived.

Gemma's hair was down instead of in her customary pony-tail, and she was wearing blush and lipstick. She smiled as I approached. "Ah, Tuppence, how does it feel to be off-duty?"

*Neither the time nor the place to tell her I'm not convinced I am.* "I'm just happy Caryn's well enough to be back in her cottage. Wendy and I are taking her dinner tonight, and she's looking forward to yoga in the morning."

Carrying two glasses of wine, Wendy joined us. "Gemma, do I deduce correctly that you have a date tonight?"

Gemma blushed. "Can't put anything past you, can I? Yes, I'm meeting Jake in Truro for a quick bite. It will be a day or two before he's free for more than that." She touched Rhiannon on the arm. "Rhiannon, will you excuse us for a moment? I need to speak with Tuppence and Agatha alone."

She led us to the yoga studio down the hall. "I don't want to spread these details about, but Jake wanted me to update you two. Why, I'll never know."

*I knew there was a reason I liked the man.*

"If Jake's predecessor had listened to Caryn sooner, he would have solved his drug case for sure and had a line on Arthur's death. She kept mentioning the concern about arti-facts, and she was right. There was something fishy going on there, and it was to do with drugs."

Wendy gasped. "Drugs? What did I tell you, Leta? Mum suggested drugs as a possibility, but we thought she'd watched too many police shows on the telly. The idea kept coming back to me, and just today, I raised it again."

I wondered whether she was pretending for Gemma's sake or she'd made up her mind our conclusions about Dylan were wrong. "Is it drug smuggling, Gemma? What?"

"Do you recall Colin from Saturday night? He works at the warehouse where the artifacts are cataloged and packed, and you can imagine the care that has to be taken to ensure they arrive in London undamaged. Jake hasn't gotten to the bottom of how Martin came to hire Colin Carmody to pitch in with the daily operations, but the Carmodys are major players in the drug trade. Martin likely had no idea about that connection when he hired him. What Jake's gleaned so far is that Colin came on as a volunteer in the winter. He's older than the university students who typically sign on for summer stints and proved a reliable worker."

Reflecting on my conversation with Caryn, I remembered the Museum announcement in late December. "You mean he was sent here so he'd be on the scene when the work for the Tintagel exhibit took off?"

Gemma nodded. "That's what Jake thinks, and it worked like magic. The man went from unpaid volunteer to being paid as a photographer and jack-of-all-trades, including working at the warehouse. There's a lot more detail, but the short story is drugs come into ports in Cornwall, they're transported to Tintagel, and Colin has a crew packing them into crates after hours for distribution in London."

I murmured, "Just like on TV. But how did Arthur know?"

"Jake doesn't think he cottoned to the drug angle—he just asked one too many questions, and the Carmodys couldn't risk him exposing their operation. The drugs were hidden in crates of souvenirs destined for the Museum gift shop and nearby Carmody shops. The family henchmen took care of them on that end. Unfortunately, a mislabeled crate wound up with Arthur.

According to what Caryn told Jake's predecessor, Arthur was worried that if he received souvenirs, a crate of relics might have gone missing, and he was already put out over some sloppy packing. Turns out what they were sloppy about was labeling the crates."

Wendy asked the obvious question. "So, did Colin kill Arthur?"

"Jake thinks he did. He has Colin dead to rights on the drugs, but not the murder. Now that he's lawyered up, Jake's desperate to uncover a witness or another lead."

A case involving drugs was out of my league. "Wow! This is hard to absorb. And, how does Caryn's poisoning fit in?"

"Well, we know from Caryn that Gareth delivered the poisoned tea, but since he claims he merely *found* the envelope, we don't know all the whys and wherefores. It may have nothing to do with Arthur's death, but it certainly puts him in the frame for poisoning Caryn. We've told him to stay put."

Squinting, Wendy scrunched her mouth to the side. "Why would Gareth poison Caryn? It doesn't make sense to me."

Gemma had a ready answer for that. "When it comes to crime, things don't always make sense. For example, we don't know yet who else at the warehouse was actively involved in the drug smuggling. Jake is still digging, but getting people to say anything about a Carmody is nigh unto impossible. He's checking financials now."

*But how does all that connect to Gareth?*

What she shared next was nothing new to us. "Unfortunately, much of what Jake's predecessor did was superficial at best. It will all need to be checked over." She looked at her phone when a text came in. "That's Jake checking to see if I've left. I'll see you later, and I'm trusting you not to share what I've told you beyond Ellie and Belle. None of it's top secret, but there's no need to broadcast it."

When Gemma departed, Wendy whispered in my ear. "You know I was acting, right? I still think Dylan is involved in this, somehow, some way."

I whispered back. "That's why you and I say great minds think alike—because ours always do."

Dinner was a quiet affair. None of us seemed inclined toward small talk, and we didn't linger long. While Wendy prepared a plate for Caryn, I escorted Belle and Ellie to their cottage. We hadn't felt comfortable sharing Gemma's information in the dining room where we might be overheard, so I spent ten minutes with them at Igraine Cottage giving them the news. Much like Wendy and me, they felt a need to digest the information. Both were worn out after our long day and looking forward to an early night. I could have done with one of those too, but I was also eager to chat with Caryn. *This detective work can wear a girl out.*

# CHAPTER EIGHTEEN

DICKENS HAD REVIVED WHEN I stopped by Iseult Cottage to fetch a bottle of wine. "Where are you going? Can I come?"

"Are you sure you wouldn't rather find your friend Merlin? I'm starting to get jealous, you know."

With his paws on my thighs, he barked, "It's your turn tonight."

We knew we'd disturbed Christie when she appeared in the kitchen, yawning. She stretched one front paw and then the other. "I'm feeling a bit peckish, Leta. I need food."

I cracked up. "Peckish? You've been hanging around Archie too long. You're beginning to sound like a Brit."

Her response was a demanding look. She was a master at standing by her dish and looking at me as though I were her servant—one that was falling down on the job. I managed to slightly redeem myself by putting a dab of food in the center of her dish and freshening the water bowl.

When I arrived next door carrying the wine, Wendy greeted me. "We wondered what had happened to you. We're parched."

She and Caryn laughed as I explained that I had to attend to my prissy cat before I could join them. As we made small talk and poured the wine, Dickens assumed his belly rub position next to Caryn. It was a relaxing start to a more serious conversation.

Wendy took the lead in recounting what had transpired at the police station with Colin, and Caryn's only reaction was to alternately frown and nod.

When Wendy finished, I covered Caryn's hand with mine. "None of this is easy, and there are still unanswered questions. If you're uncomfortable staying here on your own, I'm happy to bunk in the extra bedroom—with Dickens the guard dog."

Caryn grasped my hand and took a sip of wine. "I'm not sure how I feel, Leta. I can't quite accept that it was Gareth who tried to hurt me, even though he brought me the tea. Why would he do that?"

Wendy started to speak until I kicked her beneath the table. She was quick on the uptake. It was time to work the pregnant pause and nod encouragingly. We were quiet while Caryn rubbed Dickens's belly and murmured something unintelligible.

I leaned closer. "I'm sorry, Caryn, what did you say?"

Looking up, she took a deep breath. "I didn't do a very good job of explaining my misgivings to Gemma. She questioned me about my activities Sunday, who I spoke with, who I saw. I told her how comforting it had been to spend some time with Morgan by the pool, just the two of us. We hadn't done that since her miscarriage and Arthur's death. Gemma listened patiently to my timeline—yoga, eating alone in my cottage, taking a long walk, and Gareth knocking on my door with the envelope after that. She must have a sixth sense, because her ears perked up and she asked if there was a bag of tea in it."

*The girl is good at her job, no doubt.*

"I said yes and described the sticky note on the bag of tea from Arthur, and how touched I was that he'd thought to get it for me. After that, she didn't seem to hear anything else. The wheels were in motion before I could say more."

Wendy spoke softly. "Why don't you tell us?"

"Leta, do you recall my saying that the title of Dylan's book sounded like something Arthur would have come up with? Something about our conversation prompted me to think of a request from Arthur, and I took a trip down memory lane. I looked at the last few emails he and I exchanged. So many were silly sweet notes, like, 'Found my keys. Yet another reason I can't live without you.' Some were related to his book or museum work. In one of the last, he asked me to locate some articles for him."

Neither Wendy nor I said a word as Caryn continued. "One thing led to another, and I wound up reading emails between Arthur and Belinda, his publisher. Before I knew it, I was at the front desk in my pajamas printing off scholarly research and a handful of emails." She closed her eyes. "I still can't believe what I discovered."

As she attempted to explain, Wendy stopped her. "Caryn, hold on. This conversation would be easier if we had what you printed, and we do. It's next door in our cottage. I'll be right back."

We spread the pages on the kitchen table, and Caryn studied them. "This is it. My brain is still fuzzy, but I was right about my recollection. It was well after midnight when I fired off an email to Belinda asking if the book referenced in the emails was *Archaeology and Arthur*. I didn't expect an answer in the middle of the night, so before breakfast, I texted Dylan."

I gasped. "You did what? What did you say to him?"

"Not much. I simply texted, 'Clifford Vere?' I thought his reaction might tell me something, but it wasn't all that revealing. He put me off with 'Huh?—Need to talk but swamped today. Monday?' I even asked Morgan a question or two, in a general way, while we were at the pool that day. You know, like how the book was going. She knew it was on schedule, but not much more. I shouldn't have expected she would, since she's never been much involved with Dylan's scholarly pursuits. And they've had such a hard time of late with her suffering another miscarriage, his book would be the last thing they'd discuss."

Wendy nodded. "Yes, she told me about that. What a heart-breaking time for the two of them. Are you and Morgan close?"

"That's the sad part. We were until Arthur died. My anger with Martin and Dylan about the whole artifact issue spilled over into my relationship with Morgan, and I know I shouldn't have let that happen."

"Caryn," I said, "did you hear back from Dylan that day?"

"No, only that one text, which I wasn't sure how to take, and I was more confused when I got a reply from Belinda after lunch."

"Why? What did she say?"

"I thought her response was odd. She said yes, that was the book, but it was old news, that Arthur had resolved it."

Wendy looked from me to Caryn. "The text message from the phone dump. That's back in our cottage too, but if I recall correctly, Arthur said something like he was wrong and every-thing was okay."

Shuffling the papers, Caryn stabbed her finger at highlight after highlight. "How could he say that? This is blatant—not a single quotation mark anywhere. Dylan would have to footnote every bit of this chapter or completely rewrite it, and I don't think either option would have made Belinda happy. I think this is why Arthur came down to Tintagel. He might have taken the opportunity to speak with Martin about the artifacts while he was here, but Dylan's book was the trigger for the trip."

I thought I knew the answer but asked anyway. "Caryn, I don't know anything about writing books, but why wouldn't Belinda be happy with a rewrite?"

Again, she found a page and stabbed her finger at a section. "It's right here in this email. Because Dylan sent the manuscript to the editor as final, it should have had only minimal adjustments based on earlier suggestions—that's how the process works. A rewrite at this point would disrupt the publication schedule. I don't know for sure, but maybe the Vere material was new to the editor."

Chewing my bottom lip, I thought about the phone dump. "Wendy, remember what we said about that last text message? Are you thinking what I'm thinking?"

Wendy nodded. "Arthur didn't send it."

Tears streamed down Caryn's face. "If it wasn't Arthur, it could only have been one other person. It had to be Dylan."

*This is why I don't feel right about Jake's conclusions.* "Caryn, talk to me about Dylan. Can you imagine him hurting Arthur?"

"I don't want to think he did . . . but maybe I can. He was always a bit jealous of Arthur's accomplishments, as though it all came too easily to him. But maybe DI Nancarrow is right. Maybe it was this Colin person. Maybe it was about drugs."

*She's grasping at straws.* "Except a drug dealer has no reason to send a text about a book."

Wendy grimaced. "Forgive me, I know this is hard to hear, but I'm afraid the more likely explanation is Dylan had something to do with Arthur's death—over a book, for goodness' sake. And, if that's the case, it follows he was also somehow involved in the attack on you."

Caryn stood, her chair toppling behind her. "We have to do something. The police have it all wrong."

*Sometimes I think Wendy and I do a mind-meld.* She put her arms around Caryn and took her to the couch in the sitting room. Our eyes locked as I pulled out my phone and rang Gemma. The only problem was my call went to voicemail.

By now, Caryn was sobbing. I grabbed the canister labeled *K'night* and brewed a large mug of tea. When I placed it in Caryn's hands, she breathed in the steam before taking a sip.

I knelt in front of her. "Caryn, there's nothing we can do tonight. Why don't we get you to bed, and we'll figure out what to do in the morning. Do you want me to stay with you or leave Dickens here?"

She gulped. "No, I'm exhausted, and I'll be fine on my own. Can we talk before breakfast?"

We agreed to come by for tea before heading to the barn, and Wendy helped her to bed while I straightened the kitchen. My mind wandered as I washed and dried the three wine glasses and wiped down the counters. It was then that I noticed the brass keyring tossed in the corner near the fridge.

*Why on earth does she have so many keys?* Almost without thinking, I picked them up and flipped through the collection. The bulk of them had labels, and I quickly surmised the ones labeled *LON* were for places in London. The ones labeled *TIN* had to be for something here.

Keyring in hand, I walked to the bedroom. "Caryn, I just have to ask, why do you have so many keys?"

She smiled and held out her hand. "They're Arthur's. He was forever losing his keys so I got this as a joke, but he liked it and kept most of his keys on it in his briefcase. I told him I imagined jailers in Victorian England carried something similar. You can see his whole life on this thing. The ones labeled *CARD* are for the office and file cabinets in Cardiff. Then there's *KR* for the family cottage here and *TIN* for the building in Tintagel where he had his office. And, of course, he had several for the museum in London."

She laughed about how he was so organized except for this one area of his life. Her yawn was our signal to say goodnight, so we turned out the light, promising to see her in the morning.

When Wendy closed the bedroom door, she all but ran to the kitchen. "Leta, I have an idea. Give me those keys and let's go. I'll tell you why when we get to our cottage."

Double-checking to be sure Caryn's door was locked, we walked next door. Wendy was opening our door when I grabbed her arm. "Shh. Don't look now, but Dylan and Morgan are embracing in front of her cottage."

She jerked me inside and closed the door, almost catching Dickens's tail. As soon as we were inside, she turned off all the lights, even the one outside. "This couldn't be more perfect. Let's watch to see if he stays."

I wasn't sure why we were whispering and standing in the dark until Wendy enlightened me. "I want it to look like we're going to bed. We're going to the village—to the office."

"Have you lost your mind? Why would we do that? There's no one there. It's closed." *Uh-oh. That's exactly why she wants to go.*

Her next statement confirmed my worst fears. "That's precisely why we need to go tonight."

"And break in? Do you know what kind of trouble we'll be in if we're caught?"

Wendy continued to stand vigil by the window, staring at Morgan's cottage. "We won't be breaking in if we use Arthur's keys. We'll just be paying a visit."

"And why? Why would we pay a visit?"

Crossing her arms, Wendy frowned. "Don't be so obtuse. We need proof that Dylan is the killer, proof that he poisoned the tea and left that envelope at Caryn's door."

"Are you serious? Do you have any idea what form that proof might take? What are we looking for?"

"We'll know it when we see it. Oh! Look, you can see lights glowing from the bedroom in Morgan's cottage. They've turned out the other lights, and I think that means Dylan is staying the night."

I stomped my foot. "Wendy, this is a bad idea. There's no way we're doing this."

"Fine. I'll go without you. Let me have the keys to your taxi."

*I can't believe my ears.* "Absolutely not. No way, José."

Wendy was making my point—that she was the one who took risks, who came up with bold ideas. She stood her ground, literally. Tapping her foot, she extended her hand as in 'hand over the keys, now.'

"All right, already. I can't let you go on your own. I know this is stupid, but I feel like I need to change clothes like they do in the movies."

She laughed. "Good idea. Let's put on our black yoga duds, but I draw the line at smearing black stuff on my face."

To my usual pants and top, I added my long-sleeved yoga wrap, my red Coach crossbody bag, and my black canvas cloche. *Look at me. You'd think I did nighttime sleuthing all the time.* I tucked my small travel flashlight into my bag.

When I handed Wendy a black ball cap to cover her short platinum blonde hair, she laughed. "Are we prepared or what? I think we're very fashionable cat burglars. The hats are a nice touch."

Trust Wendy to have a plan of sorts. She wanted to tell Ellie and Belle where we were going and why, so she left first and jogged to Igraine Cottage. As directed, I waited five minutes before exiting the cottage and was pulling the door to when Dickens squeezed out behind me. I tried in vain to push him back inside. "You need to stay here, boy."

*How is it he's not barking? It's as though he knows we're on a secret mission.* He ignored my plea and ran to the parking lot. Throwing up my hands, I locked the door and followed him. A glance at Morgan's cottage told me all the lights were out.

I was wondering whether Wendy was giving chapter and verse to our partners when she finally appeared. Pointing to the dirty Land Rover covered in Tintagel decals, she whispered, "See, his car is still here. Even if he doesn't stay the night, he'll go to his flat in the village. There's no reason for him to visit the office."

We didn't speak until we hit the main road. Dickens sat up straight and Wendy bounced in her seat, as though we were on a lark. Frowning and grumbling to myself, I drove on.

Wendy chuckled. "Don't look so grumpy. Let's think about what we need to look for." She ticked off a list on her fingers. "Any loose tea—probably shoved in a drawer or a filing cabinet or who knows where. And he mentioned he had a box of his books. We should grab one of those for proof he didn't change a thing . . ."

I hissed. "But what if he did? That blows our theory. Maybe he and Arthur talked it over, and he rewrote that chapter."

"Don't be such a Debbie Downer. You know we're on the right track."

*Great image. I'm a grumpy Debbie Downer following the Pied Piper.*

# CHAPTER NINETEEN

Driving along the dark roads to the village, I glanced at Wendy. "Do you honestly think Dylan killed Arthur? His best friend?"

"I'm not sure. We know he and Arthur liked to visit Merlin's Cave. Dylan mentioned he did his best thinking there, so I can see the two men standing on the landing talking despite it being high tide. But that doesn't get us any closer to proving Dylan drowned Arthur. It's like a jigsaw puzzle. We need all the pieces in front of us to get started."

When my phone rang, I jumped. *Oh my goodness. It's Dave.* Before I could think, I hit answer on the dashboard screen, and then I hesitated.

"Hello, hello, Leta? Are you there?"

*Now, what do I do?* "Um, yes. How are you?"

"I'm good. Are you in the car? It's late for you. Are you and Wendy doing a pub crawl?"

Wendy piped up. "You got it, Dave. We're touring Tintagel pubs, and we've got Dickens with us."

Dave chuckled. "Well, before you overindulge, tell me how your afternoon was. Has the Little Old Ladies' Detective Agency closed the case yet?"

*Whoa boy, we're entering dangerous territory.* Between the two of us, Wendy and I updated Dave on our conversation with Caryn. I felt as though I was on stage trying to remember my lines. If he asked what we planned to do next, what would I say? We weren't lying to my boyfriend, but we weren't being aboveboard. Subterfuge in pursuit of a killer was one thing. Withholding information from Dave was another. If he had any idea what we were up to, he'd be furious.

His next line gave me pause. "Hmmm, you sound funny, Leta. Must be the Bluetooth connection. Anyway, please tell me you've got your protection devices in your purse and the car. Two lovely ladies out on their own can't be too careful."

Thankfully, Wendy took over. "She's focused on the road, Dave. And, yes, if anyone bothers us, we'll be sure to paint 'em purple. It's so like you to give Leta a defensive spray in one of her favorite colors."

I smiled at my friend and mouthed 'good job' before wrapping up the call. "We'll say goodnight now, sweetheart, and I'll call you tomorrow with a report on our evening."

Wendy looked at me. "You're terrible at dissembling, but it doesn't matter. He's an ocean away and will never know."

"And you call me a word nerd. Who uses the word dissemble? Why not just say it plainly—I, or we, lied to my boyfriend. If you'd been there when we argued about me putting myself in danger, you'd be squirming too. But at least you told the truth about my protective doodads. The alarm is attached to my bag, and the spray is in my wrap."

A memory of Henry flashed into my brain. "I should give credit where credit is due. Henry worried about me running by myself or cycling with girlfriends, and I carried pepper spray everywhere I went, so I guess I was well-trained before Dave came along. Maybe it's not as much about me as it is about the world we live in."

I was looking for an out-of-the-way place to park when the phone rang again. *What is it tonight? Does the whole world know we're up to something?*

Wendy yelped. "Why's Gemma calling?"

I automatically reached to answer the call when Wendy grabbed my hand. "Don't answer that. You'll give us away for sure."

The call rang through to voicemail and almost immediately a text came in. I couldn't look at my phone and the road, so I handed it to Wendy.

"Bloody hell. She's looking for us. She's texted, 'WHERE ARE YOU TWO?' Uh-oh. I think the fact that she used all caps means she's not happy."

*How did I let myself get talked into this?* "You do realize we had a conversation with Gemma about putting ourselves in danger, right? If she finds out about this, she's going to kill us, no two ways about it."

"What is it that Mum says? In for a penny, in for a pound? We're not stopping now, so I'm ignoring this text."

I chose to park near the Beach Café. The waterfront was quiet and deserted with only a delivery van by the restaurant. As I unhooked Dickens's harness, I whispered in his ear for him to be quiet, no barking. A wet tongue on my face was his response.

"Leta, do you have a torch in the boot? An extra one could come in handy."

She was right. I handed her the flashlight from my trunk or, in Brit speak, the torch from the boot. She carried it along with the keyring. I took charge of Dickens.

We stuck to the shadows as we trekked uphill, and our dark clothing kept us somewhat hidden. Even my red bag was covered by my wrap. Had anyone been looking, though, they would have noticed Dickens. *It's probably my imagination, but I swear his white coat glows in the moonlight.*

The further we climbed, the more my knee bothered me, and I was having difficulty keeping up with Wendy. She must have realized I wasn't close behind her because she turned and waited for me. "Is it your knee? I'll slow down. There's no rush."

"I guess not, but I'd feel better if we could move quickly and get this over with."

When Wendy disappeared into an alcove on the left, I breathed a sigh of relief. We were across the street from the small stone building with the English Heritage sign above its door. On the day we met Martin for our tour, we learned that Arthur and now Dylan used the office as their headquarters for the dig. I was relieved to see there were no outdoor lights, and from inside, there was only a dim glow.

Tucked in the alcove, Wendy crouched and shined her flashlight on the keyring. She found the three keys labeled *TIN* and gripped them in one hand with the flashlight in the other. Motioning me to stay put, she crept across to the door.

I almost had a heart attack when she dropped the keyring but convinced myself the sound could be mistaken for a cat or a dog rummaging in a trash can. When she pushed the door open, I limped across the street with Dickens.

In front of us was an open area with two desks. Racks of brochures stood beneath the front windows, and a large open area formed a pathway to the counter centered on the back wall. Posters and framed photographs hung above it. *I wonder if those are Colin's photos?* On opposite sides of the wall were doors to two offices.

Wendy pointed to the desk near the right side of the front room. "That's where the light's coming from. Someone left their monitor on. Let's check the offices first. It's a cinch one of these is Dylan's."

Together, we moved to the left office. I almost tripped over a box on the floor and belatedly clicked my flashlight on. "Look, it's Dylan's books. You can tell they're advance copies because of the grey banner across the top—*not for resale*." I pulled one from the box and put it in my bag as I whispered I'd search the desk while Wendy took the file cabinet.

Dickens was snuffling in the trash can beneath the desk. I was still amazed he was following my directions not to bark and wasn't sure what I'd do if he suddenly let out a yelp. Still, I felt safer with him by my side.

I started with the jumble of papers scattered on the desk. I wondered whether Dylan could easily put his hands on things or was completely lost. *Intuitive and absent-minded. That's how Caryn described him.*

I unearthed two notepads, a yellow legal pad, a spiral notebook, and a handful of loose notes. I found hearts with 'Morgan' written on them, stick figures, and his name written in elaborate script. He had better handwriting than I'd ever had.

A third scratchpad emerged from the pile. "Oh my goodness, Wendy, look at this." I held up the small pad where Dylan had scrawled *Vere* in the center of the page. He'd drawn a jagged circle around it, and lines extended from the circle to several names—Caryn, Ellie, Belinda. They all had question marks next to them, and two more lines ended in question marks with no names, as if he were still brainstorming.

Wendy's eyes grew wide. "Is he trying to figure out who knows?"

I nodded as I snapped a photo. "That's what I think, but it's not proof of anything. I want to look through the book to see if anything's changed from what we read in the original manuscript."

"Later, Leta. What we need is some trace of jimson weed. Whether or not he had anything to do with Arthur's death, I'm convinced he had a hand in poisoning the tea."

I stuck out my tongue and saluted my taskmaster as I began methodically searching drawers. Nothing fit the bill in the three on the left. When I opened the shallow kneehole drawer, Dickens stuck his nose in it and whined, "Smells funny."

Pulling it as far out as it would go, I spied a tin of mints tucked in the back. I opened it and put it beneath his nose. "I was hoping it had tea concealed in it, Dickens, but it's only peppermints. What else should we look for?"

Wendy must have heard my whispered question. "The jimson weed could be disguised as tea, tobacco, potting soil, who knows. I'm almost done with the files. Wouldn't it be lovely if one were labeled *Clifford Vere* or *Stolen Material*? They're so disorganized, I don't know how he keeps track of anything. If you don't come up with something in the desk, we'll check the other office too."

Suddenly, we both froze. There was no mistaking the sound of a car creeping down the road. *Is it my imagination? Is it stopping?* The sound of tires on the rutted road faded as the car continued downhill.

Looking at me, Wendy uttered the word I was thinking. "Phew!"

I moved to the drawers on the right side of the desk. The top one held pens, pencils, name badges, and a muddle of business cards. Ellie's was among them. Next, I searched the file drawer beneath it. Nothing beyond schedules, correspondence with English Heritage, and what you'd expect.

I sat back and thought. "Wendy, I'm going to look in the other office."

Tilting my flashlight to the floor, I made my way to the office on the right. It was much neater than the first one. A nameplate on the desk read Martin Pascoe. *Did the boy who wanted to be Indiana Jones ever imagine he'd sit in an office?*

The desktop held neat in- and out-boxes and a pottery mug with pens and pencils, not a single scrap of paper. I searched the drawers in a left-to-right pattern as I had before.

It wasn't until I pulled out the bottom right file drawer that Dickens whined. He trotted to my side and stuck his nose in the drawer. In it were four hanging files labeled *Photos*, *Clippings*, *Correspondence*, and *Events*. Stuck in the Clippings folder were advertisements and articles. Several of them were about Arthur's death. Others were writeups about the new Tintagel bridge and the relics that continued to be unearthed at the dig. The Correspondence folder was a mixture of cards and letters. None seemed relevant to my search. *A recipe for Jimson Weed tea would be nice.*

Behind the folders was a grey metal box, the kind found at flea market stalls and jumble sales to hold money and tickets. There was a lock on the front but no key.

When I lifted it out, Dickens stood on his hind legs and whined more loudly. "I know that smell."

A white label was stuck to the top with the name *Arthur Knight* typed on it. Those words were struck through with a red pen and Martin Pascoe printed below.

I went to grab Wendy. "Wendy, bring the keys. I've found a locked box."

Joining me in Martin's office, she held up the keyring. "I bet it's this small key. I wondered what it was for." Sure enough, it fit. "Whoa! Tea! And some papers."

*Thank goodness we have the key. It's not like we know how to pick locks.* I handed Wendy two small brown bags with the English Heritage logo on them.

She opened one labeled *English Heritage Breakfast Blend* and dumped out six triangular teabags. "I doubt these individual bags have jimson weed in them." She sniffed the bags and held one to Dickens's nose for good measure, but he shifted his nose to the metal box.

"Those don't interest him," I said. I opened a bag with the same logo but labeled *English Slurp Organic Tea*. "Would you drink something called Slurp?" This bag held loose tea. "If there's jimson weed hidden somewhere, it's more likely to be in loose tea, don't you think?"

With Wendy holding the torch, I poured a small amount in the palm of my hand. There were a few crinkly chunks of red but no seeds or purple particles. I raised it to my nose. It had a pleasant aroma, nothing like the tea we'd found at Caryn's.

Dickens whined again and this time, he stuck his nose in the box. "Smell this, Leta."

Wendy touched his head. "What is it, Dickens? Is there something else in the box?"

I lifted the pieces of paper to reveal a small black satin pouch with a black ribbon drawstring. By now, Dickens was wagging his tail and whining nonstop.

Loosening the ribbon, I poured the contents of the bag into my palm. *Jackpot.* "This is it—the same concoction we took to Merry. See the seeds and purple bits?"

Dickens sat back. "Told ya."

I held it up for Wendy to inspect, and she nodded. Mission accomplished, I suddenly felt nervous. I laid my open palm on the desk next to the tiny pouch and asked Wendy to take a picture with my phone. Next, I carefully poured the jimson weed back into the bag, tied it, and returned it to the metal box.

Wendy touched my shoulder. "What are those papers?"

They were 8 ½ x 11 pieces of paper folded to fit into an envelope as a letter would. The first was a printout of an article from the *Ottawa Citizen* titled "Health officials issue warning about dangers of jimson weed."

I read aloud "About 15 teenagers were treated at the Cornwall Community emergency department, with some being admitted to the intensive care unit."

Wendy's jaw dropped. "Cornwall on a different continent? With jimson weed?"

Unfolding the next piece of paper, I uttered, "Oh my gosh! This is a similar article but from the *Daily Mail* explaining it's become popular with teenagers in the UK. The kids describe hallucinating and hearing music coming from the walls. Some users merely hallucinate or get sick, but the article also says jimson weed kills hundreds of people a year."

"What's on the last piece of paper?" Wendy read the headline aloud when I unfolded it. "Why herbal tea made with jimson weed is dangerous brew." It was from an American medical organization called ACEPNow. At the bottom of the page was a scribbled note—*check on amounts.*

*Why would he keep these printouts?* I was flummoxed. "This is pretty damning evidence, don't you think? Except it's evidence against Martin, not Dylan. It tells us he had the means and the know-how to poison Caryn. But why? Why would he want to do that? And what does it have to do with Arthur's death?"

Neither of us had a ready answer. I snapped photos of the papers, carefully folded and placed them in the box, and locked it.

When I put it back in the drawer, Wendy held out her hand for the keyring. She turned in a circle as she scanned the office. "I think it looks like it did when we got here. What else should we check?"

"Nothing. We need to get out of here. We need to figure out how the heck all these dots connect—Colin and drugs, Dylan and his book, Martin and poison. We've got enough to convince Jake and Gemma we've found the poisoner, but we don't have anything else. I'll go ahead with Dickens while you lock up, okay?"

She nodded, and I tiptoed to the front door. *Now, why am I tiptoeing?* I looked out the window. Seeing the coast was clear, I carefully turned the knob and exited with Dickens. We moved across the street and stood in the dark alcove.

I held my breath as Wendy locked the door and jogged across the street. She grinned. "Ready? We'll be back at Knight's Rest in no time and we can show Gemma what we found."

"You realize she's not going to be happy with us despite the fact we've uncovered evidence of who poisoned Caryn."

"She'll get over it. And we've cleared Gareth too. That makes me happy."

Dickens trailing behind us, we started down the hill. My knee hurt worse going in this direction, much as it hurt more descending the stairs in my cottage than climbing them.

I grimaced as I saw Wendy getting farther and farther ahead of me. She must have missed me because she turned around.

When she rejoined me, she frowned. "Why don't you wait here and let me get the car. You trust me to drive your prized taxi, don't you?"

"Sure I do. Hold on, let me find the keys." I pulled my bag from beneath my yoga wrap and dug around for the keys. "I'll rest a minute and then see how far I can get, so look for me. And you know what, I think I'll text Gemma the photos we took so she can digest our discovery. Maybe she'll simmer down before we see her in person."

It was dark, so I couldn't see well, but I imagined Wendy was rolling her eyes. "Right. Not likely, but we have to tell her sooner or later, so go ahead. Hopefully, your phone won't explode when she texts back."

She took off downhill, and I found a low stone wall to perch on. Dickens leaped up beside me and nuzzled my hands as I texted.

Attached to the photos of the Vere note, the baggie, the jimson weed, and the three articles, I wrote, "Note found in Dylan's office, the rest in Martin's."

The immediate response was "BH, are you there now? I'm coming." I took BH to be short for bloody hell, her favorite expression. Coming from where? I wondered.

I didn't get a chance to ask before I got another text that said, "Leaving the Malthouse."

*Rut-ro.* I tapped out, "Headed to the Beach Café" and whispered to Dickens as I stood. "I wonder what she's doing at the Malthouse. We'd better catch up with Wendy so we can present a united front. I'd rather not get read the riot act by myself."

Dickens jumped off the wall. "Hey, you're not by yourself. You've got me."

I soon saw the Beach Café and my car. The van I'd seen earlier was still there plus another vehicle I couldn't make out. *But where is Wendy?* A gleam on the ground near the driver's side of my car caught my eye. *My keys?* I picked them up and circled the car before walking toward the restaurant. No sign of her.

Dickens gave a soft yip. He started in the opposite direction toward the steps to Merlin's Cave.

"What is it, boy?" I whispered as I followed him.

He yipped again, and I saw movement partway down the steps. *What's she doing down there?* I hobbled as fast as I could but slowed when I heard voices over the sound of the waves—a man and a woman. They were about halfway down the steps to the pebbled beach, except there was no beach tonight. The tide was coming in, and in the moonlight, I could see the railing along the cliff, and beyond that the cove filled with water.

"I'm not buying it. Where's your sidekick?"

"She's not here. She's at Knight's Rest. You know, we're not joined at the hip."

*That's my gal.* Dickens and I crept closer. Who was the man?

"I saw you two sneaking off, and I followed you. I know she's here somewhere."

I recognized the voice as Martin's.

Wendy spat back. "I don't care what you think you saw. It's just me. I drove down to Merlin's Cave to see it in the moonlight."

I heard keys jingle. "And you brought Arthur's keys? I don't think so. Tell me where she is."

Wendy yelped. "Stop it. You're hurting me."

Gravel moved beneath my feet and rolled downhill. I could see Wendy's platinum blonde hair gleaming in the moonlight, a man gripping her arm. She must have lost her ballcap.

"Don't play games with me. Why were you two snooping in the office?"

*Please, Wendy, don't say anything stupid.* I couldn't hear her reply, but Martin's response told me she wasn't cooperating.

He drew back and slapped her, and she would have gone down if he hadn't been holding fast to her arm. "This is your last chance. Why are you here?"

Without thinking, I tried to run down the uneven steps. *Bad idea*. I slipped and slid partway down on my backside. Still holding on to Wendy, Martin looked up. "What the hell?"

That's when it dawned on me that I had the alarm gizmo on my purse and the spray in my pocket. I fumbled for the button and a piercing sound ripped through the air. Martin froze. Wendy broke loose. Dickens charged.

When Dickens hit Martin below the belt, he grunted in pain and fell back onto the railing. He would have gone over with Dickens attached to him if Wendy hadn't grabbed my boy. All three fell in a heap, and I got there in time to give Martin the coup de grace with a burst of purple spray to the face.

Dickens panted and looked at his paws. "Leta, you painted me purple!"

And that's when Gemma arrived.

# CHAPTER TWENTY

To say Gemma was fit to be tied wouldn't do justice to her reaction. "Bloody hell" was the mildest thing she uttered as she helped Wendy up and handcuffed Martin. *Doesn't she ever leave those things at home?*

Martin wasn't going quietly. "You need to arrest these two. They broke into my office tonight, and their dog attacked me. Why aren't you handcuffing them?"

Dickens growled and Wendy spluttered. "Dickens attacked you?! You attacked me, you stupid git. Like you attacked your best friend."

"The hell I did. He was drunk. He fell. I couldn't get to him in time."

In rare form, Wendy continued her verbal assault. "We know he wasn't drunk. And why didn't you tell this tale when he was found dead on the rocks? Huh? What do you have to say to that? What's your next lie?"

Gemma held Martin's handcuffed wrists in one hand and put out the other to move Wendy away, to no avail. It was almost comical to watch my five-foot-nothing friend stand her ground with Dickens bristling beside her. Together, they looked like some kind of dynamic duo.

Hands on her hips, Wendy got in Martin's face. "Nothing to say, big guy?"

That last taunt did the trick. He put his face in Wendy's and shouted. "I'm not lying. I didn't kill him. I tried to save him, but I was too late!"

*What did he mean—he tried to save him?* It was my turn to interject. "Right. You were here but you didn't kill him?"

He lunged toward me, but Gemma held him back. "And you! You stirred up Caryn. You fed her suspicions about the artifacts."

*Boy, does he have the wrong end of the stick.* "Are you kidding? Caryn's a bright woman. She didn't need me to figure out something was up—much like Arthur did. Is that why you killed him?"

As though a switch had been thrown, he slumped to the ground. "All I wanted was to keep him from getting hurt. But the stubborn sod wouldn't let it go." He hung his head.

When DI Nancarrow and his constable drove up, I could only imagine what they thought of the sight framed in the headlights—a cowed man, a feisty dog, and three angry women. I'm sure we were a striking tableau.

Relieving Gemma of her prisoner, the constable hauled him up the steps and placed him in the back of the patrol car as Jake and Gemma conferred. By now, I was out of steam and sat on a step with Dickens snug against my side. Wendy's rush of adrenaline had dissipated, and she leaned against my other side, trembling. I looked at the waves surging over the boulders in the cove and shuddered.

As I'd come to expect, Gemma gesticulated and spoke in hushed furious tones while Jake attempted to calm her. I couldn't help smiling at the sight of him with his arm around her, walking up toward the patrol car. *She'd never tolerate that from her DCI back home.*

Leaving Gemma by the car, Jake returned to where we three waited. "Now, ladies, would you care to explain yourselves?"

I looked at Wendy, seeing for the first time the tell-tale mark of Martin's handprint. When I started to speak, she placed her hand on my arm.

Looking up at Jake with her tear-streaked face, she murmured, "It was all my idea. Leta tried to stop me." She paused and took a deep breath. "But you know what? It was a *good* idea. It paid off, even if my jaw hurts like the devil."

Jake shook his head. "Really? I can't wait to hear this."

And so, as we sat huddled on the steps, she took him through our day. She emphasized that if he'd only listened to us at the police station, we wouldn't be here now—we wouldn't have been forced to take action. I thought that might be a stretch, but Wendy plowed on.

When she reached the part where we used Arthur's keys to unlock the office, he held up his hand. "Arthur still had his keys?"

I piped up. "I thought that was odd too, but Caryn explained he made it a habit to 'accidentally' take keys from the temporary offices he occupied during his digs. He considered them his mementos and invariably, the folks left behind simply had new copies made. She said you could read the story of his life from his keys."

"Okay, you two, since we have the keys, let's continue this tale at the office."

He helped us to our feet. Though Wendy was a little unsteady, she seemed fine as she climbed to the parking lot. I flexed my knee a few times but faltered when I tried to follow her.

"Leta," Jake asked, "Are you hurt? I didn't think you were involved in the wrestling match."

I managed a chuckle. "I wasn't. It's nothing quite that exciting, only a sprained knee from yoga. Never fear, I can make it to my ride."

Wendy and I walked to my car with Dickens and watched as Jake waved the constable on his way and took Gemma's car to the office. I hugged my friend hard before loading Dickens in the back seat. "Goodness, Wendy, I was scared half to death. Were you?"

"Not in the moment. I was too angry to be scared, but when he said Arthur fell, it suddenly dawned on me what he might have in mind for me. Heck, he could have tossed me over that railing and no one would have been the wiser. I think that's exactly what he did to Arthur."

Sighing, I put my taxi in gear. "I'm not sure. That part about trying to save Arthur puzzles me. Anyway, it's the firing squad next with Gemma giving the command to shoot. Especially after she was so clear that we were not to put ourselves in danger."

"But wasn't it Gemma who quoted Shakespeare at Ellie's last party? As in, 'All's well that ends well?' I mean she can't argue with that, can she?"

All I could do was shake my head. Wendy knew the answer to that question. DI Nancarrow was waiting for us with the door already unlocked when we parked in front of the building, and Gemma was inside with the lights on in Martin's office.

Dickens bounded in ahead of us, barking as he ran to Gemma. "I can show you."

When Wendy and I made it to the office, my boy had his nose pressed against the drawer that held the metal box. His bird dog act even got a smile from Gemma.

She petted Dickens's head. "I take it this is where I'll find the evidence?"

Jake stood in the doorway as Wendy expounded on our methodical search. She's getting into this, I thought.

Gemma let Wendy prattle on while she carefully bagged the contents of the box. Looking up at the two of us, she sighed. "Tuppence, this time it was Agatha who led you astray? Is that what I'm hearing?"

Wendy gave a crooked smile. "Yes. If it weren't for me, Tuppence would be tucked up in bed sound asleep. And a killer would be on the loose."

We both jumped when Gemma slammed her palm on the desk. "Don't get carried away with yourself, Wendy. Jake could have done this tomorrow in broad daylight if only you'd been patient. You don't know how lucky you are Ellie called me. From what I saw when I arrived on the scene, Martin might well have gotten his wits about him and done serious harm to you two despite the injuries your attack dog inflicted."

Dickens barked at her. "Hey, I had him. He was down for the count."

Gemma's glance at my purple-stained dog made me think she was struggling to remain stern. I knew she'd correctly interpreted my surprised look when she said, "Yes, Ellie called me. She and Belle talked over your plan and realized just how ridiculous it was! It's a good thing the senior members of the Little Old Ladies' Detective Agency have some common sense. I was planning to catch you in the act and set you straight. What were you thinking?"

I expected a sassy retort from Wendy, but she was oddly quiet. *Maybe she's running out of steam.*

Gemma, however, was on a roll. "And another thing. Those devices from Dave are all well and good, but someone has to be around to hear the alarm go off and alert the police. Someone like Martin with murderous intentions isn't long deterred by a blast of sound. Not that I don't like the purple paint, but Martin could have *killed* you—do you hear me? *Killed* you. He could have escaped before anyone showed up and stayed out of sight a few days until the stain was gone." She glared at us.

Jake knelt to pet my attack dog. "I bet Dickens is happy to hear the stain fades."

His comment lightened the tense atmosphere and gave me the gumption to ask why, if Gemma was so worried about us, she went to the Malthouse and not the office.

She inhaled sharply. "Not that it's any of your concern, but I drove by the office and didn't see your car. So, I turned around and drove to the pub, thinking you two may have needed a mite of Dutch courage and had stopped by there first."

Wendy looked at Jake. "And you, how'd you turn up so quickly?"

"My constable and I were speaking with the bartender at the Cornishman Inn to suss out more info on the drug trade. Bartenders always know." He put his hands on his hips. "Now, are you two done with the questions?"

I was sure I could think of a few more, but I was exhausted and my knee hurt. "For now, yes. Does that mean it's okay for us to leave?"

Thankfully, he gave us his blessing, and we three crime-busters were on our way.

\* \* \*

Meowing plaintively, Christie climbed on my chest. "Get up. Archie is at the door saying it's time for yoga."

I groped for my phone. She was right. "Is feeling like I've been run over by a truck a good excuse to skip class?"

"For you, maybe, but I'm in fine shape. At least open the front door for me."

As I groaned and sat up, the ice pack I'd applied to my knee fell on the floor, and Dickens rolled over and stretched. When Christie darted out the door ahead of him with no mention of milk, I thought surely someone had done a personality transplant on my prissy cat.

I made coffee and sat with a steaming mug in my hands as memories from the night before flooded in. I should have put my foot down. I should have hidden the car keys. *Woulda, coulda, shoulda.*

Wendy wandered listlessly into the kitchen, her cheek still puffy, and poured a cup of coffee. "I see we have the same idea—no yoga this morning."

"I told Christie and Archie to make our excuses. I feel as though I'm a wayward teenager waiting for the ax to fall—like Gemma's going to show up any moment to tell us we're grounded. If we're lucky, maybe she'll go to yoga and we'll get a reprieve."

She peered at me over her steaming cup. "I know we have loose ends to tie up, but this morning feels a bit anticlimactic, doesn't it?"

"Wendy, we don't tie up loose ends. Jake does that. Hopefully, all will be revealed in good time. At least, that's been my experience in the past."

"Now, Leta, that's the difference between us. I'm much more impatient than you are. I want answers *now*."

*Ya think?* "And how do you propose to get those?"

There was a gleam in her eye when she replied. "It happens I spoke to Ellie last night after you fell into bed, so I already have some answers. Let's start with those."

"Please proceed, Agatha."

"Ellie and Mum were reluctant to call Gemma, but they were worried about us. When they alerted her to our 'risky jaunt,' as she and Mum call it, they made sure to explain we'd taken the precaution of watching Morgan's cottage to be sure Dylan was there and not in town. She also told her our latest conclusions about the book."

"I can well imagine her reaction to that bit of news, but I don't understand what prompted her to come after us."

Wendy held up her hand. "You heard her last night. She wanted to catch us in the act. When she used the phrase 'set us straight,' I couldn't help thinking of that documentary from the 70s, *Scared Straight*."

"Hey. It's not like we're juvenile delinquents! Regardless, it's a darned good thing she was there. I still can't believe I let you talk me into last night's escapade."

My friend was unabashed. "Now, now, wasn't it your General Patton who said, 'A good plan today is better than a perfect plan tomorrow?' I think that applies."

I stretched and yawned. "You know you're incorrigible, right? Do you have any other updates?"

"No, but I have an idea as to how to get some. I say we put Mum and Ellie to work on Gemma. They can tag-team her with their little old lady act. After all, they're the senior members on our team—the true little old ladies. What do you say?"

"If it means I can avoid Gemma and lie by the pool, I say go for it." That would free me up to ponder how to explain all this to Dave.

Refilling our mugs, Wendy went to her room to call her mum and shower. I let Dickens in and sat on the couch with my feet up surfing Facebook and playing Words with Friends. Sometimes, if I pushed a problem to the back of my mind, an approach or a solution would work its way to the surface. I hoped that would happen in this case, that the words for telling Dave about our 'risky jaunt' would spring to mind. At least I had several hours before I had to worry about speaking with him, as it was the middle of the night in New York.

When I heard a knock on the door, I groaned. *I can't deal with Gemma yet*, I thought, and was relieved to see it was Caryn.

Her eyes brimming with tears, she thrust a plate of scones at me and explained she needed to know what had happened the previous night—what Martin had told us. "I saw Belle and Ellie as I was leaving breakfast, and when I asked where you were, they exchanged a strange look. Belle whispered that Martin was in jail and I should speak with you and Wendy, that the two of you confronted him last night. Why Martin? What about Dylan?"

*Oh my, she doesn't know we rewrote the script.*

She followed me to the kitchen. "I know it's going to be hard for me to hear, but I have to know what's going on. And I think it may be easier to hear from you two than from DI Nancarrow or Gemma."

I sat her down and went for Wendy. "I'm not sure I'm ready for this, but Caryn's here wanting information. I at least need to be dressed to have this kind of conversation."

After throwing on clothes and splashing water on my face, I joined them in the kitchen. Thankfully, they'd saved me a scone. Wendy took the lead on how Dylan had been our quarry, how we searched the office, and how we discovered we were wrong when we searched Martin's desk—at least about the tea. When she got to the part about leaving me behind on the trip to the parking lot, it dawned on me I hadn't yet heard how Martin got her to the landing.

Wendy's expression sobered. "I was so focused on juggling the keys and unlocking the car, I didn't hear him come up behind me. Plus the sound of the surf hid his footfalls. He grabbed me, spun me around, and shoved me against the car."

I thought back to last night. "Is that when he grabbed the keyring, Wendy?"

She paled. "Yes, he knocked the torch from my hand and snatched the keyring. He all but dragged me down the steps, firing questions all the way, until I tripped and almost fell. I guess that's why he stopped midway where you found us."

"This is about where I came in," I said. "I shudder to think what would have happened if Wendy'd been on her own, but that's not what you want to hear, Caryn. You want to know whether he confessed to anything."

Caryn whispered, "Please tell me he's in jail not only because he attacked you, but also because he confessed to . . . killing Arthur. It was him, wasn't it?"

Wendy and I hadn't hashed it all out yet, but I told her what I thought the situation was thus far. "I think last night, they arrested him for attacking Wendy, but with the evidence they collected from the office, I'm pretty sure they have enough to charge him with attempting to poison you. He admitted he was at Merlin's Cave when Arthur died, but didn't fully confess. Is that your read, Wendy?"

She nodded. "Yes, but now that DI Nancarrow knows Martin was there at the scene and withheld that information, I think it's only a matter of time before he gathers the evidence to charge him with murder."

I sat forward. "I wonder whether they're still holding Colin Carmody? Well, I guess they must be, at least for the drugs."

Caryn looked from me to Wendy with a puzzled expression. "How did we get to Colin and drugs?"

Wendy looked at me. "Oops. We're not supposed to talk about that. Leta, what are you thinking? What do you mean about the drugs?"

"I'm trying to piece it together. It's just odd that Martin said he tried to save Arthur. Save him from what or who? Given we were wrong about Dylan, I don't much trust my judgment right now."

That comment got a frown from Wendy. "The only way we're going to find out is to speak with Gemma, or preferably DI Nancarrow."

I could tell we'd lost Caryn. She wiped the tears from her face and went back to Dylan and Martin. "Last night, I didn't want to believe Dylan could hurt Arthur, but it's even harder for me to believe Martin would. They've been best friends since they were lads. And . . . why poison me?"

I looked from Caryn to Wendy. "Wendy's right, Caryn. We can't fully answer your questions because we're in the dark too. I wonder whether Gemma would tell you more than she'd tell us? She was pretty peeved with the two of us the last time we saw her."

This was the first time Wendy'd been hurt in the line of duty, as I thought of it. *Gemma would be horrified if she heard that reference!* I could tell the only thing keeping my friend from ringing Gemma that instant was that she was running out of steam. Reminding her that Gemma had never failed to update me in the past—perhaps not as quickly as I'd like, but soon enough—I suggested we be patient. After a weak protest from Wendy and some sniffling from Caryn, the two eventually accepted my suggestion we wait a few hours before bugging her.

"All right, ladies, I plan to lie by the pool with my dog. I hate to miss today's tour to Land's End and St. Ives, but I just can't face

it. Maybe Belle and Ellie will give us the highlights over dinner."
*And maybe by then, we'll have news from Gemma.*

# CHAPTER TWENTY-ONE

Spreading my towel on a lounge chair, I opened my Peter Wimsey book. He and Harriet Vane were getting close to solving the crime, and I was eager to learn the identity of the villain. I hadn't seen Christie since she left for the barn, but Dickens kept me company lying beneath my chair in the shade. Despite my desire to read, I soon succumbed to a nap in the sun.

I opened one eye when I heard voices. It was Wendy and Caryn stretching out on two chairs, and Wendy had Dylan's book with her. *Fine. Let her play detective.*

A loud exclamation woke me. "Caryn, look, he *did* fix it."

*Huh?* "Fix what?"

"Oh, you're awake. I was showing Caryn that Dylan made changes to the Vere passages. All the material is in two chapters, one on Stonehenge and another on Glastonbury, and he wrote a lovely introduction in each chapter, crediting Clifford Vere for the insights, plus he footnoted it."

Caryn added, "Boy, do I feel like an idiot. What does it say about me that I was ready not only to believe Dylan was guilty of plagiarism but also that he had a hand in Arthur's death?"

Groaning with the effort, I sat up. "It says you were overcome with grief and grasping at straws, nothing more. If the police had done their job and pursued the case, you wouldn't have overthought it."

Echoing my sentiment, Wendy added, "One mystery solved. We'll have to ask Dylan if we want to know what his doodles meant, but I bet he was wondering how anyone beyond his editor knew he'd referenced Clifford Vere in his book since it's not out yet. First, Caryn texts him the name, and then Ellie mentions it. He must have been scratching his head over the sudden interest. That's the only explanation I can come up with for his scribbling the names Caryn, Ellie, and Belinda on his scratchpad."

I yawned. "Well, now that I'm awake, I realize I'm hungry. That scone I had for breakfast wasn't nearly enough. Shall we grab lunch at the barn and bring it back here?"

We were in agreement we preferred to enjoy the outdoors, and Dickens seemed happy with that plan too. Once again, I found Christie stretched out on the reception desk in the barn, though Archie was missing this time. "Are you contemplating taking up residence here, little girl?"

When I stroked her belly, she meowed and stretched. "I don't think so. I miss our garden."

"What about Watson? Do you miss him too?"

"Maybe a little."

Passing me, Wendy asked whether we were going to leave Christie behind at Knight's Rest when we left.

Christie bolted off the desk and meowed. "Not on your life."

*Gee, I guess in her sassy little way, she loves me.*

Guin and Rhiannon had their heads together in the dining room. Probably planning the final session for this afternoon, I thought.

Rhiannon motioned us over. "How's your knee? I missed you this morning."

It dawned on me she had no reason to know what Wendy and I had been up to the previous night. Even Guin probably only knew Martin was in jail but nothing more, unless Morgan had additional information. As always, Guin exuded calm, so there was no telling how much she knew.

I flexed my knee. "Much better. If the afternoon class isn't standing poses again, I should be able to handle it."

Guin explained they had planned a pranayama class to wrap up the week but wondered whether the ladies might prefer something more active after their drive up and down the coast. "They may need something to energize them instead."

Rhiannon smiled as Wendy walked up. "What would you two vote for?"

It took only seconds for us to weigh in. "Inversions," we said simultaneously. That settled it. Inversions it was.

Thankfully, there was no mention of the police or arrests as we assembled sandwiches and chatted with our two yoga instructors.

By the time we finished lunch, Wendy had reached her sun quota for the day and retired inside to read. Dickens must have felt the same way, because he followed her.

Caryn yawned. "I'm not sure I know what to say to her, but I think I should check on Morgan. She must be beside herself."

*And I don't know what I'm going to say to Dave.* I avoided the issue by checking on Harriet Vane and her wealthy husband and was about to learn the killer's motivation when Caryn returned.

She sat on the edge of my lounge chair and whispered, "One mystery solved."

"Huh?"

"Who knows whether Morgan would have told me sooner, but this is the first I've seen her since I returned from hospital. She's a bit embarrassed."

*What on earth?* "Well, don't keep me in suspense. What's going on?"

"It was Morgan who searched my cottage. Dylan was beside himself with worry over my text. It was all about his publishing schedule. He knew he and Arthur had resolved the attribution issue in *Archaeology and Arthur* but was horrified that there might be something else he'd overlooked, and time was of the essence. Since he couldn't talk to me after I was taken ill, he persuaded Morgan to search my cottage hoping she'd find some notes on whatever prompted my text. In the scheme of things, it was innocent enough."

"And here I was thinking it had to be Martin. Instead of things becoming clearer, they're getting more convoluted by the minute."

It wasn't long before I was left on my own at the pool, my book lying open on my lap. When the phone rang, I knew it was Dave, and I hesitated before I answered, "Hello."

"Hi there, sweetheart. Did you survive your pub crawl?"

I got to my feet and walked to the cottage. This was a conversation best had in private. "In a manner of speaking. Even my knee is better."

As I made myself comfortable on the couch, I did a grand job of avoiding the news of the hour. Since Dave didn't know about my knee, I spent some time explaining that before I broached the subject of what Wendy and I had been up to.

As I began the story, he groaned. "How did you get from a pub crawl to breaking into an office? Did alcohol have something to do with that bright idea?" *So far, so good.*

He was quiet as I described our discovery. "So, if I'm hearing you correctly, your book idea led you down the garden path? You broke into an office only to find *Archaeology and Arthur* had nothing to do with Caryn's poisoning or Arthur's accident?"

"Right. Given we found the jimson weed and the articles about teenagers using it in Martin's desk, it had to be Martin who dosed the tea."

His tone grew stern. "And what did Gemma have to say when you told her what you did? Did her head explode?"

I hesitated. *This was the tricky part.* "Well, we, um, we had an encounter . . . with Martin . . . and when she got there—"

"You what? Don't tell me you confronted the man."

We went back and forth with him interrupting me and starting sentences with "I can't believe you . . ." until I was able to get the whole story out. I'd never seen Dave angry, and he'd never raised his voice to me, but there's a first time for everything.

An ominous silence echoed down the line. "Dave? Are you there?"

"Yes."

"What are you thinking?"

"I'm not sure you want to know what I'm thinking."

"But Dave, we had no idea it was Martin we needed to worry about, and Dylan was here the whole time . . ."

That's when he exploded. "Leta, listen to yourself! Can't you hear what a stupid idea this was? What a dangerous idea? Do you know what—?"

I hung up. It was the word *stupid* that did it, even though I knew he was right. When my phone rang, I almost didn't answer it.

"You hung up on me!"

"You called me stupid!"

Silence. On both sides of the Atlantic.

"Leta?" I heard him take a deep breath. "You know I love you more than anything in the world, right?"

"Yes."

"But you're making me crazy. How am I supposed to deal with you taking these kinds of risks, time after time? You're breaking my heart."

My voice cracked. "I'm sorry. I never set out to worry you."

We continued in a conciliatory vein for a few minutes, but this rupture in our relationship wasn't going to be quickly repaired. Maybe it was a matter of getting through our first major argument. Our April discussion of my risk-taking was merely a mild disagreement compared with this. Never had the limitations of our long-distance relationship been more apparent. *Words on the phone are a poor replacement for a hug.*

I didn't want to hang up, but I was out of words. "Talk later?"

"Yes. And, Tuppence?"

"Yes, Tommy."

"Never doubt how much I love you. I'm not going anywhere."

I gulped as I said goodbye.

Since I couldn't shake my sadness at my argument with Dave, I was thankful the afternoon session was an active one. There was no way I could have cleared my brain for a pranayama class. Focusing on headstands and attempted handstands distracted me long enough to improve my mood. Ignoring Gemma's presence took a bit more effort, but I told myself she was Wendy's problem.

Guin and Rhiannon reminded us that tonight was the final group meal of the retreat. While the Astonbury contingent had booked an extra night, the Dartmouth sisters and Lilith and Lily would depart in the morning. I wondered what tomorrow would bring for those who remained.

Clusters of women walked toward the semicircle of cottages. With the addition of two cats, our foursome included me, Gemma, Caryn, and Wendy. The two younger women trailed behind talking quietly, and I hoped Caryn was getting the latest on Martin.

When Gemma strode purposefully past us without a word, I heard Caryn call, "Leta, I did it."

Wendy and I stopped in our tracks and turned. Caryn beamed. "Good news, ladies. Gemma's agreed to meet us for a late breakfast in the morning after the other guests have cleared out. She said she might as well update the LOLs at the same time she did me, since she knew I'd turn right around and tell you."

As I uttered the expected words of good job and congratulations, I realized there was a pattern as to how I dealt with our sleuthing situations. Each time I became involved in an investigation, I wound up in danger. When that moment passed, my senses seemed dulled. Of course, on several occasions, I'd been injured, so I was in no shape to be sharp.

Unlike me, Wendy was tuned to a high pitch and was ecstatic. "Wow, Leta, I can't wait to hear what's happened with the case. Can you believe Gemma's going to share? She must be over being upset with us."

Fortunately, she didn't require an answer, as she continued to enthuse over meeting with Gemma. In the aftermath of the confrontation, I felt emotionally drained and physically exhausted, and it didn't help that this time, an argument with Dave came next. Whatever the cause, I wasn't as excited as she was at the prospect of getting answers. Sure, I wanted to know, but I wasn't hopping up and down in anticipation.

I chose cropped leggings, a cherry-red top, and a brightly patterned scarf as my attire for the cocktail hour. My reflection in the mirror told me the perky outfit did little to camouflage my somber air. *C'est la vie.*

Morgan, understandably, didn't join us for dinner, but the rest of the women were there. The six who'd traveled to Land's End regaled us with tales of what they'd seen. The Dartmouth sisters and Lily and Lilith had visited the area previously, but without a tour guide. They agreed having one for this trip made the experience infinitely more enjoyable. Guin beamed at their enthusiasm, and Wendy and I discussed making the drive before we returned to Astonbury.

As the meal drew to a close, I wasn't surprised Sue passed a sheet of paper around to collect emails. On my many bicycle trips, someone always did. Only a small percentage of people typically stayed in touch, but keeping up with those who did was a joy. Many had become Facebook friends as well as pen pals. I particularly treasured the annual New Year's email I received from our Normandy tour guide, as that had been my last cycling trip with Henry, and touring the WWII sites had been a dream come true for him.

When I no longer had the dinner chatter to distract me, my thoughts returned to Dave, and I was quiet as Wendy and I walked to our cottage. Seeing Dickens lolling by the pool with Merlin made me smile, if only briefly. I'd told Wendy about my argument with Dave, and when I said I'd be at the pool for a bit, she understood I wanted to be by myself.

True to form, I reflected on what I'd done wrong, what I could have done differently to prevent our disagreement. I might get defensive in the heat of the moment but never failed to blame myself afterward. The obvious answer was to be more cautious, to avoid risky situations. Yes, Wendy had instigated this one, but I could have said no. *Right, like I could've lived with myself if I'd let her go off on her own.*

Our unfortunate sleuthing adventures, as my sister Sophia dubbed them, were always triggered by a need to help someone. In one instance, we ensured the wrong person wasn't arrested. In another, we cleared an estranged spouse who was the strongest suspect. When I struggled to articulate to Dave how rewarding the feeling was, he eventually understood. Admittedly, I also enjoyed finding the puzzle pieces and laying them out, and I liked ferreting out anomalies others missed. And, after he'd helped solve a murder in Chipping Camden, Dave was hooked too.

*So, why did we argue about it?*

*Because he loves you, you fool.*

I scratched Dickens's ears as I whispered, "I don't know what to do."

Along with Christie, we two called it a night, and coward that I was, I texted Dave goodnight rather than call him.

# CHAPTER TWENTY-TWO

I WAS SOUND ASLEEP when Christie meowed in my ear. "Your phone made that funny noise. What do you call it? A ping?" When I ignored her, she tapped my nose with her paw.

Stretching and yawning, I reached for my phone and my red cheaters. Later in the day, I could manage to read texts and emails without them, but not first thing in the morning. It was a text from Dave. *It's the middle of the night in New York? What's he doing up?*

He'd sent two texts minutes apart. The first read, "Thoreau was a wise man when he wrote, 'There's no remedy for love but to love more.'" The last read, "Call me, I'm up."

As I closed my eyes and sighed, Christie crawled on my chest. "You're smiling. Do you feel better?" She was an intuitive little thing. Dickens was too, when he was awake, but he was still snoring softly on the rug by the bed.

Dave answered the phone in his usual chipper fashion. "Good morning, sweetheart."

"Good morning to you, too. Now tell me why you're still up. I assume you haven't been to bed yet?"

"I couldn't go to sleep without talking to you, so I worked on my book until it was late enough to text you. I didn't wake you, did I?"

"No, my furry black alarm clock did that. The Thoreau quote is sweet. Does that mean we're on solid ground again?"

I pictured him shaking his head with a smile. "See, Leta, that's the difference between you and me—I never thought we were on shaky ground. We argued. Couples do that. But I knew you thought it was more than that when you texted me last night instead of calling me. And I had to make it right."

"Well, quoting Thoreau worked. That and a good night's sleep. I hate arguments. And I hate that silly *Love Story* quote, 'Love means never having to say you're sorry.' Of course, we have to say we're sorry, but it's not like waving a magic wand. It's not like 'poof' and the awful feelings disappear. I can't shake it off that way. It's as though I have an emotional hangover."

He gave a soft chuckle. "And instead of two aspirin, the right quote is the cure?"

All was once again right in my world, and his parting words sealed the deal. "Tuppence, I'm not sure I can love you more than I already do, but I promise to try."

Wendy looked up from her book when I wandered into the kitchen. "Does that silly grin mean you and Dave made up?"

Pulling my phone from the pocket of my robe, I showed her the quote. She rolled her eyes. "The man does have a way with words. Unbelievable, a good-looking perceptive wordsmith. Should I add caring and, more important, single? Too bad he doesn't have a twin."

I poured a cup of coffee and glanced at Dickens prancing by the door. Tossing him a treat, I let him out. "Wendy, are you up for a walk through the lavender fields before breakfast? It's a beautiful day."

She begged off, and Christie wasn't interested either, even when I offered to take her in the backpack. "No. Today's my day off," she meowed.

The scent of lavender wafted through the air as I meandered up and down the rows. Merry had explained that they'd soon harvest the plants, as late August was when the soil temperature would be at its warmest. Pruning the plants then would give new shoots the chance to grow before winter and bloom well in spring. Guin and Rhiannon had picked the perfect time for their yoga retreat.

We walked to the cliffside where Dickens stood with his nose in the air, the wind ruffling his fur. *He looks so majestic in that stance.* I heard a distant bark, and soon Merlin joined us. The two ran along the top of the cliff, playfully dodging and darting, before they headed inland.

In no hurry to catch up with them, I strolled toward the garden shed where I'd seen Merry puttering as we passed earlier. When I said hello, she motioned me over and asked me to wait as she ducked into the garden shed. She returned with an index card and a small cobalt blue spray bottle. "This recipe for lavender scones is for Wendy. I hear she's hooked on them, and this catnip oil is for Christie's mouse so you can refresh the scent as it fades."

Laughing, I described Christie's antics with her new toy. "She's never experienced catnip, so I didn't know what to expect, but she's quite taken with it."

"I'm glad. Now, Leta, how are *you* doing? I hear you and Wendy had something to do with figuring out it was Martin who poisoned Caryn. I'm having a difficult time digesting that."

Though Guin had told her of our presence at Martin's arrest, I could tell she didn't know the details of the confrontation. *Best left that way,* I thought. If there were additional charges, she'd hear about them in good time. I suspected his friends and family were devastated at the news it was Martin who poisoned Caryn. Whatever the ins and outs of his involvement in Arthur's death, that story would be an additional blow. I didn't let slip any details, just expressed my relief Caryn was no longer in any danger.

When I said I needed to be on my way to breakfast, I was taken aback by Merry's response. "Guess I'll see you there. Guin phoned to say DI Nancarrow requested our presence at the barn."

*He must have more concrete news about Arthur's death.* As I hurried to corral my dog, I wondered whether Martin had confessed or DI Nancarrow had found a witness. I looked forward to getting some answers.

Dickens and Christie followed me and Wendy to the barn, but Christie deserted us when Archie leaped from the top of the reception desk. He chased her to the yoga studio, and I chuckled, wondering what they were up to.

In the dining room, Belle and Ellie sat together, sipping tea and speaking quietly with Gemma. Gareth, Guin, and Merry were eating at another four-top, and Rhiannon had a nearby table to herself. The buffet was piled with the tasty dishes that make up a full English breakfast—eggs, rashers, beans, tomatoes, mushrooms, and toast. Our yoga meals had been lighter. *Good thing I'm starving.*

Fixing our plates, Wendy and I joined Rhiannon. I dug in, assuming the show would start when Jake arrived. The minutes seemed to drag until he entered the room followed by Caryn. He surveyed the room as they continued to talk.

I whispered at our table. "I bet Gemma suggested he have this Poirot-like gathering. Why else would he invite the Knight family and all of us?"

My comment got a concerned look from Rhiannon. "Surely he's not planning to arrest someone in front of us!"

"No, I think this will be more of a recap, like what we did at Ellie's after the murder in Chipping Camden. It will save him the time of updating everyone individually."

Caryn looked around the room until she spied me and Wendy and made a beeline for our table. Nodding at Gemma, Jake poured a cup of coffee before joining her.

After a few minutes, Jake stood and cleared his throat. "Most of you know that I've been taking a fresh look at Arthur Knight's death in light of the poisoning case here at Knight's Rest." He motioned toward Gemma. "Though she's here on vacation, DI Taylor was quick to offer her assistance, and with her help, things have progressed quite quickly. I'll let her start."

When Caryn dabbed her eyes with her napkin, Dickens went to her side and put his head in her lap. I smiled at my intuitive dog.

Gemma stood. "I'll start with the poisoned tea. You're all aware Martin Pascoe was arrested Wednesday night." She turned toward our table. "Caryn, late yesterday afternoon, he confessed to poisoning the tea delivered to your cottage, though he claims he intended only to make you sick enough to stop asking questions about your fiancé's death and artifacts, nothing beyond that. That confession came easily once DI Nancarrow told him he was arresting Gareth and Merry for the crime—which of course, he wasn't."

*It's just like the TV crime dramas where the police lie to the criminal.*

When Ellie asked how Martin knew about jimson weed, Gemma looked at me and explained about the articles stashed in his desk. As for finding it, that was easy enough as it grew wild locally.

We listened intently as she continued. "To understand why he needed to silence Caryn, we have to go back to the death of Arthur Knight. DI Nancarrow recently reopened an investigation into a drug-smuggling enterprise known to be operating in the area. It turns out it was run out of the warehouse in Tintagel where artifacts from the dig are housed along with souvenirs destined for London shops and English Heritage sites. Martin Pascoe wasn't actively involved in the operation, but when he stumbled across a crate with drugs tucked among the souvenirs, he made the mistake of asking his employee, Colin Carmody, if he'd noticed any unusual activity, thinking they would both go to the police."

I heard a sharp intake of breath and realized it came from Guin. "Mistake? You mean Colin Carmody is involved in drugs?"

Gemma nodded. "It's worse than that, Guin. He's the coastal kingpin. He coerced Martin into turning a blind eye with bribes and threats of harming his sister if he didn't play along, and that was all well and good until Arthur complained about the shoddy packing of artifacts coming to the British Museum and one shipment going to the wrong place. For Arthur, that misplaced shipment was the straw that broke the camel's back. For Colin Carmody, that reaction is what sealed Arthur's fate. Your brother had no idea drugs were involved, but he was bringing undue attention to Carmody's business."

Caryn gasped. "So it wasn't Martin at Merlin's Cave that night?"

"No, he was there, but DI Nancarrow believes his story that he was trying to save Arthur, not hurt him."

Taking a quick drink of coffee, Jake picked up the story. "When Arthur let it be known he was coming to Tintagel to discuss his concerns and tour the warehouse, Colin pressed Martin to shut him up and reminded him it was easy enough to harm Morgan if Martin didn't solve the Arthur problem."

Gareth spoke up. "This sounds like the plot in a DCI Banks episode, not something that happens in real life, and not in Tintagel."

Shaking his head, DI Nancarrow responded. "I wish I could tell you it's fiction. Instead, it played out here. The two met at the cove as I understand they often did. Under the gun, Martin tried his best to convince his friend the warehouse problem was taken care of, that there was no need for him to get involved, but Arthur was like a dog with a bone. Martin felt he had no choice but to tell him about the drugs and his complicity, as a last-ditch attempt to dissuade him."

Wendy commented, "But Martin couldn't stop him. Arthur wouldn't let it go, right?"

"Correct. He even told Arthur about the threat to Morgan, but that made Arthur all the more determined to go to the police. Little did Martin know that Colin Carmody leaves nothing to chance. He lay in wait hidden near the steps that night when the two friends met. Who knows whether he'd have been satisfied simply to hear Arthur agree to keep quiet. Maybe he planned all along to kill Arthur because he couldn't risk him continuing to ask questions. It doesn't matter. When Martin threw up his hands and left Arthur staring into the sea, Carmody took matters into his own hands."

I gasped. "So it was Colin Carmody who killed Arthur, not Martin?"

"Yes, though Martin didn't see it happen. When he heard a shout and a splash, he turned around to see Colin leaning over the railing. Martin ran to save his friend, but, as he says, he was too late. He clambered down the stairs, but he couldn't do anything as Arthur disappeared beneath the waves. No one could have done anything at that point."

Raising her hand, Belle asked a question. "Do you have enough to charge him with murder if Martin didn't see the act?"

"I hate to say it, but probably not. The man hasn't said word one since we picked him up. We've got him on the drugs, and we're working to connect him to a man who's gone missing in Boscastle, someone who also worked at the warehouse. Martin said that was a factor in his believing Colin when he said he'd harm Morgan."

Ellie posed a question. "I know real life isn't always like what we see on the telly, but why didn't the coastal kingpin, as you call him, just do away with Arthur from the get-go? Why involve Martin at all?"

"Lady Stow, that's not a bad question. I wondered that myself. My theory is that if he could get Martin more entangled, possibly even push him to commit murder, he'd have him permanently under his thumb."

I could tell from the expression on Wendy's face that the wheels were turning in her brain. "What was Arthur doing at Merlin's Cave in the first place? Everyone we spoke to said he never would have gone there at night."

Gareth nodded. "Except Arthur and Martin called it their thinking spot, and I recall being thrilled as a small boy when they invited me to tag along. Visiting at high tide scared me until I realized they weren't going to make me go to the water's edge.

The attraction was listening to the pounding surf and watching the waves from as close as they could get, though for me, about midway down the steps was far enough."

*The thinking spot!* "That's right. Dylan even mentioned that he and Arthur worked out knotty problems there. And that makes me think of the text from Martin to Arthur—the one that said 'See you at eleven.' We took it to mean eleven in the morning, and, heck, Martin even told us that's when they agreed to meet. But, in reality, Martin must have asked to meet Arthur at night."

*What an awful betrayal.* I wondered aloud about the need to silence Caryn. "But Martin and Colin hadn't planned on Caryn asking questions, so doing away with Arthur didn't solve the problem. Did Martin poison her on Colin's orders?"

Gemma shuddered. "No, he came up with that all on his own, as a way to deter Carmody from doing worse. Fed up with Caryn stirring up doubts about Arthur's death and her constant reference to the artifacts, Carmody worried the police might decide to listen to her. Martin claims he'd already asked his London partners to take care of her in London, but called them off when Martin begged him to let him try another route."

Caryn winced. "So it was Martin who propped the envelope outside my door? With the tea in it? And then poor Gareth was blamed for trying to poison me."

Gemma fielded that question. "That would be the simple answer, but that's not what happened. Bear with me on this. Dylan put the other stuff in the envelope back when he took over Arthur's desk, planning to get it to Arthur—the Merlin hat, the keychain, things Arthur had left behind. After the accident, as the condolence cards started coming in, he added those, thinking you'd like to have it all. It was a lovely thought."

Jake chimed in. "Martin's inspiration for the poisoned tea came from reading a newspaper article, but he had no plan for how to get it to you. He's not a criminal mastermind, by any means. When Dylan mentioned taking you the envelope, it was a stroke of luck for him. He already had the tea ready, so he slipped it in the envelope, and reminded Dylan about giving it to you. He was convinced you'd drink it while you were here and his problem would be solved."

Holding up her hand, Gemma interrupted. "Dylan told us he knocked on your door with it Sunday evening, but when you didn't answer, he left it propped outside."

Caryn stroked Dickens's head and gave a wan smile. "Martin never was much of a planner, and Arthur called Dylan the absent-minded professor. Between the two of them, it's a wonder the tea ever made it to me. But one thing's for sure. Martin was a good enough judge of character to know I'd brew it right off once I saw the note from Arthur on it."

I whispered to Wendy, "Good grief! Is it any wonder we couldn't figure this mess out?"

DI Nancarrow looked around the room. When there were no further questions, he recapped the case. "I must apologize that this case wasn't investigated as it should have been from the beginning, and I hope the answers we've provided this morning will bring you some peace. Colin Carmody may or may not be charged with Arthur's murder, but he will serve a lengthy sentence for his role in the drug smuggling operation."

He cleared his throat. "Several charges are pending against Martin Pascoe, and I know you must have mixed emotions about that because he's a long-time family friend." He hesitated, as though trying to find the right words.

Guin came to his rescue, and though this turn of events had to be especially hard on her, she seemed her usual calm self. "DI

Nancarrow, thank you for all you've done to find the answers about our brother's death, even though they weren't easy for us to hear. And Caryn, you were right all along. I wish I could have seen it sooner. None of this will bring Arthur back, but knowing the answers will help us move on."

DI Nancarrow nodded. "Thank you. And I'd like to thank Gemma Taylor for her unstinting support on this case." He grinned and looked towards my table. "And, of course, the Little Old Ladies' Detective agency was instrumental in ferreting out a few key bits of information. With Merry's help, they wasted no time pinpointing the toxic ingredient in the tea. They also identified the poisoner, though that was more of an accident."

When he mentioned the LOLs, Belle and Ellie whispered to each other, and then Belle spoke up. "I was just saying how disappointed I am our conclusions about Dylan's book turned out to be misleading—a red herring, if you will."

Jake shook his head. "Yes, the confusion over those parts in the book led you astray. When we followed up with him, Dylan explained he was fortunate that Arthur brought the issue to his attention. He had written glowing introductions to the material but forgotten to insert the paragraphs into the final manuscript. It was absentmindedness, not some malicious intent."

Ellie chuckled as she looked at Gemma. "We understand DI Nancarrow lost a bet to you over our tendency to see everything as a literary mystery."

Those comments got a smile from Gemma. "I suppose I should be thankful you didn't add a king, a wizard, and a sorceress to the mix. I'm still waiting for a tall, dark, handsome knight to appear in my bedchamber, though."

Leave it to Wendy. She looked directly at DI Nancarrow. "Oh, I think a tall, handsome detective in the dining room could be a start, don't you?"

Gemma blushed. Jake blanched. And in the blink of an eye, the dishy DI made a remarkable recovery. Turning to the fair maiden, he bowed, grabbed her hand, and planted a kiss on it.

The smattering of applause told me he'd succeeded in striking just the right note. The mood seemed less somber, the faces a bit brighter, the spirits more hopeful.

Guin smiled. "Thank you, DI Nancarrow. As Dumbledore says, 'Happiness can be found, even in the darkest of times, if only someone remembers to turn on the light.' I think you just did."

*The End*

**Book VI**

**A major cycling event. A high-profile murder. Can the Little Old Ladies' Detective Agency stop a killer from riding away scot-free?**

Read ***Bicycles, Barking & Murder*** to find out!

Want to learn more about Leta's life before she retired to the Cotswolds? Curious about how Dickens & Christie became part of the family? Find out in *Paws, Claws & Mischief*, the prequel to the Dickens & Christie mystery series. Join my newsletter today for exclusive access to the subscriber-only area of my website, where you'll find your complimentary copy of the prequel, plus much more! Enjoy behind-the-scenes content, recipes from my books, and an ever-growing list of books mentioned in my stories. New content is available every month—don't miss out!

Would you like to help others discover the world of Dickens & Christie? If so, please leave an honest review on Amazon, Goodreads, and/or BookBub. Readers depend on reviews to help them decide what to read next. It doesn't have to be a book report! A short I loved it is all it takes.